CLUES TO LOVE

Failing to sense the danger that lurks about her, expatriate Kate Stanhope converts her deceased husband's Lake District mansion into an upscale hotel. The first weekend the hotel is open, a Cornish guest is found dead in his room. Detective Chief Inspector Nick Connor soon concludes that Kate was the intended victim. But who would want to kill her? While Nick struggles to find the elusive killer, he falls in love with Kate, in spite of his vow to never love again. Can Nick catch the killer before he finds Kate?

NANCY MADISON

◆

CLUES TO LOVE

Complete and Unabridged

ULVERSCROFT
Leicester

First published in Great Britain in 2003

First Large Print Edition
published 2003

This book is a work of fiction. Names, characters, places, and incidents are either the product of the author's imagination or are used fictitiously, and any resemblance to actual persons, living or dead, events, or locales is entirely coincidental.

British Library CIP Data

Madison, Nancy
    Clues to love.—Large print ed.—
    Ulverscroft large print series: romance
    1. Romantic suspense novels
    2. Large type books
    I. Title
    813.6 [F]

    ISBN 1–8439–5042–1

Published by
F. A. Thorpe (Publishing)
Anstey, Leicestershire

Set by Words & Graphics Ltd.
Anstey, Leicestershire
Printed and bound in Great Britain by
T. J. International Ltd., Padstow, Cornwall

This book is printed on acid-free paper

Dedication
This book and its predecessor, Never
Love A Stranger, are dedicated to my
faithful, talented critique group —
Jo Anne McCraw and Chris McKeever
who have offered me friendship,
advice and encouragement.
Many thanks and happy writing, ladies.

1

'Mrs. Stanhope! Anybody! Help! Help!' The shrill cry cut through the quiet May morning, startling everyone in the King's Grant Hotel dining room.

'What in the world!' Kate Stanhope, the owner, jerked and set the coffee pot down with a bang on the table.

Recognizing Mrs. Penmar's agitated voice, Kate's stomach muscles clinched as she fought down panic. Just when things were going so well. They'd just opened Kate's home as an upscale hotel that weekend. The gracious old mansion perched on a ridge over Lake Windermere in Cumbria, northern England. She'd expected a few minor glitches, every new business had some. But hysterical guests? That she wasn't prepared for.

'Please excuse me,' she said to the six guests enjoying their meal then darted from the room. A few minutes earlier, Mrs. Penmar, another guest, had left the table to go upstairs and locate her husband, the last straggler to breakfast.

Once out of the dining room, Kate dashed

1

into the front hall. Glancing upward, she saw Mrs. Penmar draped like a rag doll over the railing of the next floor. Why was she so upset?

Holding up her long denim skirt, Kate ascended the broad, oak-panelled staircase. Before she reached Mrs. Penmar, the old woman slumped to the floor.

'Chris.' Kate leaned over the railing and summoned a member of her small staff from the dining room where he'd just served breakfast. 'Would you come up here for a moment?'

Kate knelt and rubbed Mrs. Penmar's icy hands. Seconds later, the old lady's eyelids fluttered, and she moaned. Chris and Kate eased her guest into a chair.

Mrs. Penmar immediately burst into tears.

'What's wrong?' Kate leaned over her guest.

The woman babbled, her words incoherent. She sobbed and waved her arms around like a windmill out of kilter.

'Let's help her to her room,' Kate suggested to Chris. She glanced downstairs, hoping the other guests hadn't heard them.

'No, I can't go in there.' Mrs. Penmar reared back and clung to the chair's arms with unexpected strength.

Bewildered, Kate stared at Chris.

'All right, we'll go downstairs to the living room,' she said, trying to pacify the older woman. Kate and Chris tried to help Mrs. Penmar walk but her legs buckled under her.

'Let me carry you downstairs, ma'am,' Chris offered. With no apparent effort, the husky young man picked up Mrs. Penmar and carried her to the lower floor.

Kate followed, praying her other guests' patience would hold just a bit longer.

'Thanks, Chris,' she murmured. Her heart raced. 'If you'll put her in that armchair, she'll be comfortable.' She indicated a large upholstered chair in one corner of the living room.

'Go see to breakfast,' she whispered after he set the older woman in the chair. 'I'll handle Mrs. Penmar.'

Kate knelt by her guest and asked, 'What's wrong?'

'It's Giles.' Mentioning his name produced another torrent of tears.

Miss Alden, a retired school teacher, walked into the room. Kate hoped the other guests didn't follow. She watched the teacher take off her heavy shawl and place it over Mrs. Penmar, then Miss Alden hugged the distressed old lady.

'There, there.' Kate sympathetically patted her guest's shoulder. 'Maybe it's not so bad.

3

He can't have gone far. Why, I imagine he'll turn up any minute now.'

Tears formed in Kate's eyes, distress for the other woman and also worry about the hotel's success. She'd used almost all of her capital to get it started. If it failed, she'd have to go back to the States. No one waited for her there.

Kate turned to Miss Alden. 'Let's find Mr. Penmar. Will you stay with Mrs. Penmar while I go and see if her husband's still upstairs?'

Her heart beating furiously, Kate raced up the stairs, not sure what she'd find. At the Penmars' room, she knocked. No answer so she turned the door knob slowly, and stepped inside. Mr. Penmar was there, not missing after all. He lay on his back, asleep on one of the twin beds. Kate let out her breath. She hated to wake him, but his wife needed to know he was all right.

'Mr. Penmar?' He didn't speak or move. Kate edged closer to the bed. 'Mr. Penmar?' Thoughts swam around in her head when he remained still. Why didn't he respond? His chest wasn't moving up and down, as it should. No movement. Was he dead? What should she do? Find out if he's alive or dead. Right. Kate gingerly took his thin wrist between her fingers. Touching his cold

4

skin, she shivered, then she felt for a pulse. There was none. She placed her ear to his chest, no heart beat. Keeping her gaze on the still, quiet body, she reached for the telephone, perched on a night stand crowded with prescription bottles, large and small.

Kate fingered one, then another and another. They were all labeled 'for Giles Penmar.'

The names of two of the prescriptions looked familiar. Her mother had suffered from heart disease and took those medicines for years. Had Mr. Penmar died of a heart attack during the night?

Kate dialed 'o'.

'Operator. How may I direct your call?' A woman's voice echoed on the other end.

'Hello, this is Kate Stanhope at King's Grant Hotel and we need help. I believe one of our guests has died.' At the sound of her own voice, harsh reality struck and Kate began to shake. A mental image of Mr. Penmar's round, sunburned face, telling jokes and laughing with the other guests the previous night, flashed before her. It brought tears to her eyes. In seconds, she reached the local police headquarters.

'Windermere Constabulary.' A male voice answered.

The voice on the other end of the line made her feel she wasn't totally alone with the corpse on the bed. Kate repeated what she'd said to the operator and gave directions to the hotel. Hanging up the telephone, she wiped her eyes and left the room.

As she walked down the corridor toward the stairs, a door clicked shut behind her. Nerves taut, she whirled around and found nothing except the empty corridor. It must have been the wind.

The two women waited for her in the living room.

'I'm afraid Mr. Penmar is . . . ' Seeing Mrs. Penmar's and Miss Alden's anxious faces, Kate stopped. 'They'll send an officer right over.'

Crossing the room to Mrs. Penmar, Kate knelt by her chair. 'I'm so sorry. Please tell me what we can do to make you more comfortable.' She spoke in a low voice, wishing there were something she could do to lessen Mrs. Penmar's grief.

The older lady shook her head as tears ran in rivulets down her wrinkled face. She slumped in her chair, her plump hands lay limp in her lap.

Two uniformed officers walked into the room. One of the policemen checked his notebook then addressed them in a brisk

6

voice. 'A Kate Stanhope called the Constabulatory, reporting a death.'

'I called.' Kate told them what had happened.

The next arrival was a stocky, middle-aged man who entered the living room and tossed his rumpled trench coat on a chair.

'I'm Dr. Walton from Windermere Constabulary. Would one of you be Mrs. Stanhope?'

Kate stepped forward and introduced herself. 'Mr. Penmar, a guest, appears to have . . . ' She hesitated.

'If you'll take me to him.' Dr. Walton picked up his bag.

'Please follow me.' Kate again climbed the stairs, this time with the doctor at her heels. Reaching the next floor, she led him to the Penmars' room, then moved aside to let him enter.

The doctor searched for signs of life in Mr. Penmar, then 'I'm sorry, but he's gone.'

She inhaled sharply at the finality of his words. 'The poor man. What in the world happened to him?' Kate stood, riveted to the floor for a moment until she remembered her responsibilities downstairs. Shaking her head, she became more alert. 'Excuse me, please, while I check on my other guests. Let me know if I can help in any way.'

7

Bewildered and shaken by the morning's events, Kate descended to the ground floor, hoping for a moment alone to regain her composure. Instead, she found Miss Alden waiting for her. The retired school teacher clutched at Kate in the hall. 'What happened to Mr. Penmar?'

'I'm sorry, but I have no idea.' Kate tried to keep her voice calm though inside her stomch churned. 'The doctor should be able to tell us something once he's completed his examination.'

After she informed the other guests of the tragedy, they filed into the living room and huddled together, speaking in whispers in respect for the dead.

Kate stood by Mrs. Penmar, her arm spread protectively along the back of the chair, while they waited for the doctor. Hearing Dr. Walton on the stairs, Kate caught him right before he entered the living room.

'Was the gentleman alone?' The doctor inquired.

'No, his wife is here. I'll introduce you to her.' She led him to the corner where the older lady sat.

'Mrs. Penmar, I'm so sorry.' Doctor Walton leaned over to pat the widow's hand. 'Was your husband a heart patient? I saw several medicines in your room that are prescribed for high blood pressure.'

'Yes,' Mrs. Penmar replied in a weak, tired voice. 'Since Giles had a heart attack six months ago, our doctor has controlled his blood pressure with medications.'

'Did Mr. Penmar complain, recently, of chest pains or have an adverse reaction to his medications?'

'No, I would have noticed. Giles felt so much better, he went back to work recently. We came up here by train from London yesterday so he could review King's Grant Hotel for his travel magazine. He is a freelance journalist.'

'He didn't complain of indigestion or an upset stomach last night?'

'No, I sleep soundly, but I would've heard him if he got up during the night. I didn't hear anything. This morning he appeared to be asleep when I dressed and went outside. I'm a birder and I've found early morning is the best time to watch the birds.' Mrs. Penmar rested her head on the back of the chair.

'I understand.' Doctor Walton reached over, took her wrist and felt for her pulse. 'Let's check your blood pressure and see how you're doing.' He knelt by her and put a monitor on her arm. 'This won't take long.'

Straightening up a few moments later, the

9

doctor announced, 'Your blood pressure is a bit elevated. That's not unusual, under the circumstances.' He touched Mrs. Penmar's shoulder. 'I have a mild sedative here I'd like you to take.' He drew an envelope out of his bag. 'It's not strong and will help you relax.'

Kate took the envelope and gave it to Mrs. Penmar, then she left the room and returned with a glass. The old lady washed down the tablet with water. A few minutes later, she appeared calmer. Resting her head against the back of the chair, she closed her eyes.

Watching Mrs. Penmar sitting, quietly, in her chair, Kate worried about the older woman. She also worried about her other guests' reaction. And she worried about the future.

* * *

Detective Chief Inspector Nick Connor admired the heavy oak doors as he entered King's Grant Hotel. Another family mansion transformed into a hotel, he surmised. The Victorian mansion was worlds removed from the lower-class Manchester flat of his childhood. He'd traveled a long way to get where he was today. Five years ago, on his twenty-seventh birthday, he'd become Cumbria's youngest DCI.

'Good morning.' Nick spoke to a young woman at the reception desk in the entry way. 'I'm Inspector Connor. Dr. Walton asked me to meet him here.'

Dr. Walton appeared a few moments later. He led Nick down a hall to a small room where they stopped, briefly, to confer. Nick viewed their images reflected in an antique wall mirror.

Seeing his own reflection, he made a mental note to get a haircut soon. No one had reason to question his ability, his competence in his profession, but personal appearance also mattered, especially when a promotion was in the works. At the present, other DCI's and he competed for the position of superintendent. His boss would retire in six months. He'd hinted he would recommend Nick for the position. And solving this case wouldn't hurt, either. Nick believed it might give him an indisputable edge over the other candidates.

'Why do you suspect Penmar died of unnatural causes?' Nick pumped Dr. Walton for information. The doctor's long career as Medical Examiner for Cumbria had made him a virtual encyclopedia on many subjects, not all related to morbidity.

'Years of experience, lad. And a feeling up here.' The older man tapped his forehead.

11

'There was an odd discoloration on the deceased's mouth. I'll need to run tests to determine the cause.'

Nick nodded in agreement, mentally reviewing other cases he'd investigated. What could have caused the discoloration? Poison? Murder by poison happened from time to time, though rarely in a hotel or other public place where people were just passing through.

Poisonings were typically commited by a relative or friend. Then what? But something didn't feel right. The doctor wasn't the only one with an instinct that talked, and Nick's had been alerted the moment he walked through those fancy oak doors.

'You'll need to meet Mrs. Stanhope, the hotel owner. If you'll come with me, I'll introduce you,' Doctor Walton said.

Nick followed the older man to the rear of the building and an elegant room full of people.

They walked over an Aubusson carpet and under a crystal chandelier, which Nick's self-educated eye recognized as Waterford. The doctor came to a halt before a young woman with auburn hair seated on a sofa.

'Mrs. Stanhope, let me introduce Detective Chief Inspector Connor. He's the investigating officer,' the doctor informed the hotel owner.

'Thank you for coming.' As she gazed in his direction, Nick's senses vibrated. Then she extended her hand and he took it in his. The moment their hands touched, his fingers tingled. His surprise must have shown on his face since she immediately jerked back her own hand.

'Mrs. Stanhope.' Nick nodded. 'Is your husband away?' He glanced at the others in the room.

'He died last October.'

'I'm sorry, ma'am.' Nick paused, then continued. 'I'll need to speak to you in private for a few minutes. Is there somewhere we can go?'

'Of course. If you'll come with me?' She excused herself to the others and led him toward the front of the hotel.

As they walked, Nick scrutinized the woman. Simply dressed in a long denim skirt and quilted blouse, she was stunning, about 5'7, 30 maybe, thin and graceful. His nostrils inhaled the scent of an unknown fragrance. Definitely out of his league, the perfume and its wearer. Her cool tone irritated him. Nick admitted she was attractive. So what? He'd known enough women to last a lifetime.

She opened the front door, paused, took a deep breath. For a moment, she slumped, then straightened her shoulders. Did the beautiful view soothe her? The aged pines by the circular driveway swayed in a cool May breeze. Bees droned in fragrant beds of golden dahlias. Looking over her shoulder, Nick saw the lake sparkling through the pines and spruces. After months of winter, spring had at last come to the Lake District. He'd been too busy with his work to notice, until now.

He followed her down the driveway. She stopped at a stone bench. As he watched, she ran her fingers over its surface, took a seat, and gestured for him to do likewise.

What was there about this woman that alarmed him? His keen glance took in her slender figure and auburn hair. Only the pallor of her skin and her clenched hands betrayed her shock at the situation. So she did feel badly about the man's death. Otherwise, she appeared calm. Her self-control was admirable, under the circumstances.

'I hope you don't mind coming outdoors?'

'Not at all.' Nick sat down beside her and stretched his legs. 'Have you lived in this country long?' He'd picked up on her American accent.

'Four years, since my husband and I met and married in New York City. I was assistant food editor with the New York Times. It was interesting work.'

'And when did you move to the Lake District, Mrs. Stanhope?'

'About two years ago, after Stephen's first heart attack.'

'I see. Prior to Mr. Stanhope's death, did your husband help you run this hotel?'

'No, we've just converted the house to a hotel and opened for business this weekend. Speaking candidly, Inspector, King's Grant Hotel has to show a profit if I am to keep the estate. My husband left me the property, but not enough capital to maintain it.' Worry creased her brow. Her lips clamped together in a thin anxious line.

'I should tell you, we haven't determined what killed Mr. Penmar, but we will, soon.'

As they sat talking, he couldn't help staring into her jade green eyes. They sparkled in the sunlight in spite of her worry and went well with her auburn hair and creamy skin. He admired beauty in any form, but he reminded himself that it didn't always go hand in hand with honesty or trustworthiness.

Totally disenchanted with the opposite sex since a failed marriage two years ago, he'd resolved to avoid serious relationships. Ultimately, women disappointed him. Today he found it difficult to stick to that resolution. With effort, Nick dragged his attention back to the case.

'Did Mrs. Penmar leave the living room before I came? I didn't meet her.'

'Diane, my assistant manager, persuaded her to lie down in another room for a few minutes.'

'Had you met the Penmars before they stayed here?'

She appeared to hesitate before answering. 'No. We met for the first time yesterday.'

'I saw several other people in the drawing room, two Chinese gentlemen, a young couple and two older ladies. Are they all guests?'

'That's correct.'

The mansion and its beautiful grounds exuded tranquility and peace, but as a policeman, and a good one, Nick knew that a serene environment could be deceptive. In his years of police work, he'd investigated murders in many places just as peaceful as this one. 'I'll have to talk to everyone who was here last night. Could you find me a room I can use?'

'Of course.' She paused and bit her full bottom lip. 'Do you have any idea how long it will take your labs to determine what caused Mr. Penmar's death?'

'It depends on how backed up they are. Also, they may have to run several tests.' Seeing a frown on her face, he was thankful she wasn't crying. Weepy women made him nervous. He'd take a frothing, hatchet-brandishing lunatic to a sobbing woman any time. 'If you'll find me that room?'

The muscles in his arms and legs grew taut while he fought his attraction to this intriguing woman with her green eyes. His brain sent him a warning. Stick to the case.

'Of course you realize that we'll have to shut down your hotel if Mr. Penmar didn't die of natural causes?' He glanced in her general direction. He hated to add to her dismay, but it was part of his job.

'I'd assumed he died of a heart attack. What evidence makes you think otherwise? Please tell me.' Confusion reigned on her face as she leaned toward Nick as if to plead with him.

'We don't know anything definite yet.' In an attempt to ease her anguish, he added, 'I'm sure it's a shock, having a guest die in your hotel. We'll do all we can to solve this case as soon as possible so things can get back to normal.' And get him out of there before she bewitched him.

2

'Madam, let me express my condolences.' Nick's tone was patient, even gentle as he interviewed the widow. 'We're just going to talk for a few minutes now. And, as soon as possible, we'll find out what caused your husband's death. To start, I'd appreciate your reviewing your schedule since you arrived.'

Mrs. Penmar blew her nose, a bewildered expression crossed her face. Confusion and grief filled the air while she twisted a white lace handkerchief back and forth in her wrinkled hands, and began to weep again.

Better try a different tactic with her. 'I'll tell you what I know already, and you can correct me if I'm wrong. Please feel free to add anything I've left out. All right?'

She nodded her head and wiped her reddened eyes.

'Good. According to Mrs. Stanhope, you came up here from London so your husband could review King's Grant for his travel magazine. The trip was a combination of business and pleasure since today you were going to take the train to visit your family in Carlisle.'

Her sad expression lightened for a moment and she nodded. 'We have a new grandchild we wanted to see.'

Nick smiled, then consulted his notes and continued. 'You got here about four o'clock yesterday and went upstairs to your room. An hour later, both of you joined the other guests for appetizers and wine. Later, a staff member noticed you'd barely touched your plate and inquired as to whether your dinner was all right. You replied that you've been suffering with a stomach disorder. Correct so far?' Nick waited for her response.

'That's right.'

★ ★ ★

'I see.' He waited and hoped she'd continue. She didn't, so he glanced at his notes and went on. 'Early this morning you took a short walk around the grounds. Mr. Penmar didn't meet you at breakfast, so you went upstairs to get him. It was then that you found his body.' She began to sob.

'If you'd bear with me another minute. I only have two more brief questions I'd like you to answer.'

The old lady wiped at her eyes and nodded.

'Do you remember meeting Mrs. Stanhope

or her staff in the past?' Nick recalled Kate's hesitation when asked about the Penmars.

'No, I wouldn't have forgotten her. She's been lovely.'

'I see. Finally, has Mr. Penmar ever mentioned the Stanhopes or King's Grant prior to your booking your reservation to stay here?'

She thought a moment. 'No, never. But why do you ask?'

'Just part of my investigation, ma'am.' Nick made a note to have Mrs. Stanhope and her staff checked out. From Dr. Walton's comments about the dead man, it could have been poison. 'I'll need to talk to the other guests and the staff now. In the meanwhile, please try to remember if there was anything unusual about last evening.' Then he added, 'Dr. Walton has requested the names of any medications your husband took which weren't in view in your room.'

★ ★ ★

Kate saw Mrs. Penmar's gaunt, strained face when she re-entered the living room. 'Why don't we go upstairs and find a room where you can rest?'

The elderly woman nodded and accompanied her to the next floor and the only

20

unoccupied guest room. Kate waited while the old lady went in the bathroom.

Standing by the half-open window, Kate inhaled the fresh spring air and surveyed the rose gardens that spread out below her, a shower of early blooming antique roses in a dozen hues. A breeze brought their fragrance to her and blended it with the scent of purple wisteria growing up the corners of the house. She heard the soft calls of a pair of resident mourning doves nesting under the eaves of the residence.

Turning down the covers, she ran her fingers over the soft rose satin duvet. As soon as Mrs. Penmar reappeared, Kate found a foot-stool and helped the chubby little woman climb onto the four-poster bed.

The old lady yawned as if worn out from the morning's events.

Kate yawned in response. She'd answered a call on her personal line after midnight. The moment she picked up the phone, all she could hear was the sound of breathing on the line. Vaguely disturbed, she'd had difficulty going back to sleep. 'Why don't you try to rest? This room isn't used as part of the hotel yet, so we haven't installed a telephone but I'll bring you a cordless phone in a few minutes so you can call your daughter. You'll feel better after you've talked to her, and I'm sure she'll come for you as soon as possible. Until then, let us know of anything we can do to help you.'

She sympathized with Mrs. Penmar, certain that her guest must feel lost and bewildered. Kate remembered her own husband's death. The worst had come following the funeral service.

While Mattie, her housekeeper and friend, patiently held an umbrella over her, Kate had stood by Stephen's grave. For some reason, she felt she shouldn't leave him alone there. Raindrops mingled with tears on her cheeks as she inhaled deeply of the sharp, clean scent of the spruce trees in the cemetery.

Had it been eight months? The realization of time's passing brought fresh tears of regret to Kate's eyes. But she wept for what might have been. She'd loved, or thought she loved the older, charming British banker when they married, or was it gratitude for his kindness at the time of her mother's death?

Stephen Stanhope had appeared out of the blue. An old dear friend of the fantastically successful, vivacious, raven-haired authoress of gourmet cookbooks sold around the world. Her fame had rivalled that of Julia Child, a contemporary and friend. Kate always felt she lived in her mother's shadow, no matter what she did.

On their brief honeymoon in Venice, Kate discovered the charm and gallantry of Stephen's whirlwind courtship masked a coldness beyond imagination.

He considered her a charming addition to the objets d'art gracing Middleton, his ancestral home in Kent. Like his Ming Dynasty vases and antiques, she would show well to his banker friends who came to visit.

He'd suffered his first heart attack the day she told him she was leaving. Kate stayed. He was her husband, after all. Shaking her head, Kate dismissed old memories and came back to the present. She patted Mrs. Penmar's shoulder, tucked the duvet around her and closed the flowered draperies, blocking out the bright May sunshine and the chirp of birdsong. Then she tiptoed out of the room and pulled the door closed.

⋆ ⋆ ⋆

Downstairs, Nick continued his interviews. Sgt. Kennedy, his fresh-faced young Scot assistant, stepped into the hall and called, 'Miss Murf, would you please come now?'

The Sergeant led a tiny olive-skinned lady in a red and purple dress, into the room, closing the door behind her. Nick blinked, rubbed his eyes. She was the spitting image of

Miss Fontaine, a Manchester neighbor who'd read tea leaves and told fortunes when he was a youngster.

'I'll be brief, ma'am. What was your impression of the deceased man? And his wife?'

She stared at him over the top of her schoolmarm glasses until Nick felt eight years old again and caught in a mischevious deed by his teacher. Nonsense. He was full-grown and definitely not subject to a whack on the knuckles or paddling on his rear end.

'We met, of course, but I wasn't seated next to them so I didn't get a chance to talk to either Mr. Penmar or his wife during the evening, Inspector.' She wiped away a tear that ran down her withered cheek. Why would the death of someone she didn't know upset her? A flash of insight told him that any death might upset the elderly. Perhaps she saw Penmar's death as proof of her own mortality?

'My goodness!' She gasped as if shocked. 'Is it possible that you think he didn't die a natural death?'

'I'm conducting a routine investigation, ma'am. What about dinner? Did everything taste all right?'

She ignored his questions and asked, doggedly, 'What caused his death?' She licked

24

her dry, cracked lips.

'We don't know yet, ma'am. Did everything taste all right?'

'I didn't hear any complaints.'

'I see. That's all the questions I have for you. Would you ask Miss Alden to come in?'

Alone for a minute, Nick stood, stretched and thought again of Kate. That was her name. He'd found it on hotel stationery in the room. Kate kept popping up in his mind. Why did she tantalize him? He didn't even know her. Get hold of yourself.

You will not become infatuated with another woman. Nick reminded himself that his ex-wife had enchanted him until she revealed her true nature. Kate might be just as bad.

Forcing his concentration back to the case, he told himself he might not find out anything additional from the other guests. But a clue could appear where least expected.

In the other interviews, he heard the same refrain, again and again. It had been a pleasant, uneventful evening. But no one came forward with any useful information.

Later that day, Nick brought his Sergeant up-to-date. She'd returned to the constabulary while he talked to Kate's staff.

'Mrs. Stanhope's assembled a pleasant group to work with her,' he said. 'They all seemed anxious to help, but didn't add anything new to what I'd already heard from the guests. In our talks, I found each of her staff thinks of Mrs. Stanhope as a friend as much as an employer.'

Rubbing tired eyes, he scanned his notes one more time. It had been a long day. 'We'll need to see the two temps from the agency. Please call Lakeside Temps and ask their office to contact the girls. Have them get in touch with us as soon as they can,' Nick directed his Sergeant.

★ ★ ★

Kate came downstairs that afternoon after settling Mrs. Penmar for a nap. Kate's head throbbed. With one hand rubbing her temples, she headed toward the kitchen to brew some herbal tea. A soothing mixture, it relaxed her without causing drowsiness. She couldn't afford to fall asleep on her feet. There was still a lot to do before she could relax. She'd help Mrs. Penmar contact her daughter and see that her family came for her. Also, they must consider the other guests. Would they want to stay the rest of the weekend in a hotel where death lurked?

In the kitchen, Kate glanced across the

counters for the glass pitcher she used to make tea.

She'd brewed tea the previous afternoon before things got hectic with dinner preparations. But she hadn't been able to stop and take even a sip of the lemon balm tea, they were so busy.

Kate scanned the kitchen and spied the pitcher tucked away behind several large pans. Picking it up, she looked inside. It was still almost full. The help had missed it when they cleaned up the kitchen. She took a seat at the table to catch her breath before going back to Mrs. Penmar. The old lady needed a nap after this morning. The shock of her husband's death must have drained the poor woman's strength.

Sitting there, Kate's thoughts strayed, idly, to DCI Connor. She couldn't remember meeting anyone else so self-confident, so sure of himself. And the lean, rangy detective was handsome with that thatch of slightly unruly black hair and dark brown eyes. He was the first man she'd found attractive since Stephen died.

She shrugged. Nick Connor wasn't her type. A handsome man with bold eyes was the last thing she needed. Better concentrate on her business and leave Nick to the more experienced members of her sex. Anyway, with his looks and self-confidence, he'd probably find her too inexperienced for his taste and quickly move on to more likely prospects.

Rested, Kate got up, picked up the pitcher, and reached out to pour the old tea down the drain. Dr. Walton burst into the kitchen. Jumping, she thumped the pitcher down on the counter top and spilled some of the liquid.

'I'm sorry to disturb you, Mrs. Stanhope, but we've received preliminary lab results on Penmar. He ate or drank a substance that contained poison! The lab hasn't identified the substance, but the old gentleman ingested it last night.'

'What?' Kate's knees turned to rubber. She grabbed onto the edge of the counter and gasped as she fought frantically for her next breath. 'Poison? Here, in my kitchen, my hotel?' In her mind's eye, her hard work and dreams flowed away, like the spilled tea trickling down the cabinets to the tile floor.

On automatic, Kate went through the motions of taking a dish towel and dabbing at the spill. All the while she listened, intently, to the doctor's words.

'The lab tests show Mr. Penmar died of poisoning,' the doctor informed her. 'But, based on his interviews, DCI Connor informs me that Penmar ate and drank the same as the other guests. Until we find out what killed the man, I'm afraid we'll have to close King's Grant Hotel to business as of now.'

Before she could react, a police courier came to the kitchen door and handed a message to the doctor. He read the note, then turned to Kate and spoke briskly. 'I need to return to the constabulary on another matter, but I'll contact you as soon as I can give you more information.' Turning on his heels, Doctor Walton rushed out of the kitchen.

'Wait a minute! You can't close the hotel. I have guests. I've . . . ' She spoke to the air. The doctor had gone. Kate stared, helplessly as two lab aides walked into the kitchen.

One technician opened the pantry while the other took over the refrigerator. Kate watched them box up all of the foods and beverages in the kitchen, even her pitcher of tea.

The younger technician brought out a large sign. He walked to the front of the hotel. Following on his heels, Kate saw him tape the sign on the front doors. When he stepped away from the entrance, she read its message, 'Closed Until Further Notice.'

3

Kate grabbed the telephone and dialed the police station. 'Put me through to Chief Inspector Connor.' Waiting to hear the Inspector's deep voice, her hands frantically twisted the phone cord back and forth. Fear galloped across her mind like a wild stallion racing free across a mesa. He had to help her. They'd go under if the hotel didn't re-open soon.

The operator came back on. 'Sorry, ma'am. His line's busy. Can Sgt. Kennedy, his assistant, help you?'

'No. This is an emergency and I need DCI Connor. Can't you break in on his call?'

'Hold, please.'

'Connor.' The Inspector barked into the phone.

'Inspector, Kate Stanhope. Please help me. I don't know what to do . . . ' She broke into tears.

'What's the matter?' There was real concern in his voice.

'They've shut us down, and who knows when we'll be able to open again.' Taking a deep breath, Kate regained her composure and wiped her eyes.

'I'm sorry,' she tried to explain. 'It just hit me hard, seeing that 'Closed Until Further Notice' sign on the hotel's front door. Please forget I called you.' Kate hung up. As she stepped outside, the phone rang twice, then stopped.

She paced up and down in front of the hotel, trying to think logically. What should they do? Her savings wouldn't last long. Her mind whirled in search of a solution while the birds sang overhead, oblivious to her dilemma. Their chirping grated on her nerves. Irritable, she yelled, 'Shut up.' and glared upward.

Minutes later, a green Rover sped up the hotel driveway, stopping abruptly. Kate jerked with surprise when the Inspector jumped out.

'I had a break in my schedule.'

She must have sounded frantic on the telephone for the Inspector to take the time to drive over and check on her. Now that he was there, she felt calmer. 'Thanks for coming. Diane and Chris are in the hotel. If you don't mind, we'll talk here.' Kate led him down the drive to the same stone bench they'd used.

She tried to explain what had upset her. 'I know you warned me the police might shut us down, but I didn't really think it would happen. Now we're closed. God knows for how long. It'll ruin our business. Can't you speed up things so we can re-open?'

'I can't do that. The lab technicians have their job just as I have mine. What — .'

Clutching the edge of the cold stone bench beneath her, she interrupted him. The calmness she'd felt with his arrival slipped away. Panic spurred anger and she spoke abruptly. 'In case you haven't noticed, we depend on the hotel. Other than my savings, which won't last long, it's our one source of income. We've got to re-open soon.'

'Sorry, but you'll have to wait until the labs determine just what killed Penmar. Then you can resume business.' The Inspector raised his chin stubbornly.

'How can they be so sure that poison killed him? Couldn't it have been something else?' Kate knew she was clutching at straws, but it was all she had. 'Maybe the labs mixed up the test results with another case.' Her future was slipping between her fingers like grains of sand.

'No.' The Inspector scowled. The fierce expression distorted his handsome features. At that moment she pitied the criminal this angry man pursued.

Kate sucked in a deep breath, then another then asked, 'How long will the labs take?'

'I don't know. A few days, perhaps.' She watched as he got his temper under control. His tone was milder a moment later when he added, 'I'll let you know the moment they release the information. Now I've got to go back to work.' He got to his feet and turned to go.

'You have to go back to work?' The bile of rage rose in her throat. 'That's what we want to do here, but your stupid police department shut us down.'

'I sympathize with your feelings, but I don't know what I can do.' Opening his hands, he held them out in front of his body, palm side up, gesturing his powerlessness. 'Wait for the labs to do their work. We'll call you the minute we have the test results.'

Still frowning, the Inspector jumped into his car.

He revved the motor then sped through the open wrought-iron gates. In his haste, he almost hit a HRM postal service truck. Tires screamed as the Rover navigated a sheer curve further down the road.

He was in a big hurry to leave. Too bad there wasn't a policeman on a motorcycle handy to give him a speeding ticket. But he was a policeman. Fat chance of any uniformed officer giving him a ticket.

Angry and frustrated, Kate kicked the base

of the stone bench. When she scraped her toes, she yelped in pain. Then her anger turned inward. It wasn't the Inspector's fault, he was just doing his job.

Inside the hotel, Kate checked the hall clock. Time to go upstairs and see Mrs. Penmar. She carried her cordless phone with her to the next floor. When she tapped on the door, the lady was awake and waiting for her. Kate fluffed up the pillows on the bed, making Mrs. Penmar more comfortable. 'Here's a phone if you'd like to call Cecily now,' Kate handed her a cordless phone then helped the old lady dial her daughter's number.

'Cecily, it's Mom. Dad died last night, dear. I . . . ' Mrs. Penmar's voice broke and tears came in a torrent. The phone fell on the bed while she fumbled for a handkerchief.

'Mother, Mother? Are you there?'

Kate could hear a woman weeping when she picked up the telephone. 'Cecily, this is Kate Stanhope at King's Grant Hotel. Your parents stayed with us last night. I'm sure this comes as a great shock to you. We don't know yet what happened, but Mr. Penmar died during the night. Now your mother needs you and I'm sure you'll want to be with her.'

'Of course we do,' a husky voice responded. 'How do we get to your hotel?'

'Let me give you directions. You'll be coming south on A6. Exit at Penhurst. Go west to Ambleside, then take Lake Road south to the Methodist Church. Kendal Road is on the left across from the church, and we're up Kendal Road one mile east of the lake.'

'We'll see you later today.'

'I'll be expecting you.'

Three hours later Dr. Walton, the Inspector and Kate met Cecily and her husband in the living room.

'The police lab found poison in Mr. Penmar's stomach,' the Inspector informed the young woman.

Kate could see pain and disbelief on their faces. Cecily appeared to have difficulty accepting this new information on her father's death. She turned pale and her eyes filled with tears. Her balding husband blinked several times, then he removed his wireframe glasses and studiously wiped them with a handkerchief.

After a few moments of silence, Mrs. Penmar's daughter cleared her throat. 'Poison?' Doubt distorted her pleasant features. 'Do you mean food poisoning?'

'We don't think so. To be honest, we don't know what the poison was.' The Inspector hesitated. 'Please don't take offense, but I must ask . . . You were both at home on Friday evening?'

'Why in the world?' Cecily appeared confused. 'Oh, I see. You want to know if we have alibis? Yes, friends came in for bridge last evening. There're six people who can vouch for us.' She sounded a little insulted. 'I'll give you their names and phone numbers before we leave.'

'Thank you. I'm just following procedure. Now you'll want to see your mother. And as soon as the lab has the test results, I'll contact you so you can arrange for the funeral.'

'My father didn't have an enemy in this whole world. He was a well-liked man.' Cecily glared at Nick, then at Kate. 'I can't believe anyone would have wanted him dead.'

Cecily and her husband decided to wait and tell Mrs. Penmar about the poison when they got home. Kate helped them pack up the Penmars' possessions and walk the old lady to their car. She waved to Mrs. Penmar as the old lady's grim-faced son-in-law slowly drove their family car out of King's Grant grounds.

★ ★ ★

The next day Nick listened as one of the Lakeside temps told him what had happened in the kitchen the night of the murder.

36

'I was cleaning the stove Friday evening when Mr. Penmar walked in. He must have been thirsty because he picked up a glass, poured himself some herbal tea and drank it.'

'He didn't ask if he could have the tea?' Nick queried.

'No, he didn't say a word.' The young woman stared, wide-eyed at Nick. 'Could the poison have been in the tea?'

'We haven't heard yet. The lab's analyzing the contents of the food and beverages here Friday night.' Thanking the girls for their help, Nick let them go, then he picked up the phone and called the Lab Director.

'This is DCI Connor. I've just interviewed a Lakeside Temps employee here last night. Please check out the herbal tea, if you haven't already. I've a hunch that's where you'll find the poison. Let me know.' Nick hung up the receiver and thought about the case. He hoped Kate hadn't been involved in Penmar's poisoning. So far, a background check on her revealed nothing criminal. It was possible the poison had been meant for her.

He'd been furious with Kate the last time they met. Now Nick put himself in her shoes and rationalized that he might have reacted just as strongly if his livelihood was threatened. He liked her direct manner. Also, she'd handled herself well in a grim situation.

Nick shook his head. No involvements. I won't take that route again.

* * *

On Monday, Kate gazed out the kitchen window at the gray somber sky. 'The place's too quiet today.' She glanced at Mattie, Diane and Chris. They all sat gathered around the kitchen table.

'Anyone want another cup of tea?' Mattie stepped over to the sink, re-filled the copper tea kettle, and placed it on a stove burner.

'Our guests got off all right.' Diane's cheerful voice sounded encouraging. 'And no one appeared upset. Maybe we'll be able to re-open in a few days.'

Kate hadn't nicknamed Diane Little Miss Sunshine without reason. She always looked for the brighter side of things. Kate wished she could be so optimistic.

When the telephone on the counter rang, Kate jumped and spilled her tea, grabbing for the receiver.

'Hello,' she responded. 'Yes, speaking.' She gazed at her friends sitting quietly at the table. A moment later, she gripped the phone with both hands. 'Thank you for calling me.' Her hands were unsteady placing the telephone back in its cradle.

'Don't keep us in suspense!' pleaded Diane.

Tension filled the air. Chris fidgeted with the sugar bowl lid and Mattie wiped a dish towel back and forth over a table which was spotless already.

'That was Dr. Walton's office.' Kate stopped to clear her throat. 'The lab found an herb called cowbane in my tea. That's what killed Mr. Penmar. But what in the world is cowbane, and how did it get into my lemon balm tea?'

Then Kate realized what she'd just said and began to shake. Her legs went limp, and she sat down at the kitchen table, afraid she'd fall otherwise. Dizzy, she rested her head in her hands for a few moments, then sat up and brushed back the hair which had fallen over her face.

'I almost drank that tea while we were cooking dinner.' Her cup rattled against the saucer as she shakily raised it to her lips.

'You know what that means?' Diane bit her already short nails. Her voice quivered, a sure sign she was upset.

'Yes,' Kate spoke before Diane could. 'Someone expected me to drink the tea.'

'But who'd want to hurt you?' Chris's boyish face looked puzzled.

'That's a good question, and one I'll have

to answer,' a deep voice called from the doorway.

Surprised, Kate turned and found the Inspector leaning in the open Dutch door.

'Could we talk for a few minutes, Mrs. Stanhope? Outside on the terrace will be fine.' He pulled the kitchen door open and waited for her.

When they stood together, the Inspector frowned.

'Mrs. Stanhope, . . . ' He stopped and raked his fingers through already unruly black hair.

Gazing in Nick's direction, Kate felt an unexpected warmth flow through her body. Then she remembered their last meeting and flushed. He must think she was a horrible person. Feeling embarrassed, she considered how to make amends. How could she put it so he'd know she was ashamed of her poor behavior.

'I owe you an apology for the last time we saw each other. My behavior was completely unreasonable, and I do apologize.' Her stomach clenched. Everything she'd worked for was falling apart. Could he possibly understand that?

'It's all right. I shouldn't have lost my temper. Let's forget it and start afresh.' He accepted her apology with grace.

She smiled in agreement. Glancing his way, Kate couldn't help but admire his extraordinary brown eyes, flaked and ringed with gold.

'I expect we'll see each other on a regular basis until the case is solved,' she said. 'You can call me Kate if you like.'

He hesitated, then nodded. 'All right, and I'm Nick.'

'You received the lab report saying they found a poison called cowbane in my herbal tea, didn't you?'

'Yes. Who do you think it was meant for?' His dark eyes bore into hers as he moved so they stood closer to each other.

Kate hoped he didn't notice the tremor in her voice. Being in such close proximity to the man was unnerving. 'I'm so confused,' she stammered, almost afraid to put her thoughts into words. When he didn't respond at once, she explained. 'The Penmars were only here overnight so that rules them out.

'Besides, from what his daughter says, the man was easy going and well-liked and had no enemies. All of the others were strangers except Mattie, Diane and Chris.'

'Go on.' Nick seemed to be absorbing every word she spoke.

'Diane and Chris are newcomers. She and I worked together in New York City.'

Nick leaned forward. 'Just how well did you know her?'

'Reasonably well, though we weren't best friends. The paper hired us both as assistant food editors the same month six years ago. Diane and I worked on a number of assignments together for the two years I was there.'

'Did you see her outside working hours?'

'Yes, on occasion.' Kate felt him probing for information. Surely he didn't suspect Diane? 'She liked to party. Diane always had a boy friend and he would have a friend who she wanted me to date.' Kate smiled, remembering.

Nick spoke up. 'Excuse me. I hope you won't think I'm being too personal, but someone as attractive as you wouldn't need a 'Diane' to get you dates.'

She smiled, pleased with his compliment.

'You married a well-to-do, older man, a British banker. Did you detect any jealousy on Diane's part? Did you part as friends when you left New York?'

'No, she wasn't jealous, and yes, we parted as friends.' A little annoyed, Kate reminded herself Nick had to ask questions. It was part of his job. 'She hasn't harbored a grudge because of my marriage. I'm sure of that.' She glanced down at the stone terrace for a moment. How could she convince Nick about Diane?

'Maybe this will help you understand our relationship. We shared a dream, of opening and running a small, select hotel in which we would serve exquisitely prepared meals in just the right setting.' Feeling his eyes move across her face to her lips, she looked away.

'So after your husband's death . . . ' He waited for her to continue.

'Right. I called Diane and we made plans. That was after I found out how little my husband had left me other than the property. I had to do something in order to keep King's Grant.'

'I understand. And there was no obstacle to her coming, no husband or fiancé?'

'No, the only people unenthusiastic about our venture turned out to be Diane's parents. Of course, she's their only child. They just didn't want her to come to the U.K. But she's promised to visit them as often as possible.' Kate leaned on the stone wall around the terrace and gazed down on the gardens.

'All right, you've convinced me that Diane is no Nellie Borden.'

When an unexpected smile lit up Nick's face, Kate could have applauded. He was handsome, solemn-faced. But he appeared

43

warmer and more attractive the second he smiled.

'On to Chris Lewis.' Nick moved to Kate's second staff member. 'All I know about him is he's British, and judging from his physique, he must be into physical fitness.'

Kate grinned. 'I guess. He's bright and hard-working, a little younger than Diane and me. We're both thirty. I believe Chris's twenty-six or twenty-seven. He appeared out of the blue one day after I'd received poor response to my ad in the local paper.'

'What are his skills?' Nick leaned on the wall next to her and she picked up a trace of his cologne, a light, citrus scent.

Concentrate, she told herself, entranced by the man. 'I advertised for a 'dogsbody' or jack of all trades. Chris fits our needs for that position perfectly. He can do everything, from landscaping to repairing my old Rolls. He's our Mr. Fix-It and doesn't mind rolling up his sleeves and scrubbing floors, painting or wallpapering or anything else.'

'Sounds great. Does he have any formal education?'

'By profession he's an engineer, but he got burned out by the layoffs in the defense industry. When we met him, Chris was hiking through the Lake District. He was staying at a youth hostel on the lake when he saw my ad in the local paper. He immediately applied and I hired him. In fact, I interviewed him in my gown and robe.'

Seeing Nick's eyebrows go up, way up, Kate grinned. 'It's not like that. Chris was so eager to apply, he came over without calling ahead and turned up about five in the morning. I was still sleeping here in the house. Mattie's yelling and her Scottie's barking woke me. She was about to take a broom to Chris when I came downstairs. I guess she thought he was up to no good.'

When Nick smiled again, his lop-sided smile tugged at Kate's heart.

'And you hired him on the spot?'

'Right.'

'With references, of course?'

'I didn't need any. I could tell Chris fit our requirements.'

Out came a frown telling her Nick didn't agree or approve. 'I see, so you don't really know the man?'

She sighed, trying to be patient. 'I know all I need to know. He's not only hard-working but loyal to the core.'

'You're very trusting, Kate. I hope no one disappoints you.' A wistful tone slipped into his voice.

Looking at his face, all serious again, she thought . . . If you only knew. Stephen disappointed me beyond belief, but that was only one experience.

'And Mattie?' Nick moved down his list.

'She's been housekeeper for the family off and on for many years, came here as a young woman from a village outside Glasgow and never went back home, except to visit. She's completely trustworthy. I count on her, depend on her and love her dearly.' What more could she say about the woman who'd filled the gap left by her own mother's death?

'I see. So, we're left with you, Kate.'

Kate's heart thumped hard and fast, then she asked the question which plagued her, one she was almost afraid to ask.

'Was the poison meant for me?'

'Why would anyone want to kill you?' His voice was husky.

'I don't know.' A lump rose in her throat. Who could want her dead? She resolved not to cry. She'd never met a man who felt comfortable with a woman's tears. Nick was probably not the exception.

'Am I in danger?'

Nick didn't answer, but his serious expression didn't reassure Kate.

'I hope you aren't trying to frighten me.' The hairs on the nape of her neck prickled. 'Why me? Why would anyone want to kill me?'

'Do you have any enemies?' Nick frowned.

'If I do, they've kept their feelings to themselves,' she retorted.

'Anyone who might be envious of you?'

'No, I don't think so.'

'Does your husband have any family living besides you?'

'Only a niece and nephew. Everyone else is deceased.'

'Let's sit down and you can tell me about the Stanhopes.'

They pulled together two rustic chairs. When they were seated, side by side, Kate continued. 'Stephen was 56, thirty years my senior, on our wedding day. Before we met, he'd spent all of his free time with family. During those years, tragedy struck the Stanhopes twice.'

Nick raised an eyebrow, looking restless and appealing. She looked away, afraid to gaze in those dark brown eyes, afraid he'd see her yearning. Years ago her mother had told her not to lie, that her face gave her away every time.

What was she telling him? Oh, yes, about the family.

'First, his brother Alex, a nature photographer, died with his wife and son in a small plane crash in the Amazon. And ten years later, Charles, Stephen's other brother, hanged himself in his cell after being sent to prison for his role in a kidnapping.'

'This all happened before you met your husband?'

'Yes. His father and mother had died years earlier. In a ten year period, Stephen lost both of his brothers. Only Charles and Clarissa, his brother's children, survived. Stephen named them his heirs.'

Nick's eyes flickered with interest.

'Two years ago, after Stephen and I moved to King's Grant, he abruptly changed his will and named me his heir. He cut his nephew and niece out of the will, except for token gifts.'

Kate rose and walked to the end of the terrace. She stood gazing down on the rose gardens.

'How did they take the news?'

'Clarissa didn't seem to mind, but Charles became upset. I remember he pouted for weeks.' Nick's eyes burned into her back until Kate turned to face him. 'But he's over that a long time ago. We're all friends. Besides, they're wealthy and don't need King's Grant.'

Nick shrugged but didn't disagree.

As they went back inside, one thought persisted. Was there someone who wanted her dead? And why?

4

Early Tuesday morning, Nick pulled into Nolan's Greenery parking lot. He spotted the owner hosing down a shipment of flame red geraniums.

'Good morning, Pat.'

Pat Nolan, a stocky, bearded, jean-clad man, turned around. 'Morning, Nick.'

Nick and Pat had met at a picnic last fall. When time permitted, they got together for supper and a game of darts at the Black Swan Pub down the hill from Nick's condo.

'What can I do for you? Want an antique rose bush? They're on sale this week.' Pat scratched his beard and looked hopeful.

'Thanks, but this's a business call,' replied Nick.

Pat turned off his hose and gestured for Nick to follow him to the pre-fab shingle structure he used for his office. 'Sit down and tell me what brings you out here so early this morning.' Pat flopped on a rickety chair by a desk loaded down with small, wooden bird houses and kids' gardening kits.

As usual, Nick found no other chair in the room. Shooing off a large orange cat that hissed at him, he took a seat on a barrel labelled Bunny Trails by the window. 'This won't take long. Do your employees know much about herbs?'

'Well, there's Gregson. He's not in yet, has an appointment with the dentist. His tooth hurt so much, he finally agreed to go. He'll be here around 11 o'clock.'

Nick sensed his friend's mounting curiosity. 'When he gets to work, could you spare him for a couple of hours? I need an herb expert to take a look at the King's Grant Hotel gardens.'

'Isn't that the Stanhopes' old place on Kendall Road?' Nolan stroked the new beard that had taken him months to grow.

'That's right. I guess you heard a tourist got himself a dose of poison and died there last weekend?'

'Yes. I read an article on it in the papers.'

'If you'd ask Gregson to examine the hotel gardens. I need to know if there're any unusual herbs or plants, especially an herb called cowbane.' Nick handed Nolan a copy of a drawing Sergeant Kennedy had located at the library. 'It's a member of the carrot family, but you wouldn't want to feed it to your pet rabbit. It's quite deadly.'

'I'll get Greg over there when he comes to work.' Pat took the sketch, folded it and put it carefully in his shirt pocket.

'Great, I appreciate your help. Let me know what I owe you for his services,' Nick said.

'No charge. You can buy our drinks next time.'

'Thanks a lot.' Nick stood and shook Pat's hand, then Pat's phone rang. Picking up the telephone, he waved goodbye. Nick climbed into the Rover and headed back to work.

★   ★   ★

That afternoon Kate walked the grounds, extra alert since Penmar's death. Walking by an overgrown boxwood hedge near the herb garden, a ripple of movement caught her attention. She looked away, then saw it again, out of the corner of her eye. Chris walked out of the hotel through the kitchen door, so she put a finger over her lips and gestured silently toward the boxwood.

Chris nodded and crept quietly toward the hedge. After a brief pause, he lunged.

'Gottcha,' he barked.

'Let me go,' a frightened voice cried out.

Chris brought Kate his trophy. A smallish man in overalls wiggled in his unrelenting clutch. Kate bit her lip to keep from laughing.

'Look what I've found, crawling on his

belly, like a worm, through our boxwood.' Chris shook his prisoner like a dog shakes a bone.

'I can explain. Please put me down.' The man's tremulous voice rang with fear.

He looked like a toy, the way Chris dangled him. 'Better put him down, Chris.' Kate could sense the small man's fright.

Dumped on the ground, he straightened his clothes, pulling the remaining shreds of his dignity around himself. 'It was DCI Connor. He wanted me to — .'

'To snoop around my property?' Kate exploded with rage. 'What did he expect you to find? A patch of cowbane I grow to poison selected guests?' The man was unbelievable. To pull a stunt like this. How could he? Nick and she had talked several times. By now he should have some idea of the kind of person she was. Did he see her as a murderess?

'Get in my car. What's your name, anyway?' Her anger mixed with disappointment. Nick obviously didn't trust her. Who did he trust?

'We're going to see DCI Connor. You can tell him what you found in person.'

With the nurseryman beside her, Kate navigated the busy streets, driving slowly. Lunchtime and blue skies had brought out crowds of office workers, each in search of his own patch of sunshine. Tourists with more time to spare, drifted languidly, drawn to one or another attraction. How pleasant to have nothing more demanding on your schedule than a visit to the attractive shops or a ride on the lake.

Reaching the Constabulary, Kate parked in the rear of the building and guided the nurseryman through the revolving doors to the front desk. 'We're here to see DCI Connor if he's in.' Her nostrils twitched, inhaling the spicy fragrance of pastrami in the constable's sandwich. Her stomach growled, a reminder that she'd left King's Grant before lunch.

'Yes, ma'am. His office is down that way.' The constable directed them to one of the long corridors radiating from the front desk.

As Kate and the nurseryman walked down the hall, she found the constabulary built like a rabbit warren. Looking closely, she could see where the new structure had been added to the old.

Turning a corner, Kate spotted Nick, loping along, his nose stuck in a report. She stepped around the corner, out of sight.

'DCI Connor.' Gregson's voice trembled a bit.

'Yes?' Nick turned and glanced at a man in Nolan's Greenery shirt and overalls. 'Gregson? What did you find?'

'Nothing, not one single poisonous plant on the place.' The little man puffed up his chest and sounded as pleased as if he alone were responsible.

Then Kate burst forward. 'Did you think I was the murderer? We caught this man snooping in our gardens. He's lucky Chris didn't shoot him for trespassing.' She felt her anger fade, looking at Nick. She had to admit she enjoyed looking at him.

'Kate, I'm sorry.' Nick seemed shaken at her sudden appearance. 'We needed to be sure.' He turned to Gregson. 'Thank you for your help. Let me reimburse you for your time.' He fished in his pocket, pulled out a £20 and handed it to the other man.

'You're quite welcome, sir.' The £20 rapidly disappeared into Gregson's pocket. 'If you ever need any more help with plant or herb identification, feel free to call on me.' He handed Nick a soiled card from Nolan's, his own name carefully printed in the lower right corner.

'If you need a lift, Mr. Gregson, wait outside. I'll give you a lift back to the nursery in just a minute,' Nick offered, politely.

The nurseryman thanked Nick and walked toward the exit.

Did she have a dirty face? Nick kept staring at her. Maybe it was a new method of police intimidation, staring.

'You've checked out our gardens now, so I expect you'll need to find other places to look. Here's a suggestion. Why not visit the herbal shop over on Lake Road? Maybe the owner can help.'

'Thanks, I plan to.' There was a curious glint in Nick's dark eyes.

'Well, I won't keep you.' He was making her nervous. Kate turned and walked away. She felt his eyes following her until she left the building.

That evening, Kate helped Mattie and Diane prepare dinner.

'And Mattie, . . . you should have seen the look on Nick's, I mean, the Inspector's face, when I stepped out in front of him. He looked like a kid caught with his hand in the proverbial cookie jar.'

'If I didn't know better, I'd say you like the Inspector.' Mattie teased Kate.

'You couldn't be more wrong.' Kate scoffed at the idea.

* * *

After work, Nick drove to the Herb Shop a few blocks away and found a closed sign on the front door. He knocked, just in case the owner hadn't left yet, then he rattled the door knob. There was no response. He pressed his face against a window and peered inside. The small shop was dark. He'd go home and call. As he unlocked his front door, the living room phone rang. Picking it up, he was surprised to hear his ex-wife's voice.

'Valerie? Is everything all right in Manchester?'

'As all right as it can be with you in the Lake District. Isn't it about time you came home?'

She just wouldn't accept the facts. Nick strained to remain patient. 'Let me remind you again. We've divorced and we both have new lives.' From her slurred speech, he could tell she'd been drinking. She still wanted him back, but that marriage had died years ago, even before he'd applied for a divorce.

'Nick, are you seeing someone now?'

'Not really. But you should try to meet someone, yourself. You're a young woman. You shouldn't waste your life, waiting for something that won't happen. Have you considered going back into therapy? It could help you to feel better about yourself.'

She didn't reply.

'Well, I need to go. Next time I hear from you, I want to hear you're in therapy. Have them send me the bill. Goodbye, Valerie, and good luck to you.' Nick hung up the phone.

Out of the blue, a hunger attack drove him into the kitchen where he dug in his almost empty refrigerator. Eying its meager contents, he realized he needed to grocery shop soon or stop eating. Beer, one avocado, several slices of deli ham and a loaf of rye bread didn't constitute a nutritional diet. Nick created an avocado and ham on rye and opened the remaining bottle of beer.

Fred, his golden canary, burst forth with a brief aria, reminding Nick to feed him, also.

Slipping off his loafers and removing his tie, Nick munched his sandwich in front of the television set in the living room and thought again of Kate. Suspicious by nature and wary of women, he'd concluded the poison had no doubt been meant for Kate instead of Penmar. But he could find no motive. Under Kate's warm, pleasant exterior, he sensed strength, a self-sufficiency that he found refreshing. And she seemed unaware how attractive she was with that auburn hair and those green eyes. Stop thinking about her. She can't mean anything to you.

Again at bedtime, Kate's face flashed in front of him. He could see her fighting back tears while she struggled with the idea someone wanted to kill her. Nick admired her courage. Even faced with danger, she didn't fall apart.

Nick was becoming increasingly uneasy. His policeman's instincts were alerted. If he wasn't mistaken, there'd been one attempt on Kate's life. But that didn't mean the killer wouldn't try again.

5

Kate lay quietly in bed next morning, watching the early sunbeams weave a pattern on her bedroom wall. Outside, a breeze toyed with her windchimes. Now and then she'd hear a tinkle. She admitted she was drawn to Nick, but she'd keep that information to herself. He must have a girl friend. The man was extremely attractive.

Later, as she pedaled her exercise bike, Kate realized it'd been a week since she heard from Clarissa. She picked up her cellular phone and punched in their number.

Kate's niece by marriage answered the phone.

'It's Kate, dear. If you're not busy this morning, I'd like to come by for a few minutes.'

After a long pause, Clarissa replied. 'We may not be home. Could you call me back? Charles isn't here, and I don't know what he's planned for the rest of the day.' An unaccustomed reserve rang in her passive voice.

'All right. I'll talk to you later.' Kate hung up and frowned at her tousled image in the mirror. Clarissa and she'd become good friends since Kate married Stephen. What'd happened to cause this coolness?

Charles burst through their foyer and slammed the door as he called out to Clarissa. Not finding her on the ground floor, he stamped upstairs.

'Clarissa, where are you?' He yelled, getting madder by the minute.

At the top of the stairs, he almost collided with his sister as she ran into the upper hall.

Grabbing her thin shoulders, he gave her a good shake. 'You fool!' he snarled, then he managed to curb his temper.

'What's wrong with you, Charles?' Her voice squeaked.

'You've really done it this time. I just heard what happened at King's Grant. An old man died there last weekend after he drank a glass of Kate's herbal tea. And we know who concocted that tea, don't we?'

'Died? An old man? What are you talking about?' A look of horror streaked across her face.

'I forgot,' he muttered. 'Cook's here, isn't she?'

Clarissa nodded.

Charles put his finger to his lip and peered over the banister. As if on cue, a whirling sound came from the vicinity of the kitchen. Charles led his sister into the spare bathroom she used as her 'workroom' when she puttered with herbs, and shut the door.

'I believe the paper said it was a Cornishman. His name was Penwithe. No, it was Penmar. He and his wife were guests overnight at Kate's hotel.'

'This isn't what you planned. Kate . . . ' Clarissa's thin white fingers clutched the counter-top.

Then she reached for her brother's hand.

Charles backed away, ignoring the plea in her eyes. 'I deposited it in Kate's tea pitcher, but you found the recipe so the responsibility is yours, too.' If the police caught up with them, he'd make sure they understood Clarissa had helped him.

'But it was your idea and you picked the herb,' Clarrisa reminded her brother.' I guess you got the wrong plant.'

'We're in a real mess.' Charles slumped against the tile wall, then stood erect.

'I only tried to help you.' Clarissa covered her mouth with a shaky hand and sobbed.

'I know, I know. But no more, please. If you want to help, don't do anything else.'

'All right, but remember, it was your idea.'

'That's my girl.' Charles touched her silky blonde hair. Clarissa greatly resembled their mother except, in the old photographs, Renata had black hair.

'Then you forgive me?' She straightened up, not clinging to him like she usually did.

'Of course. How could I stay angry with the only girl I've ever loved.' Noticing the annoyed expression on his sister's face, he drew her into his arms and planted a reconciliatory kiss on her cheek. 'But now we have to convince Kate to sell King's Grant.' The estate remained one of his two loves. His sister was the other. 'All of my life, I've waited, knowing King's Grant would be mine one day. Now, thanks to Kate, it won't be.' If only Uncle Stephen hadn't met Kate. 'We'll have to sell The Folly. I guess I should have been more careful playing the stock market.' He'd lost again and again. Not much of their fortune remained, only their home. When the hotel agent offered ten million pounds, Charles had jumped at the chance to pay their debts and start over in a new place. To do that, however, he must convince Kate to sell King's Grant to the hotel chain, also. For that he'd get a commission plus his half of the £10 million. The hotel agent had given his word.

Now Charles pulled Clarissa to him. 'You know it's us against the whole world, don't you?' He squeezed her thin shoulders. When she flinched, he hoped he hadn't bruised them earlier.

'Yes. What would I do without you?'

'And you trust me to take care of you?'

'Yes.'

Did he hear a hint of resentment in her voice? 'You know that no one else, including Kate, really cares what happens to us?'

'Yes, as you say, it's us against the world.'

By now they repeated a litany, his words and her response.

Years ago, Charles had convinced thirteen-year-old Clarissa it was all right to comfort each other. Now he waited for her to ask him not to leave her. Today she didn't ask.

Perplexed, he said nothing, then he took her hand, gently pulling her down the hall to his bedroom. As he unbuttoned her blouse and caressed her small, firm breasts, the phone on his dresser rang. 'Let it ring. It's probably just a pest call.' Charles kissed her shoulder.

'It could be Kate.' Clarissa stirred. 'I forgot to tell you, but she called earlier, wanting to come by to see us.' Pushing his hands away, she picked up the phone on its third ring. 'Hello. Yes, Kate. We'll be home the rest of the day. I've an idea, why don't you come for lunch?'

Charles thought he detected a hint of defiance in Clarissa's voice? No, it must be his imagination.

'How about one o'clock?' Clarissa frowned at him while she listened. 'Good, we'll see you then.' She hung up the phone.

He didn't imagine it. Now ice-blue eyes the same shade as his glared at him. What happened? Oh, well, at least he could pump Kate for information on the police investigation. Did they have any clues? He hoped not.

'I'll go downstairs and tell Cook we're having company for lunch. She'll be pleased. It's been a long time since guests came for a meal.' Clarissa buttoned her blouse and walked out of his room without a backward glance.

* * *

Kate hung up the phone and turned to Mattie as she entered the gatehouse kitchen.

'Clarissa's voice sounded so strained. I'll try to find out what's wrong when I lunch with them today.'

'Be careful.'

Kate knew what Mattie meant. The housekeeper didn't like the young man who reminded her of his scheming father.

Kate drove up in front of The Folly a few minutes before one o'clock. Walking up to the front door, she saw two industrious sparrows, hard at work, building a nest in a spruce in the yard.

Clarissa opened the door and met Kate halfway up the walk leading to the handsome French Provincial mansion.

'I'm so glad to see you.' Clarissa hugged Kate. 'When Cook heard you'd be with us for lunch, she suggested Cornish hens and that stuffing you like.'

'With apricots and pecans? Hooray.' Kate examined the other young woman's face. Clarissa's eyes looked swollen. Had she been crying? 'Is everything all right over here?'

'Of course. We heard about the man who died at King's Grant last weekend. What a horrible thing to happen at your hotel.'

Clarissa held the door open for Kate then led her into a large formal living room. Kate's stomach rumbled as she picked up the scent of fruit baking.

'How about a glass of sherry before lunch?'

'Lovely.' Kate looked around. 'Where's your brother?'

'Who knows? I've begun to think we're together too much.' Clarissa poured them each a glass of sherry.

Kate sipped hers, savoring its nutty sweetness as the smooth wine slid down her throat.

Clarissa had smoothed her hair and leaned forward to speak when Charles appeared in the doorway. The brother and sister were both tall, angular, with white blonde hair and blue eyes. There the resemblance ended. Clarissa was pleasant and sweet once you got past her shyness. Charles only turned on the charm when it suited his purposes.

'Secrets, secrets. You tell me yours, and I'll tell you mine, sister dear.' Charles smirked at the two young women.

Clarissa flushed. 'You know I don't have any secrets from you.'

Her brother opened his mouth to reply then Cook walked into the room. 'Luncheon is served.' Her North Country voice was as stiff as a little girl's starched pinafore. You would've thought she was announcing a formal dinner party instead of a simple luncheon for three.

As Kate followed Cook into the dining room, she admired the burgundy moire fabric which covered the walls.

Charles seated Kate, then Clarissa before he took a seat at the head of the long mahogany table. It had been the setting for many lively dinner parties years ago when

Charles and Clarissa's parents were alive.

'What did the police say killed your guest?' Charles promptly inquired about the tragedy at the hotel while his cold, pale eyes roamed Kate's face.

Uneasy, Kate shifted in her chair. 'Cowbane, a medieval herb. It's a poisonous member of the carrot family. The police inspector in charge of the investigation told me cowbane's as lethal as belladonna and mandrake's root.'

Clarissa dropped her knife onto the floor. 'Oops.' Picking it up, she wiped it on her damask napkin.

'Do the police have any leads yet?' Charles toyed with his spoon then gazed across the table at Kate. Not for the first time, he reminded her of a cat, sleek and unpredictable, even predatory.

She watched his long fingers while a chill raced up and down her spine. Why was he so interested? Perhaps because the murder took place at King's Grant. 'If they do, they haven't informed me. I hope they find the killer soon. Monsters like that shouldn't be free to prowl around and hurt innocent people.' Kate sighed. 'Also, we need to re-open.'

Kate played with the food on her plate. Talking about the murder, she'd lost her appetite but noticed the topic didn't upset Charles. For a thin man, he kept a hearty appetite. As she watched, he tore into his Cornish game hen with the gusto of a lion chewing on its kill.

'Maybe an informant will come forward with information on the killer. I wish we could offer a reward, but it's out of the question. Our funds are low.' Money was tight. Kate didn't know how long they could hold out.

'Can't we find another topic to discuss? I get chills at the mere thought of that poor man.' Clarissa pleaded.

Kate glanced at Clarissa who appeared paler than usual. She picked up her water glass and examined it, then she fidgeted with her napkin, folding and re-folding it.

'Sorry, dear.' Kate reached across the table and patted her hand. Kate didn't understand why Clarissa would be nervous. She hadn't even known Mr. Penmar.

'Let's move on to more pleasant topics.' Charles wiped his hands on his napkin then asked, 'Have you talked to the hotel agent recently?'

'No, and the last time we spoke, I told him my answer was final.' Kate raised both eyebrows. 'It infuriates me. They want to buy our properties and tear down our homes to build a resort hotel. I get ill, just thinking of it.' Gazing across the table, she saw a worried expression on Charles's face. 'You don't have to sell, do you?'

'As a matter of fact . . . yes, we do. I haven't wanted to worry you, but I've made several bad investments on the stock market this year . . . ' He shook his head. 'The Folly is all that we have left.'

'But your fortune, didn't you inherit several million?' Kate's eyebrows went up.

'It's all gone.' Charles looked sad. 'The hotel chain will give us £10 million. At first, they just wanted our estate. Now, the architects say they need more land for the new hotel. Combining the acreage of The Folly and King's Grant, it will be just enough.'

'Never.' Pressured, Kate jumped up from the table and bumped the chair against the wainscoting.

'Think about it. £10 million is a lot of money.' A hopeful smile flitted across Charles' face. 'With your half, you could buy or build another hotel or invest and live on the interest. The hotel agent asked me to talk to you.'

'I'm sorry, but it's out of the question for me to sell King's Grant.' Kate regained her seat. 'You like to have your own way, but this time you'll be disappointed. I won't turn our lives upside down to accomodate your investment losses.'

Cook brought in three raspberry mousses.

'Enough said.' Clarissa called a halt to the discussion as she pointed to the fluffy, pink concoctions before them. 'Let's eat our dessert, then you and I'll go upstairs, Kate. I have a recipe you might adapt for the hotel when it re-opens.' She tasted her raspberry mousse. 'Delicious.'

A few minutes later, Kate accompanied Clarissa up the steep staircase and down a Berber-carpeted hall to Clarissa's blue and gold bedroom.

'You're right, this could work well at the hotel.' Kate eyed a recipe for warmed scallop salad. 'Let me take it home and run a copy. I'll get it back to you soon.'

Preparing to leave, Kate turned to the other woman. 'How do you feel about selling your home?'

'I hate to leave, but Charles says we must. Anyway, I'm twenty-one and it's time I had a life of my own. Charles has cared for me and dominated me all of our lives.' Clarissa hesitated, a lone tear trickled down her cheek. 'If I tell you something in confidence, will you promise not to tell anyone?'

'Of course, but don't cry.' Alarmed, Kate

reached out and took the other woman's hand. It was icy cold.

'It's over now, but for the past eight years Charles and I've been lovers.' Her hand clutched Kate's so hard Kate winced.

'My God, did he force you?' Kate gasped.

'No, I guess you could say he convinced a plain, scrawny thirteen-year-old girl that we didn't have anyone except each other. I was afraid he'd go away like Mother and Father if I didn't let him into my bed.' Tears glided down Clarissa's face.

'The sick bastard. I don't see how you've stayed under the same roof with him all of these years.' Kate guided the weeping girl across the room to a loveseat. They sat together, Kate's arm around Clarissa.

'Where would I have gone? He would've found me, brought me home.' Clarissa mopped her wet cheeks. 'On my twenty-first birthday, I came into funds Mother set aside for me, so now I can be independent of Charles. But you see why I need to get out of here?'

'You could have come to me anytime the past four years.'

'Not while Uncle lived. I feared he'd kill Charles if he found out.'

Kate patted Clarissa's hand. 'Please don't go too far. I'd miss you.'

Driving back to the hotel, Kate was bemused by the revelations of the afternoon. Kate felt no fondness for Charles but hadn't dreamed he was evil. It was best that Clarissa leave. So much was changing right before Kate's eyes. She mentally braced herself for what would come next.

When she stopped at the gatehouse to change into jeans and a shirt, the phone ring.

'Hello. Hello? Hello?' Kate could hear shallow breathing on the other end of the line. Then her caller hung up. Who kept calling her? This was the first anonymous call during the day. The others had come late at night. Kate couldn't fathom what pleasure anyone would derive from such a pastime. She dropped the receiver. Not wanting to be alone, she stepped out on her front porch, locked the door and hurried up the sloping driveway to the hotel.

6

Alone in his office, Nick thought of Kate. The few times he'd seen her, she'd been concerned, serious. All at once, he wanted to see her smile, hear her laugh. Stop that! You don't want to get involved. He jerked his concentration back to the case. Daydreams didn't solve crimes.

After several attempts, Nick finally reached the owner of the herbal shop.

'Mel Martin, speaking.' A whispery voice answered.

'Hello. This is DCI Connor at Windermere Constabulary. I need some information on herbs. Could I see you today?'

'I'll have some free time this afternoon, say three o'clock. Do you know my business address?'

'Yes. Thank you for seeing me. I'll be there.'

Two hours later, Nick checked the clock on his dashboard. He was on time. Punctuality was important to Nick who insisted his subordinates always be on time, much to the chagrin of a few younger officers.

Parking the Rover outside the Bowness

73

Herbalist, he admired a silver Jaguar then he eyed the small shop, one of several in a cluster of stores. A hand-printed sign inside the front door and two dusty displays of books in a display window gave him the impression this wasn't a thriving business. As he stepped inside, a tiny bell rang, tinkling its silvery tones above the poorly lit entrance.

A man stepped out of the gloomy interior. 'Inspector Connor? I've been expecting you.'

Nick shook the soft, slightly moist hand Martin offered. 'If you'll come with me? We'll go back to my office. It's more comfortable there.'

In the meager light at the front of the store, Nick could barely see the man. The herbalist turned on his heel and walked ahead of Nick toward the back of the building, through a dim maze of dusty shelves full of books and dried plants.

As Nick followed Martin, the older man shrieked and raced through the aisles. Fearing his host was in danger, Nick chased after him. He rounded a corner and found Martin sitting on the floor laughing.

'That fiend of a cat.' Martin chuckled. 'We have a game we play once or twice a week. She knows where I keep the catnip and sneaks in here to raid that shelf. Then I scream and chase her. She's my best customer for catnip.' He pointed to the tip of an orange tail protruding from beneath a shelf.

Amused, Nick knelt down and heard a loud purr. The faint smell of mint wafted up to him.

Martin shrugged. 'I've got to order more. She's eaten my entire supply of catnip.' He led Nick back to his office. Pulling a rickety chair from under an antique roller-top desk, the shop owner flopped. 'You can move those.' He waved, vaguely, in the direction of an order of new books which covered the seat of the other chair in the room.

Nick stacked the books in a corner and sat down. 'Mr. Martin, I appreciate your seeing me today.' Glancing at the herbalist in the well-lit office, Nick observed Martin's drab-colored clothing blended well with the gray-green walls. Then Martin moved his arm and a gold Rolex watch flashed on his scrawny wrist.

'Not at all. I must admit I'm curious how I can help the District police.' Martin smiled, apparently glad to have company. Nick hadn't seen any customers in the small store besides the catnip thief.

The desk phone burred. 'Bowness Herbalist, how may I help you?' Martin listened.

'Just a moment, please.' Putting his hand over the phone, he hissed, 'Do you see a book called *Herbs in the Fall* in that stack?'

What an interesting visit. Now he was a book clerk. His assistant would laugh. Kneeling, Nick checked through the new titles. 'No, but you have *Herbs for Pets*.'

The herbalist relayed this information to the customer on the phone. 'Good, we'll see you this afternoon. Goodbye.' He hung up the telephone and turned to Nick. 'Sure you wouldn't like a part-time job? You just sold a book for me.'

Nick smiled, shaking his head. Back to business. He cleared his throat. 'You've heard a tourist died last Friday night at the King's Grant Hotel?' With the local news coverage on radio, tv and in the newspapers, Nick figured most people in the area knew about the tragedy.

'Of course. What a sad business.'

'The labs have determined the victim died from a dose of poison,' Nick said.

'But how can I help?' Thinly disguised impatience seeped into Martin's voice.

'We've identified the poison as cowbane, an ancient herb. I need to know if it grows in this area and where.'

'I've read a lot on herbs and have seen cowbane twice, only once as a living plant.'

Martin's chair squeaked as he shifted position.

'And where would we find it?' Was he being evasive?

'You'd have to go to a remote, swampy place to find such an herb.' Warmed up, the herbalist spoke enthusiastically.

Nick asked again. 'To your knowledge, would you find it near the lakes in this area of Cumbria?'

'Not around here. The herbalist creased his brow, thinking. 'Maybe in the less populated areas west of here around Wastwater or close to the Irish Sea. Hold on, I just remembered something.' Martin's eyes lit up. 'Earlier this year a young woman came into my business. She wanted books on medicinal herbs.'

Nick leaned forward. 'Did she inquire about cowbane?'

'No. She didn't mention any herbs by name, just the group in general. But, as an herbalist, I can tell you medicinal herbs include poisonous plants like cowbane, belladonna and mandrake's root.'

Martin turned in his desk chair and reached for a 3×5 filebox on his desk. Fishing in it, he pulled out a card. Nick looked over Martin's shoulder and read its heading, Herbs, Medicinal. Other than that, the card was blank.

'I usually write customers' names and telephone numbers on one of these cards with their requests.' Martin frowned. 'I didn't get her name, but her phone number's here somewhere. She asked me to call when my new shipment came in.'

'How long ago did she visit you?'

'Let's see, it must have been early this Spring, perhaps late March.'

'You have an excellent memory.'

'Not really.' The shopkeeper beamed at the praise. 'It's just that she was so striking, tall, with long black hair and blue eyes.' Sighing, Martin dug in his cluttered desk like a squirrel looking for autumn nuts. 'Where did I put that phone number?' He fretted.

Next, he scrambled through the papers on his desk, creating more of a mess. 'I apologize. I can't put my hands on it, but it's here somewhere, I'm sure. When I locate it, I'll call you.'

'I'd appreciate that. I doubt she has anything to do with the murder, but I have to cover all possibilities. I'd be quite interested in talking to her.'

'Leave me your card, and I'll get in touch.'

'I'll look forward to hearing from you.' Nick opened a worn, black leather address book and gave him his business card. 'By the way, that's a handsome car out front. Yours?'

'The old jaguar? I got it for a song several years ago.'

Nick nodded, shook the other man's hand and left.

A few minutes after Nick's departure, the herbalist came out and locked the door.

Instinct had warned Nick that Martin might be more than just an older shopkeeper interested in herbs. He re-parked his car a block away and waited across the street from the business, then he followed the shopkeeper to the post office and back to his shop. Oh, well. No crime for a man to visit a post office. Nick retrieved his car and returned to headquarters.

Later, Nick sat at his desk, reviewing his notes. The woman in Martin's shop was probably just a wild card, but he should follow up on her if possible. And there was Martin. The herbalist had appeared reluctant to give out information on the killer herb. Also, the business didn't appear so profitable that Martin could afford a Rolex watch and Jaguar.

Yawning, Nick stood and stretched. Peering out at the parking lot, he saw no activity. Time for a cup of coffee. He poured a steaming cup of the muddy brew. At least it smelled like coffee. As he took a sip, the phone rang on his desk.

'Connor speaking.'

'Hello. Martin here. I'm sorry. I haven't been able to locate the telephone number you wanted.'

'That's too bad. I'd hoped . . . Thank you for looking, anyway.'

A constable tapped on Nick's open door and handed him a report. He scanned the one page document. Not much information had come from his team's discrete inquiries on Kate's nephew and niece.

Nick leaned back in his armchair, mulling over what they'd learned about Charles and Clarissa. Extremely wealthy, they were reclusive, spending most of their time together. No close friends had been found. Clarissa liked to garden and Charles played the stock market. That was all Nick's team had found out about them so far . . . of course, that could be it. He sat erect while his policeman's instincts hummed.

Nick played back Martin's description of his customer. What did Clarissa look like? Could she have been the young woman in Martin's shop? If so, did she play a role in a plot to do away with Kate?

No likely motive came to mind, but Nick felt uneasy about the brother and sister. He called his Sergeant. 'I'm going to King's Grant to see Mrs. Stanhope.' He wanted to see her, anyway. 'I need to get a picture of her relatives.'

'Yes, sir. Do you want me to go with you?'

'No. See if you can dig up more information on Charles and Clarissa Stanhope. I'd like Martin to look at their picture. Maybe he'll recognize Clarissa. And call the Stanhopes and tell them I'd like them to come in to see me tomorrow.' He'd check on their alibis for last Friday night. All at once, the pieces of the puzzle began to come together. Could Clarissa be Martin's mysterious customer? Excitement coursed through Nick.

⋆　⋆　⋆

Kate heard his car drive up and greeted Nick at the hotel door. She walked ahead of him into the sitting room where he'd interviewed her guests and staff the previous weekend.

'Please have a seat.' She motioned to a pair of blue velvet chairs in front of a small marble fireplace, then sat down. 'I'm glad you called. I was about to phone you. Have you made any progress?' Her gaze scanned his features from the cleft in his chin to his black, unruly hair. A lock of hair fell on his forehead, and she resisted the urge to push it back. What would he tell her?

81

'I won't mince words with you, just get to the facts.'

'Good.' She continued to study him. His gold-flaked dark brown eyes fascinated her. Gazing at him, she felt breathless.

'I visited Mel Martin at The Bowness Herbalist this morning. Do you know the man?' Piercing, dark eyes glanced her way.

'No, I've never met him. I've seen the sign on the shop, but haven't been inside. My knowledge of herbs is limited to those we grow in our kitchen gardens.'

'Mr. Martin mentioned a woman customer who asked for books on medicinal herbs in late March. Unfortunately, he didn't get her name and he's misplaced the telephone number she gave him.' Nick paused. 'Do you have a recent picture of your niece and nephew?'

'Why, yes, but why — .'

He raised one large hand and stopped her in mid-sentence. 'I can't explain it all now, but if you do have a picture, I'd like to borrow it for a day or two.'

Icy-fingered fear clutched at Kate's heart, seeing his grave expression. 'Are they in trouble? Please tell me. They're the only relatives I have left. All of my own family's deceased.'

'I don't know yet. I'll just have to ask you

to trust me.' Nick stood, walked to the fireplace and ran his fingers along the marble mantle.

'All right. Just a moment.' Kate left the room, briefly, and returned clutching a framed portrait of her niece and nephew. 'This was taken about a year ago, on Charles's birthday.' Handing it to Nick, Kate observed, 'They haven't changed much since then.'

'Thank you. I'll take good care of it.' Nick sat down again and looked at the picture. 'Has she always been blonde?'

What a strange question. 'Why, yes, I believe so. They both get their fair coloring from their father.'

'I plan to see them tomorrow, and I'm hoping they can help me with matters relating to the case.'

Kate jerked. 'But they weren't here. I've already told you that.' In her distress, she reached across the space between their chairs and touched his hand. Immediately, he covered hers with his larger one and squeezed it. She felt warmth and security in his touch. A moment later, she felt embarrassed and removed her hand, putting it back in her lap.

'Don't agitate yourself, needlessly. I have to check out a lot of things and a lot of people. And your relatives do live next door.'

Nick paused. 'I believe you've said they're wealthy?'

His dark eyes probed, scanning her face. Kate looked across the room, pretending to examine an antique Lalique vase. Her mind raced. She couldn't tell Nick what Charles had revealed that day at lunch, deeming it disloyal to speak of family matters to outsiders, without permission. Besides, it wasn't relevant to his case.

'Their mother was Italian, the daughter of an industrialist. Since she preceded her father in death, her share of his estate came to Charles and Clarissa.' There. She'd told the truth, at least part of it.

Nick's glance pulled hers. Gazing in his direction, she found curiosity as well as sympathy etched on his features.

'I'll be right back.' He left the room, then came back to his chair. 'I've asked your housekeeper for a pot of tea. If your hand's any indication, you're cold. Hot tea will help.'

'Why, thank you. How kind of you.'

'I try to be, except with felons.'

Kate picked up a trace of amusement in his voice.

Minutes later the door swung open.

'Here's our tea.' Nick stood as Mattie walked in, then took the tray, placing it on the small table between their chairs.

84

'Thank you so much. We both felt chilled.' He smiled his appreciation at Mattie then poured two cups. 'There're some biscuits, too.'

'So, to answer your question, they inherited a fortune.' Kate avoided looking into his eyes. She hated to lie, but Charles's losses were none of Nick's business.

'I know, but there's more, isn't there?' He took one sip of tea, put down his cup and tackled the biscuits.

'When I lunched with them today, Charles admitted that he's experienced losses on the stock market.' She stopped to sip her tea. His eyes focused on her so intently she had to look away.

'But they inherited a large sum as you've said?'

'That's right. I don't know how much exactly. Millions, I believe.' That's the truth. How did Charles lose so much? 'A hotel chain has wanted to buy The Folly for months. Until recently, Charles played with their offers. Now they want both The Folly and King's Grant and will give us £10 million. They need the acreage of the two properties for a new resort hotel.'

'I see, and your nephew? Has he asked you to sell?'

'Repeatedly, and each time I refuse. If he

85

wants to sell, he can find another buyer. I won't leave King's Grant.'

'Thank you for telling me. You asked why I was interested in their picture. I didn't tell you Martin's description of his customer who asked for books on medieval herbs. He said she was a young woman, tall and thin with long black hair and blue eyes. Does that description sound like your niece?'

'Yes, except you can see from their picture that she's quite blonde. Your description would match many young women in this area, I'm sure.'

'Of course. I'm just being a nosy policeman. I have to follow all leads that appear. Still, I'd like Mr. Martin to see this picture.'

She gazed at the tea tray. 'Can I pour you another cup?'

'No, but thanks.' Nick looked at his watch. 'I better go.' Kate accompanied him from the sitting room to the door.

He turned around, without warning and bumped into her. Kate felt his tall, wiry body tense when they collided. Then Nick put his hands under her arms, steadying her until she regained her balance.

Kate blushed and explained. 'I was going to walk you to the door.' Another thought came to mind and she asked, 'When we can re-open, will paying guests come to a hotel where murder has been committed?' She frowned. 'Or will the poisoning cast a kiss of death on King's Grant Hotel?'

'Yes and no. If anything, the murder may make your hotel more popular.' Nick leaned down and brushed his fingers against her cheek.

Kate shut her eyes, wishing he'd kiss her. Instead, she heard the door close behind him.

Opening her eyes, she found herself alone. Kate touched her cheek, surprised by his caress. She trembled.

7

Nick frowned at the dark skies. What a gloomy day. Where did yesterday's spring-like weather go? The cold wind sliced through him. Shivering, he turned up his coat collar and walked quickly around the corner to his car.

On his way to work, he drove past the lake, dull and quiet today. The place looked deserted without the lines of tourists waiting for a steamboat ride. Not even any seagulls wheeling about over the lake, though a few birds huddled together on the gravelly beach.

Later that morning, a car raced by his office window, the roar of its engine bursting through the constabulary walls. Nick peered through his half-open venetian blind and caught a glimpse of a man and woman in a black Porsche. The driver zipped into an empty slot behind the building and turned off the engine.

Thanks to the photograph he'd borrowed from Kate, Nick recognized Charles and Clarissa the moment they stepped out of the car. Deep in conversation, they walked toward the constabulary entrance. Nick couldn't hear their words but observed Charles talking fast and shaking his finger at his sister. The girl nodded her head, as if in agreement.

What did they know about the Penmar murder? Without any concrete evidence, Nick suspected Clarissa and Charles. His instincts cautioned him that, at this point of the investigation, it would be unwise to rule out anyone.

Nick glanced at his wall clock, then eased back in his leather arm chair, waiting for the department secretary to bring Charles and Clarissa to him. They were right on time for their appointment.

'Good morning. Inspector Connor, I believe?' In his navy blazer and light grey slacks, Charles seemed at ease, leaning in the doorway.

'Mr. Stanhope.' Nick rose and stepped around his desk to shake Charles's out-stretched hand. He found it as cold as the smile that didn't quite reach Charles's ice-blue eyes.

'And this is your sister, Miss Stanhope?' He eyed her tall, angular frame and long blonde hair. Except for her hair, she fit Martin's description of his mystery customer. That woman was brunette, according to Martin. Nick would take their picture over to the herbalist as soon as he located the man.

'Inspector. My brother said you wanted to see us because you think we may be able to help you.'

Her light voice was so soft, Nick had to strain to hear her words. She didn't appear nervous.

'Yes, that's true. Please have a seat.' Nick gestured to the hardback chair by his desk. 'Just a moment, please.' He left the room and returned in a moment with another chair for Charles. 'I only have a few questions.' He gazed across his desk at both of them. 'Let's backtrack to the night of Penmar's death. First, just for the record, would you tell me where you both were that evening?' He directed his attention to Charles.

Were they capable of murder? You just couldn't tell. Unfortunately, killers usually looked just like the rest of the population. It was only by probing beneath the surface that you detected a twisted mind or perverted nature.

'Clarissa and I read in our library until late. What time do you imagine it was?' Charles turned to his sister sitting quietly beside him, her hands folded in her lap.

'At least ten-thirty.' Clarissa addressed her brother. 'I remember the hall clock struck the half hour, and you said it was time to retire.'

'Exactly.' Charles beamed at his sister as if he were pleased, then he focused on Nick. 'That's about all we can tell you. If there's nothing else, I guess we'll be going.' Charles pushed back his chair.

Nick motioned to Charles to sit down. 'I do have one or two more questions. You've heard that we've found what killed the man?' Watching Charles's face, Nick saw a worried expression flash across his face. Then a bland mask reasserted itself on Charles's aristocratic features.

'Yes. Kate told us yesterday. What did she call it?' Charles turned to his sister, wrinkling his brow.

'Cowbane. She said it's an old herb.' Her voice cracked as she responded. Clarissa shifted on her hard chair, then studied her shoes.

'That's it. How odd. Where on earth would you find something like that?' Charles raised both eyebrows as if he were puzzled. Then he straightened his silk tie and continued before Nick could reply. 'It's unfortunate the man lost his life. Could it have been an accident?' He glanced across the desk at Nick, his demeanor as cool as if they discussed the weather.

'My department doesn't see it as an accident. We view the act as murder.' Nick sat back in his arm chair. After a moment, he shrugged. Then he smiled at Clarissa and spoke to her in a more relaxed tone. 'By the way, I met an acquaintance of yours yesterday.'

'Really? Who did you meet?' She seemed interested.

'Mel Martin, the owner of Bowness Herbalist. I believe you frequent his bookstore? While we talked, he showed me several books you'd ordered.' What would she say to that?

Immediately Clarissa straightened, her cheeks flushed and her chin went up. Her response came fast. 'You must be mistaken. I don't remember meeting the man, and I have no idea where his business is. I buy books in Lancaster, or phone in my order to a Carlisle bookstore.' She twisted a lock of her hair.

'You may have forgotten,' Nick persisted, not ready to dismiss the topic of conversation, 'but Mr. Martin remembers you.'

'I'm afraid he's confused me with someone else. Perhaps I've a look-alike here in the area.' She smiled slightly, but her gaze wavered, slid away from Nick's.

Judging by her appearance and abrupt speech, Nick could tell he'd hit a nerve. 'I see.'

Charles jumped into the conversation. 'Are

you sure that Martin said Clarissa Stanhope? Maybe it was another woman with a similiar name?'

'Yes.' Nick turned to Clarissa. 'I apologize. I guess Mr. Martin confused you with one of his customers.'

Her only response was a weak nod.

Did she have a twin? It was possible. Nick recalled he'd read somewhere that we each have a double. On the other hand, if Clarissa was lying, how could he trap her?

Nick let them go but he'd have them watched. 'Well, I guess that's all. I appreciate your coming in.'

He rose and shook their hands as they stood by his desk. Touching Clarissa's hand, he felt a chill. She looked away and stepped toward the door. As they walked quickly out of his office, Charles placed his hand, protectively, on Clarissa's shoulder.

Nick sat back in his leather desk chair, his hands clasped behind his head. Kate had told him that Charles was relentless when he focused on a target. Recently he'd hounded her to sell her property to the hotel chain wanting both The Folly and her home.

From their haste to leave his office, Nick surmised he had caused Clarissa and Charles to worry a bit.

Kate patted her foot, checked the time and stared out a window in the hotel's living room while waiting to hear from Nick. He told her he'd call today.

Mattie turned off the vacuum cleaner. 'What's the matter, Kate? You look like you're about to fly away.'

'I'm so tired of this whole situation, Mattie. We've been in limbo since poor Mr. Penmar's death. I can't stop wondering who could have killed him. When I think about the police closing the hotel . . . I don't know what to do. Think I'll take a walk. Maybe some fresh air will help. Please call me if you hear from Nick.' Slipping a light denim jacket over her jeans and pink cotton T-shirt, Kate walked out the kitchen door.

Passing the herb gardens, she knelt and examined the bed of parsley, thyme and rosemary. These familiar herbs they used on a regular basis in cooking were harmless. The killer herb hadn't come from the hotel gardens. Where did it come from? And who plucked it?

As Kate strolled into the woods, the dry, brittle leaves crunched under her loafers, reminding her of last autumn. A lot had happened since then. First the shock of

Stephen's death, then discovering she must find a new source of income if she wanted to continue living at King's Grant. Shortly, thereafter, Charles had begun to pester her. He'd become more disagreeable each time she turned down the hotel offers. She wouldn't sell her home to cover his investment losses. He should never have played the stock market if he lacked the necessary skills.

She'd let Nick assume she was the sole reason her husband changed his will. But there was something else . . . Kate frowned, searching her memory. The week they re-located to Bowness, she was too busy getting settled to go with Stephen and drop in on his niece and nephew. Though he gave no explanation, her husband's face had been red with anger on his return home. The next day he called his lawyer and changed his will. What could Charles and Clarissa have done to turn their uncle against them?

Kate followed the mossy path deeper into the woods. The sky that had displayed a few windswept clouds earlier, grew darker, the wind more gusty. Intermingled with the scent of the spruces, Kate smelled rain in the air.

The crack of a twig snapping echoed behind her, and she froze as she realized her isolated state in the middle of the forest. An alarm rang in her brain, warning her of danger. She whipped around but found only the trees, hardwood and spruces, and the tangled undergrowth.

It wasn't the first time she'd sensed someone following her. The day before on Lake Road, she'd looked behind her, expecting to find someone on her heels. But as she scanned the busy throng of shoppers coming in and out of the stores on Lake Road, not a single person glanced her way.

Fear and anxiety built until her nerves stretched taut. First several anonymous phone calls until she hesitated to answer the telephone at night. And she'd found out someone might have intended the poison for her, not Mr. Penmar.

Kate sensed someone stalking her. A shiver racing down her spine, she pulled the lapels of her denim jacket together, and struggled to keep her fragile control.

Leaving the woods, Kate glanced over her shoulder. She imagined a figure standing in the shadows. But when she dared to look again, no one was there, just the thicket of evergreens and underbrush.

Stumbling in her haste, Kate hurried back to the house. At first she walked fast. When she reached the hotel grounds she broke into a run.

8

Fear turned to relief when Kate reached the gate house. A dark green Range Rover was parked there. She flung open the door and smiled at the welcome sight of Nick's tall frame lounging on her living room sofa. His shoes rested on the coffee table. Sipping a cup of coffee, he perused her new Bon Appetit magazine. Nick peered over the edge of the magazine and smiled. 'Hope you don't mind. I was leaving you a note when Mattie appeared with your laundry. She let me in, said you wouldn't be long.' Rising, he came toward Kate, took her hands in his.

'Come sit with me. Your hands are cold as ice. Almost as cold as Clarissa's hands this morning.' Nick surprised Kate with a light kiss on her cheek.

Her face tingling where his lips grazed her cheek, Kate sat down on the sofa and took a deep breath. Striving for nonchalance, she took off her shoes and curled up on the sofa, feet under her. She sighed with relief and savored the heat of the fire Nick had lit. The smoky sweetness of burning apple logs, crackling and hissing, soothed her nerves.

'You were going to see Charles and Clarissa today. What did you find out?' She hoped his visit with her relatives squelched any doubt or suspicion he'd had about them.

'Not much, but I've a hunch they know more about Penmar's death than they've told me. I think my questions upset Clarissa. She doesn't seem as cool and composed as her brother. I think she'll break if I prod her a little.'

He must have seen Kate flinch because he paused. 'Sorry, I only meant she'd open up and tell me if she knows anything about Penmar. Charles will take more effort. I'll return your picture as soon as Mel Martin looks at it. I've called his shop twice today, but he wasn't there. I also left messages, but he hasn't returned my calls.'

'Perhaps he's ill. Have you tried to reach him at home?'

'He lives over his shop but has an unlisted number. Even if your niece was in his shop, that doesn't mean she's played a part in the murder. Remember, at this point I'm just searching for clues.' He sat back down and sipped his coffee, his arm draped over the back of the sofa.

Sitting close to him, yet not touching, she could feel his body warmth, even through his jacket. She caught a whiff of the tangy citrus scent he wore. It tantalized her.

'In the office today, she became agitated and insisted she didn't know Mel Martin.' Nick gazed at Kate. 'She could have lied, but we have no proof.'

'I wish I'd wake up and find this has all been a bad dream. We need to put Mr. Penmar's death behind us and get on with our lives, yet we don't seem to be able to . . .' The pulse jumped in her throat, then her voice broke. Kate slumped into the sofa and covered her face. Tears of frustration ran down her cheeks.

'Kate? Can I do something?' Nick put his arm around her.

She shook her head, mutely, then brushed the back of her hands across her face and sat up straighter.

Nick gave her his handkerchief then went into her galley kitchen. He came back a minute later with a steaming cup of tea.

Kate drank the hot tea, savoring its taste.

'What you need is a change of scene. I'm on duty now, but I'd like to take you out this evening.'

On a sudden impulse she responded to his invitation. 'Isn't that against the rules? Before you answer, let me say I'd like to go out with you. It's just that . . . should I socialize with the police inspector investigating a murder committed right on my property?'

'We'll be discrete. I don't see any problem, do you?' He smiled.

'Perhaps we could drive into the country and find a quiet pub, a place where no one would recognize us?' She knew what he suggested was against the rules, but she wanted to get to know him. Just a date with no involvement. Nothing more.

'It's settled, then. I'll come by at eight. Then you can run out and we'll drive into the country.'

★ ★ ★

'Have a good time, Kate. It's a beautiful evening.' Chris spoke to Kate from the front hallway of the hotel as he helped Diane slip on a light jacket.

Kate watched the two stroll, hand in hand, down the driveway in the direction of the lake. They enjoyed walking when the weather was pleasant. She couldn't help but sigh, enviously, as they left. Judging by the star-struck expressions on their faces when they were together, Chris and Diane were in love.

Mattie waved to Kate as she and Miles, her elderly Scottie, wandered off to bed and another Margaret Yorke mystery.

Down in the gatehouse, Kate tried on one outfit after another. At last she selected an outfit which was attractive, yet not dressy. She glanced down at the dark green sweater and slacks. She felt like she was preparing for a secret rendevous. How foolish.

For a moment, she paused to gaze at her reflection in her bedroom mirror. Seeing her pale cheeks, she brushed some color onto her face. A warm glow flowed through her body.

A depressing thought broke through Kate's euphoria. Maybe Nick wanted to get her in a more relaxed setting so she'd let down her guard and give him information that might help him solve the crime. Then he could move on to other criminal cases.

It would be great to have the case solved so the hotel could re-open, but she'd be sorry not to see Nick anymore. In spite of herself, she enjoyed his company. Kate thought ahead to the days after the case was closed. She'd never see him again. Regret filled her for a moment, then she shrugged. She didn't need him or any man. Hearing his car, she descended the steep stairs and let him in when he knocked.

'Hello. Don't you look nice?' His deep voice complimented her appearance. 'Are you ready?' He stood in the living room for a moment while she grabbed her shoulder bag and a jacket.

They drove to a less populated area of the Lake District. Sitting beside him in the Rover, Kate noticed he drove fast, yet never recklessly, as much in control driving a car as he was in the investigation. His self-confidence had impressed her when they first met. She'd never met anyone else so self-assured. It was at the same time comforting, yet disconcerting. Stephen liked being in control, also.

Nick broke the silence. 'I'm curious about your niece and nephew. Has either of them ever married?'

Kate answered that they hadn't. After a brief discussion on her relatives, they reached Cartmel Fell, a tiny village nestled in a woody valley. Nick parked in front of the Masons Arms.

Nick glanced at Kate. 'Have you been here before?'

'No. It looks like a farmhouse.'

'It was a long time ago, but it's been a pub for many years. The Masons Arms is famous for its beers. It carries two hundred and fifty beers, including its own. And they have an outside bar in good weather so we find what we want and go indoors to pay.' He steered Kate to the front porch with its well-stocked bar. They selected their bottles of beer. Walking indoors, they selected one of several empty booths near the fireside.

The tension binding her muscles relaxed a bit as she sat with Nick in the almost deserted pub, watching the fire simmer on the huge, stone hearth. From across the large room, she heard two waiters talking softly while stacking glasses in the bar. In a nearby booth, a woman burst into peals of laughter at a joke her escort told.

'We've come on a good night.' Nick smiled. 'You wouldn't believe how noisy and crowded this place gets on the weekends.'

Kate asked the question which had been haunting her for days. 'You don't believe it was a horrible accident?' She knew he would understand what she referred to.

'It's highly unlikely someone would put a rare, poisonous herb in a pitcher of tea by accident. Whoever put it there meant to kill.'

'You think I was the target, don't you?' Kate waited for his response, needing to know the truth, no matter how horrible.

'It's possible, but I won't let it happen.' He paused for a moment. 'Let's talk about more pleasant topics, shall we?'

'Such as?' All at once, she understood. She wasn't the only one who wanted to get away. He needed to escape from the grim reality of the past few days, too.

Nick leaned forward. 'Why don't you tell me about yourself and your family. What was your childhood like? Were you an only child, or were there brothers and sisters?'

'I was an only child. My father was a golf pro, older than my mother. When he died of a heart attack, she had already written one cookbook. She continued writing and publishing her books and became quite successful. Her cookbooks supported us and paid for my college tuition.' She paused to drink her beer.

'You inherited her love of cooking?'

'Yes. I can't remember a time when I wasn't in the kitchen with her, trying new recipes for her books. By my mid-teens, I was an accomplished cook, thanks to my mother. She never stopped looking for new recipes, no matter how bizarre. We must have sampled a little of every culture's foods.'

'And all of that led you to your career in New York?'

'Yes. I majored in Home Economics in college, mainly in food preparation for restaurants and large hotels. Later, Mother helped me find a position as an assistant food editor on the New York Times.' Kate glanced down at the table for a moment. 'She died a couple of months before I met and married my husband and moved to London. I was twenty-six and Stephen had just celebrated his fifty-sixth birthday.' She wouldn't tell him her union with Stephen was a mockery of the word marriage. 'How about you, Nick? What was your family like?'

'Nothing out of the ordinary. I didn't have any brothers or sisters. My parents married later than most people we knew. Father was a truck driver, the son of Irish emigrants. His job took him away from Mother a lot. I spent more time with Mother, at least when I was small.' He stopped and she could tell he'd lost himself in memories. The pained expression on his face told her more than words.

'Were you close to your mother as a child?' Kate probed as gently as she could, trying to learn more about Nick's life.

'Yes, I was. There were just the two of us. I remember her as a quiet, stoic woman who worked all the time, except Sunday.

'Mother was what psychiatrists today might call compulsive. She needed to wash and iron. As soon as she put up all of her freshly ironed lace curtains, she would start taking them down to be washed again.'

'And was her ancestry also Irish?'

'No, her family was French. Her parents disowned her when she married my father, a poor young man. I don't think they spoke to her again.'

'That's so sad.' Kate sympathized with him.

'Yes, I suppose. Mother came from a wealthier family. I guess they thought she married beneath herself. She missed her parents greatly, I know. I tried to help her with the housework sometimes, but she'd just send me out to play with my friends.'

'Do you suppose she regreted marrying your father?' Kate's heart ached, hearing of Nick's unhappy childhood.

'Probably, but she never said so.' He looked away. Kate felt him shutting her out.

'I can remember my parents laughing and having fun, even over the comics in the Sunday paper.' She smiled in reflection.

'My parents weren't close at all. I always thought Father told Mother as little as possible about his life away from us. But, enough of that . . . ' He changed the subject abruptly, surprising her. 'Kate, I'd like to see you again, or am I way out of line?'

'Not at all.' She glanced down into the amber liquid and added softly, 'I haven't dated since my husband died last October.' Perhaps one day she'd tell him about the icy wasteland of her marriage.

'I'd like to be your friend.' He smiled,

taking her hand. 'I've an idea. The weather should be good tomorrow. It's my day off, and I thought I'd drive out to the coast for lunch. I don't suppose you'd like to go with me?'

'Why don't you call me first thing in the morning?' She spoke slowly, striving for a casual tone.

'Great. I'll do that.'

They drove back to Bowness in silence. When they pulled up in front of the gatehouse, Nick stopped the car and turned off the ignition. He looked at her. 'There's something I've wanted to do for several days.' His brown eyes glowed in the dark. He leaned over and kissed her.

It was a strong, yet tender kiss. Kate responded, kissing him back. But just as she was warming to his kiss, he pulled away.

'I'm sorry. I shouldn't have done that.' His voice sounded strained. Before she knew it, he climbed out. By the car light when he opened her door, she saw a worried look on his face.

When they reached the porch, he shook her hand. 'Goodnight, Kate. I'll call you tomorrow morning.'

Her fingers trembled, unlocking her door. Kate entered her apartment, baffled by Nick's behavior.

A firm knock resounded on her door. Opening it, she found the constable assigned to night duty at the hotel since the murder.

'Mrs. Stanhope, is everything all right?'

She studied the policeman's face. Had he seen his senior officer bring her home? From his polite expression, she couldn't tell.

'Yes, Officer. I'm going to retire.' She closed the door and locked it before climbing the stairs to her tiny bedroom under the eaves.

As Kate undressed and slipped on a night shirt, she replayed her conversation with Nick that evening. One remark of his stuck in her head. In the car going to the pub, he'd asked her about Charles and Clarissa's marital status.

'And they've never married, either of them?'

She replied, 'No. They've always lived together and are seldom apart.'

Kate remembered Clarissa dated a young man that spring. Nothing came of it. After two short weeks, the man vanished. Local gossips concluded that either Clarissa rejected the fellow, or her doting brother refused to let the man continue dating his sister. What did Nick say? 'I can't put my finger on it but they seem different. They certainly aren't like other brothers and sisters

I've known.' Then he'd hesitated. 'I hope this won't offend you, but they act like two young lovers!' Kate realized that his words had echoed her unspoken thoughts. Charles and Clarissa did appear unusually close for a brother and sister. But she couldn't see a man being in love with his own sister.

9

The next day Kate waited for Nick's call.

'Good morning. Did I wake you?'

'Oh, no. I'm an early riser.' Her heart beat faster hearing his deep voice.

'I am, too. Can you go today?'

'Yes, what time should I be ready?' She felt breathless.

'Ten o'clock all right?'

'Fine, see you then.' Kate hummed as she pulled on jeans. After buttoning her plaid shirt, she reached for a windbreaker and threw it over the arm of a chair.

As she brushed her hair and pulled it back into a braid, she envisioned his dark brown eyes with the pupils ringed in gold. They fascinated her. She admitted he attracted her more than any other man she'd known.

Nick arrived sooner than she expected. They left Bowness and headed west. The sun hung high overhead while they sped along a two-lane road running toward the coast. How peaceful it was to get away from the crowds of tourists, most of them crowded into the villages like Bowness and Amberside, ignoring the unspoiled beauty in the less populated areas.

When they reached the coast, he pulled off the road, parking the car. Kate looked out the car window, pretending to admire the scenery. She wondered what he thought of her. A man as intelligent, self-confident and handsome as Nick must have his pick of women.

He reached across the seat separating them and put his left arm around her, grazing her breast, then she felt the fingers of his right hand glide, idly, up and down her arm.

Her arm tingled where he touched her and butterflies fluttered in her stomach. He stared at her without speaking. The intensity of his gaze alarmed Kate. She retreated.

Fumbling with her car door handle, she stepped out on the ground. 'Let's go for a walk on the beach.' Tension crackled in the air around them when their eyes met and locked, briefly.

He inhaled, sharply and the spell was broken. Nick looked around then nodded his head. 'It is a beautiful day.' He followed her to the sunlit beach and took her hand in his. They strolled together down the windy, debris-strewn shingle.

'Kate, I need to say something.' He hesitated, frowned and appeared to search for words.

From the expression on his face, she wasn't sure she wanted to hear what he'd tell her. Kate dropped his hand and continued walking by herself down the beach.

Nick came up behind her and put his hands on her shoulders, turning her to face him. He spoke in a bleak tone. 'I like you, but I can't get involved with anyone. You need to understand that. I can't make you any promises.'

'I don't want promises.' She hoped he didn't notice how her voice quivered.

'As long as you understand.' He smiled as the wind blew a lock of hair on his face, then he gave her a brotherly pat on the back.

'There's only one thing I want.' He murmured into her disheveled locks. The wind was playing with her braids.

'And that is . . . ?' She couldn't figure him out.

'Lunch and lots of it. Why don't we find a place to eat?' He grinned, boyishly.

Was he deliberately teasing her? She felt more irritable by the minute.

Nick put his arm around her shoulder. 'There's a good seafood restaurant over that way if you don't mind a climb?' He pointed to a steep path running away from the beach.

'Fine,' Kate replied, eyeing the rough path he'd proposed they take. This guy must be part mountain goat. But she wasn't about to appear apprehensive. 'You first.' She followed him.

Once they mastered the climb, she was glad she'd come. The restaurant was worth it. The weatherbeaten old inn, built on a bluff overlooking the sea, served excellent, freshly caught prawns and scallops served with heaps of piping hot chips. Nick and Kate munched on the crusty, fried seafood, washing it down with beer since the inn lacked wine.

They drove home at a leisurely pace, allowing other vehicles to pass them. The sun was sinking behind the western fells by the time the Rover pulled up in front of Kate's gatehouse. 'It's been a fun day,' she ventured.

'I enjoyed it, myself.' At her door, Nick turned to Kate. 'I'll let you know when we have new developments in the case.' She gazed up at him, yearning to be kissed. Instead, he took her hand and held it for a moment. 'I wish . . . '

'What do you wish?' She waited.

Uncertainty clouded Nick's face. He dropped her hand.

'Nothing. Goodbye.' He walked to his car.

Bewildered, Kate unlocked her door and stood in the doorway as he drove off. 'Thanks for the excursion.' She spoke to herself. His vehicle was already pulling through the gates.

Kate closed the door softly and leaned against it, disappointed that he didn't want a relationship, didn't want her. Then a wave of frustration and anger washed over her, frustration at how he'd turned out and anger at herself for being attracted to the man in the first place. She should have known better. He'd looked too good to be true, and he was. He'd let down his guard and told her about his life the previous night. But when she thought she began to know him, up came the barricades and she found herself left alone out in the cold.

One 'emotionally unavailable' man was enough. She wouldn't fall for another like Stephen. She'd avoid Nick except for the police investigation. That made a lot of sense. But her heart told her otherwise. Sitting alone in the gathering dusk, she realized she'd been falling in love, all by herself.

10

Charles was strolling down the hall Thursday when the telephone rang. He stepped into the living room to pick up the receiver. 'Hello.' Silence hung in the air. 'Hello,' he repeated. He shook the phone a little. Probably a wrong number.

Before he hung up, a muffled voice whispered into his ear. 'The two of you tried to kill your aunt to get her estate.'

Taken unawares, Charles gasped, 'Who is this? What do you want?' He broke out into a sweat, gripping the receiver.

'You heard me. If you don't make it worthwhile for me to forget what I know, I'll go to the police and tell them all about your scheme. I'm sure they'll find my story interesting.'

'You'd better explain what you're talking about because I'm about to hang up.'

'Let's just say I've put two and two together and concluded you've schemed against your aunt. After all, you've certainly had the motive and the means to do her in. And you must have had the opportunity, judging by the article in the newspaper that mentions a tourist dying of poison at her hotel last weekend.' When Charles didn't reply, he continued. 'I'm not greedy, but I think my silence should be worth something. Let's say £50,000, in £20 and £50 bank notes. No large bills, please. Put it in a waterproof bag and leave it at the top of the falls at Stockgyll Force at twelve p.m. Sunday night.'

Charles briefly considered hanging up the telephone. That wouldn't work. Judging from the caller's tone, he would go to the police. He didn't have any choice but to cooperate. 'I don't see how we can get that much money together so fast. Won't you accept less if we can't raise the £50,000? That's a lot of money.' As he pleaded with the blackmailer, Charles tried to place the man's voice. Perhaps he'd heard it somewhere.

'I know you and your sister are loaded, so let's not quibble about the money. It's probably small change to you. Just do as I say or you'll regret it.' The call ended with an abrupt click when the caller replaced the telephone into its receiver.

Throwing the phone to the floor, Charles slammed his fist down on the table. Then he kicked a chair several times until his toes throbbed. Limping on one foot, he hobbled across the room and fell into an armchair. 'Damn, damn, damn it.' He glanced at Clarissa.

Wide-eyed, she stared back at Charles and retreated into the relative safety of a sofa, clenching the magazine she'd been reading.

'That man who just called thinks we tried to poison Kate.' Charles inhaled sharply and ran his fingers through his hair then eyed his sister. 'When you were down by the lakes looking for herbs, you didn't see or talk to anyone, did you?'

'Of course not.' Her voice shook. 'What do you think I am, a complete fool? And before you ask, I didn't give that Mr. Martin in the herb shop my name, either. I'm not stupid.' Clutching a pillow, she slid down on the sofa and began to cry. Her thumb went into her mouth as it always did during moments of stress.

'No, you're not stupid, but you aren't as careful as I am.' Charles said, regaining his composure. 'Never mind, Sister. I'll take care of this.' He tried to think how best to catch the blackmailer. A plan came to mind and he smiled.

Rummaging in their dusty attic, Charles descended the collapsible stairs, clutching a briefcase that had belonged to their deceased father. Abhoring filth in any form, he cleaned and polished the case until the old leather shone.

'Get me all of the newspapers you can find in the house, will you? Just stack them on my desk in the study.' He did need her help after all. 'I have to go out, but I'll see you at lunch.' Charles drove into the village, eased the Porsche into one of the parking lots and proceeded on foot. That afternoon he locked himself in the study.

* * *

On Sunday evening, Charles prowled the house, restlessly. He eyed the wall clock, waiting for the time to go.

Seeing Clarissa's anxious stare, he sensed what she was about to say. 'Don't even ask. I want you to stay here. You'll be better off at home. Besides, you can tell anyone who calls, I've retired for the evening.'

The grandfather clock in the hall chimed eleven. 'I need to get ready now.' He pasted a reassuring smile on his face for her benefit and went to his room where he dressed in a black shirt, jeans and sweater. The clock stuck the half-hour, and he tried to put her mind at ease. 'Don't worry. I'll take care of this. Go to bed. I'll see you tomorrow morning.'

He slipped silently out the back door. In a

few minutes, he melted into the dark blue shadows of the thicket of woods behind their property. Having noticed a strange car parked near their gates earlier, Charles suspected the police watched The Folly. He didn't want them to see him leaving the estate tonight.

Walking through the woods, Charles steeled himself for what he had to do. He had no choice but to silence the blackmailer before he contacted the police.

Uncle Stephen shouldn't have changed his will. It was all Kate's fault for marrying Stephen, a man twice her age. He had promised to leave King's Grant to Charles and his sister. Except for Kate, he and Clarissa would have lived there together after Stephen died.

Clarissa's recent change of attitude worried him, though. She had become more independent after she received that inheritance from their mother's estate. Now she locked her bedroom door nights. But he'd wear her down. After all, he was her only family. Unless you counted Kate. He sneered at the thought. Kate might not be around in the future. Charles smiled to himself.

Approaching the waterfalls a mile from The Folly, he scanned the area. The place was quiet and deserted. The nature trails were popular for walking during the day, but there weren't any lights along the trails. Consequently, no one wandered there at night, not even silly tourists.

He found a tree next to the rocky incline the blackmailer would have to take to get to the Falls. He'd use it as a hiding place. Climbing up to Stockgyll Force, he carefully laid down the old briefcase. He'd put it in a sack, as directed.

Settling back down behind the tree, he waited, his watch slowly marking off the minutes. What was keeping the man?

The minutes dragged by. Just when he'd begun to think the man wasn't coming, Charles's muscles tensed at the sound of a stick cracking. Footsteps padded down the path. He slipped on his gloves.

At moments, dark, swirling clouds hid the moon's faint light. Peering through the intermittent darkness, Charles glimpsed a slender figure dressed in blue jeans and jacket.

He waited until the blackmailer passed his hiding place and located the package by the Falls. Peering through the evergreen's branches, Charles watched the man kneel and open the package to check out the money in the briefcase. Charles had packed the case carefully, so it would appear full of neat bundles of currency, £20 and £50 notes.

Now he allowed a few moments for the blackmailer to admire the money.

When he heard the case snap shut, Charles sprung into action. Silently, he skirted the trees and ran up behind the blackmailer. Lifting a large rock high above his victim, he paused for a fraction of a second, then slammed it into the back of the blackmailer's head. The man cried out once, then lay, face down where he'd fallen.

Charles hesitated a moment. Fumbling in the dim light, he checked the man's pulse and found none. Certain he'd killed the blackmailer, Charles located the man's wallet and tucked it into his own jeans pocket. The police would think the assailant had robbed him.

When the clouds parted briefly, Charles looked down on the man's face. Hmmm. Where had he seen him before? He fumbled to identify the man. Extracting a wallet from his pocket, Charles gasped in shock, reading the name on the driver's license. Melvin Martin. Clarissa had visited him in his herbal shop back in the spring.

Charles picked up the bank notes his victim had dropped, then he scanned the area. Only one weak park light illuminated the spot where he stood. Outside its range, night lay dark and still. His nerves taut, he jerked when a jetliner roared across the sky on its way to Lancaster Airport.

Scanning the rocky surface, he saw nothing to help the police pick up his trail when they found the body. He tossed the rock into the falls. It crashed down and rolled under a mass of ferns. The water would wash away any blood. He'd carry the briefcase home and return the money to the bank in a day or so. No one would ever know he'd been there.

Charles crept back into The Folly, as quietly as he'd left, by the back door. Feeling his way through the darkened kitchen and dining room to the living room, he squinted to see the time. The grandfather clock that stood quietly ticking near the foot of the stairs chimed once.

In his bathroom, he pulled a damp hand towel from a rack and wiped the briefcase to remove any fingerprints. Next, he removed his running shoes. Barefoot, he climbed the fold-down stairs to the attic and stuffed the briefcase behind boxes of old books. Back in his bedroom, he tucked the blackmail money into the secret drawer of his antique chest-of-drawers.

Finally, Charles deposited the running shoes in the back of his closet, careful not to wake Clarissa in the next room.

Pressing his ear against their connecting

door, he heard nothing. She must be asleep. Annoyance flooded him when he turned the knob. She'd locked him out again.

Weary beyond belief, he stood in his shower stall and let the needles of hot water relax his tense muscles. Still damp, he crawled into bed and fell asleep almost immediately.

★ ★ ★

Walking in the front door of the constabulary, Nick savored the quiet of early morning. The sharp odor of ammonia burned his nostrils as he stepped around a maintainence worker's pail. The man dragged his mop over the stained domino tiles of the reception hall. Nearby two secretaries chatted, their bosses not in yet.

In his office, Nick poured himself a mug and sipped the hot muddy brew his co-workers called coffee. Picking up a report on his desk, he came across a brochure he'd picked up at the coastal inn where Kate and he'd lunched. He wondered if she was awake yet. She'd said she liked to get up early. As if with a will of its own, his hand slid to the telephone. Pausing, he decided he might wake her. Nick imagined the kiss they'd shared. How soft her lips had been. Kate's rose fragrance had enveloped him while he held her. He'd wanted to continue kissing her, but something told him to be wary.

Nick jerked at the sound of the ringing phone. 'DCI Connor.' He spoke automatically, one hand around his mug of coffee.

Hearing the caller's message, Nick sat up straighter.

'You say you just got the call, Constable? Yes, I see. Have officers been sent to Stockgyll Force yet?' He listened again, then replied. 'I'll be there in ten minutes. Be sure the area is roped off. Thanks.' Another murder. It was a long shot, but could this death be related to Penmar's?

Fifteen minutes later, Nick and Sgt. Kennedy drove up at the Force.

Dr. Walton was kneeling to examine the soggy body. Nick recognized the dead man. The last time he'd seen Melvin Martin, the man had chatted about new books and a catnip-stealing cat.

Nick had hoped Martin might identify Clarissa as his mystery customer. Now that was impossible. At least Nick could visit Clarissa and Charles and get their reaction to Martin's death. She'd denied any knowledge of Martin. Nick wondered, wearily, what was the truth?

One hour later, Sgt. Kennedy drove Nick

through The Folly's gates. Looking up at the stone mansion, Nick recalled an article on The Folly and other stately mansions of the area. 'This is probably before your time, Sergeant, but Charles Stanhope's father won The Folly playing blackjack with a British lord. He renamed the estate, explaining the name. Charles Senior said it was folly for the lord to play with him since he had the reputation of being the most skilled card player in Cumbria.'

'How long ago was that?' The younger officer frowned.

'About twenty years, I expect. Stanhope moved his family to The Folly a year before he went to prison. Charles would have been quite young, probably no more than five. I imagine Clarissa was just an infant.' Nick rang the doorbell.

Clarissa opened the front door. Seeing Nick, she stepped back, an apprehensive expression crossed her face.

'Sorry to trouble you so early, Miss Stanhope, but we'd like to talk to you.'

'Of course, Inspector. Please come in.' She led them into the living room and offered them a seat. Wrapping her light blue robe around her more snugly, she pushed the long pale blond hair out of her face, then crossed the room and opened the heavy drapes, letting in the morning light. 'What's happened?'

'There's been another murder.'

All of the color drained from Clarissa's face. She swung around and stared at Nick.

'We're talking to residents in this vicinity to see if they heard any strange sounds last night. Did you hear anything?'

'No. My brother and I stayed home all evening, but our home is off the main road. King's Grant's our nearest neighbor and it's half a mile away.'

'I see.' Nick made a note. 'Would you mind telling me what you did last night?'

'Not at all. I read a new book on summer lilies. Charles studied his investments.'

'Mel Martin, owner of Bowness Herbalist, was murdered last night.' Nick eyed Clarissa.

Clarissa clutched the arms of her chair. 'Was it a case of robbery?'

'It's possible.' Nick thanked his lucky stars Charles hadn't come to the door. If either of these two broke down under examination, it would be the girl.

'Was Mr. Martin in his shop?'

'I don't believe I said where the crime took place.' Nick watched the girl. He could see the pulse beating in the hollow of her throat. Listening intently, he heard her sigh.

'Actually, all signs indicate Martin died in

126

the woods near Bowness. A tourist out for an early walk this morning spotted his body floating in the water near the Falls at the Stockgylls. The police doctor estimates the death occured late last night.'

Nick watched for Clarissa's reaction to his words. She stared at him in silence as if dumbfounded by what he'd told her. 'It's also possible the killer wanted the police to think a robber killed Martin.'Clarissa looked down at her slippers and wouldn't meet his eyes.

'What's going on here?' Charles strode into the room, tying the belt around his robe. His pale blonde hair sleek from the shower, he stationed himself behind his sister's chair, his hands went to her shoulders. 'What's this all about?'

'We were talking about Mel Martin's murder last night. I'd appreciate your both coming down to Headquarters this afternoon to make a statement about your activities yesterday. We're asking all Bowness residents in this vicinity to come in. Maybe someone saw or heard something last night which will help us catch the murderer.'

Charles looked puzzled. 'Of course we'll do anything we can to help you, but we keep to ourselves. And as we told you in your office, neither of us knew the victim.'

'I know, but we're really stumped this time. First that poor tourist, and now another murder in the same area.' Nick shook his head, as if baffled by this latest crime. 'Things like this just don't happen in our quiet little community. At least it's quiet when the tourists leave.'

Charles nodded. 'Exactly. You may have hit on the answer.' He sat down beside his sister and leaned forward, seemingly eager to help. His pale eyes gleamed. 'Have you considered the possibility of a deranged transient?'

Nick raised both eyebrows. Where was this conversation heading, anyway? 'No, I haven't.'

'I saw an article last month which said the mentally ill can kill without motive. You might want to follow up on that.' Charles flashed a sympathetic smile Nick's way.

'I believe you've given me a new direction.' Nick strived to keep a grateful expression on his face. 'But if it wasn't an insane person, the killer must have had a reason for killing Mel Martin.' He studied Charles's face.

Charles shifted in his seat. 'Personally, I can't think of anything which would make me act in such a barbaric manner.'

Nick detected irritation in Charles's voice.

He pressed his point. 'If one feared someone else enough, I'd imagine that could be a motive.'

Charles shrugged, but he wouldn't meet Nick's gaze.

11

Kate thought about Nick again Monday morning while dressing. She couldn't figure him out. She'd better concentrate on her business and not worry about the Inspector.

Birds whistled in the trees as she walked up the driveway to the mansion. Diane and Chris were already sitting at the kitchen table while Mattie cooked breakfast.

Kate again tried to release Chris and Diane. 'You know I'd like both of you to stay on here until we can re-open King's Grant Hotel but — .'

Diane's reply was instantaneous. 'Kate, don't try to get me to leave. There's no place I'd rather be right now.'

'That goes for me, too.' Chris chimed in. 'We'll be able to re-open soon. Just wait and see.' He glanced at the wall clock. 'I've had two requests for guided tours around the lakes since we ran that ad in the Bowness News. In fact, my first tour starts at ten o'clock this morning.' He wolfed down a piece of waffle. 'It's getting late. I better go and check out the Rolls. I pick up my party at the Information Center downtown.'

'And I need to get out to the garden.' Diane picked up the dishes and carried them to the sink.

'I think you have a green thumb.' Kate teased her friend.

A native New Yorker, Diane apparently enjoyed the garden and kept the household stocked with tender young carrots and potatoes. Her previously pale, drawn face was now suntanned and relaxed. Quite a change. Kate fancied Chris was partially responsible for Diane's smiles these days.

Mattie got out her trusty hoover and began to vacuum the carpeted stairs in the front hall. Kate could hear her rendition of a forlorn Scottish ballad over the sound of the vacuum cleaner. Mattie had became more cheerful since Diane and Chris joined them. Chris had won Mattie's heart the day he'd volunteered to take Miles, Mattie's elderly scottie, for his daily walks.

The four of them had melded into a team. Each supported the others. Kate planned to give them each a piece of the business once it was better established.

Later that morning, Diane returned to the kitchen with her arms full of carrots. Kate was busy, stirring a kettle of vegetable soup on the stove when the phone on the counter rang.

'I'll get it.' Diane volunteered. She removed her gardening gloves, tossed Mattie's antique sunbonnet on the counter, and grabbed the phone. She grunted a response, then hung up the phone. Cramming her hands into her jean pockets, Diane turned to Kate.

Kate stopped stirring long enough to ask, 'Who was it?' She didn't like the worried expression on her friend's face.

'That was DCI Connor. He's on his way over here. He didn't tell me anything, just said he'll be here in a few minutes. I wonder why he's coming today.' Diane wrinkled her brow.

Putting down her ladle, Kate wiped her hands on a dish towel. 'Maybe it's good news. We could certainly use some after all that's happened recently.'

She'd missed Nick. He hadn't called since their trip to the coast several days ago. It was just as well since she didn't need a relationship which wasn't going anywhere. Last week he'd told her he couldn't make her any promises. She took a deep breath. She would tell him she didn't want to go out with him again. With his conducting an investigation on her property, she probably shouldn't have dated him in the first place.

'I'll round up Chris and Mattie,' Diane offered. 'If there've been new developments

132

in the Penmar case, we all need to know.' Diane opened the kitchen door.

Through the kitchen window, Kate could see Chris puttering about the Rolls on the driveway outside. Mattie had apparently finished her vacuuming since she rolled the vacuum cleaner into a kitchen closet and sat down at the table to read the paper.

By the time Nick drove up, they'd gathered in the kitchen.

Standing in the doorway, he wasted no time with greetings. 'I thought you all should know what's happened. A tourist found a man's body floating in the waters at Stockgyll Force this morning. The deceased has been identified as Mel Martin, the owner of Bowness Herbalist.'

'But isn't that the man you told me about?' Kate interrupted his monologue. 'The one with the mysterious customer inquiring for books on old herbs?'

'Yes, that's right.' Nick paused long enough to take a warm blueberry muffin offered by Mattie. As he smiled at Kate, she felt a tug on her heart-strings.

'Just as a matter of form, would the four of you come down to headquarters this afternoon and make your statements as to your routines yesterday? We've asked all of our Bowness residents in this part of town to do so today. We're hoping someone will come forth with a clue as to Martin's assailant.' He looked at Kate's friends and smiled. 'I guess that's all I wanted to tell you.'

As if on cue, Diane tugged at Chris's sleeve, then she led him out into the garden. She winked at Kate as they passed her. Mattie also left. They'd deliberately left her alone with Nick.

'These murders . . . It's horrible.' Shivering, Kate stood and pulled her sweater around her. 'Could the same person have killed both Mr. Penmar and Mel Martin?'

'That I can't say. We've only begun to investigate.' Nick stepped closer to Kate. 'I started to call you about this new crime but I wanted to see you. I hoped we'd have a few minutes alone.'

'Yes, well, I've wanted to talk to you.' She took a deep breath. 'I've been thinking.' She paused. 'I've decided it might be better if we stopped going out.' Regret filled her heart when she saw disappointment streak across Nick's face. And she'd thought he cared nothing for her. Wrong again, Kate.

'I understand.' All warmth left his voice. When he spoke again, his tone was cold and impersonal. 'Why would you want to socialize with a policeman, anyway?'

She could see she'd hurt him. 'It's not that

at all.' Kate stepped forward.

Nick moved toward the door. 'I may see you at headquarters this afternoon.' Giving her a brisk nod, he walked out. She watched him climb into his car and drive away.

Kate's eyes filled with tears. She'd been wrong. Nick cared for her, after all. Now he'd avoid her like the plague.

★ ★ ★

Driving back to the Constabulary, Nick felt cold and empty. He'd only known Kate a few days, but he liked her. Now he'd miss being with her, more than he cared to admit.

That afternoon he caught a glimpse of Kate and her three friends at the constabulary. They sat together in an office down the hall from him, talking to a constable who took notes. Nick kept walking. No need for him in there. When he passed by again, a few minutes later, they were gone.

'Could Mrs. Stanhope and her friends give you information that might help us on Martin's murder?' He queried a constable.

The constable looked over the statements Kate and the others had given. 'No, sir. They were playing scrabble in the hotel living room until one-thirty this morning.'

When the duty officer out front called Nick

announcing Charles and his sister, Nick asked that someone direct Clarissa to his office. Charles was to wait in the reception area until Nick talked to Clarissa.

Nick offered Clarissa a chair. 'First, I wonder if I could ask you to go through your activities yesterday, everything you did?' As he spoke in a quiet, pleasant voice, Clarissa seemed to relax. She sat back on the hard chair and crossed her long legs. He'd have to be careful. Clarissa wouldn't voluntarily give him any information he could use against Charles and her.

'Well, if you'd like me to go through my whole routine. As usual, I rose first, put on my robe and called Charles to get up. We always have breakfast together. I'd gone to bed before he did and had a hard time waking him. Then we ate breakfast which Cook had prepared.'

'Did you say Charles overslept? Was he out last night?' He'd already checked with the surveillance team. The two detectives parked outside The Folly's gates had seen nothing unusual on Wednesday or Thursday. No one had left the mansion those evenings except Cook.

'I didn't say that. We both stayed home. Charles just remained in the library reading after I retired. He often does that.'

Clarissa's voice was higher and more shrill now. She perched on the edge of her small hard chair. A bead of sweat appeared on her upper lip, and she kept a tight grip on her shoulder bag.

'I see. And after breakfast yesterday what did you do?' Nick glanced at the girl. She wouldn't look him in the eye.

'Not much. We both got dressed. Charles ran errands and I read and worked in the garden. When he came back, we had lunch in the dining room.' She shifted in her chair. 'I've arranged for our gardener to move the old latticed gazebo in the gardens. And he's going to dig up part of the back lawn so I can plant new flower beds. Charles thinks we should leave the gardens the way they are. He despises change. I disagree and am determined to update the grounds.' She paused. 'The weather has been lovely lately, hasn't it?'

Nick eyed her as she played with her hair, twisting the ends around her fingers. 'Yes. I hear you're quite knowledgeable about gardening. That must be a fascinating hobby. How long have you been involved with it?'

'Just the last few months. I find new hobbies stimulating, don't you?'

'Yes, indeed I do. Unfortunately, I don't

have much free time at the present. Perhaps when I retire. I guess that'll be all for now. We'll be in touch with you if we have any more questions. Thanks for coming in this afternoon.'

Nick moved quickly to his desk, summoning his sergeant. 'I'll see Charles Stanhope now,' he directed. 'Could you get Miss Stanhope a cup of tea while Mr. Stanhope and I talk?'

As Clarissa followed the Sergeant, she looked back at Nick. A few moments later, Nick glanced up to see Charles Stanhope standing inside his office door. Charles yanked at his silk tie, trying to straighten it, and ran his fingers through already discheveled hair.

'Please come in and take a seat.' Nick pointed to the same low, hard chair Clarissa sat on a few minutes earlier.

Charles arranged his lanky frame on the wobbly chair. He pulled out a handkerchief and dabbed at his sweating forehead.

'Please run through your schedule yesterday. You can start with getting up, dressing and having breakfast with your sister.'

'Oh, very well.' Charles rearranged his lanky body on the small chair, trying to keep his seat. 'I guess the sooner we get through this, the sooner I can go home. Let me see,

138

we had a lovely breakfast.' He paused.

'Very good. Please continue.'

'After breakfast, Cook removed our dishes. Clarissa wandered off to read one of her books, and I attended to errands down in the village.'

'And where did your errands take you?'

'Just to buy some champagne, pastries and to the bank. I was home before Cook served luncheon.'

'And after lunch? How did Clarissa and you occupy yourselves the rest of the day?'

'I listened to several selections of classical music, paid a few bills, read the newspaper, and took a nap.'

'And after dinner?' Nick was still waiting.

'Clarissa and I looked at some bulb catalogs. We were both weary and retired early, about nine-thirty.'

Nick recalled Charles' sister's comment about Charles's staying up after she retired, and filed the information away for future reference.

'And you didn't hear or see anything out of the ordinary last night?'

'No. So, if you have no more questions . . . ?' He waited, rocking his chair back and forth.

'All right.' Nick let him go. 'I guess that's

all for now. Thank you for coming in.'

Charles and Clarissa got in the Porsche and drove away a few moments later. At once, Nick summoned the detectives helping him. The surveillance team at The Folly reported Clarissa had stayed at home the previous day. One member of the team tailed Charles as he went about the village.

Charles had told the truth about the champagne. And after he left that shop, a detective talked to the disgruntled owner.

Annoyed, the merchant told the detective Charles was always late paying his bills.

Next, Charles went in the local bank and came out, tucking a large envelope into his coat pocket. He then returned home.

'Did you find out what he did at the bank?' Nick queried.

'Yes, I explained the information I requested might be crucial to a murder investigation, and I would come back with a warrant if necessary. The bank manager told me Charles had withdrawn £1,000, all in £20 and £50 notes.'

Alone again, Nick wondered why Charles would want so many small bills. He sat up abruptly in his chair. Could it be for blackmail? Why would anyone blackmail Charles unless . . . Nick felt the heat of excitement race through his body.

He remembered dealing with several cool, clever criminals before this case. And he'd outwitted them. Now, he must outwit Charles, if he really was the murderer. But how to prove it?

12

Nick stopped talking to Sergeant Kennedy at a sharp knock on his office door.

A tall, thin lab technician looked in. 'Excuse me, sir. We've examined the mold of the footprint from the Martin murder scene. A large running shoe made the impression, probably a man's size 12. The tread hadn't been worn down so it could have been a fairly new shoe.'

Nick turned back to his assistant. 'Sergeant, get an enlarged photograph of the mold from the lab. Take it and visit the managers of the local stores which carry running shoes. Maybe a manager will recognize the impression. If so, I want a list of the customers who've recently bought that brand of shoes, size 12 and larger.'

'Yes, sir. I'll start on it right away.'

Nick stopped Kennedy as she left his office. 'And, one more thing, Sergeant. See if you can find out Charles Stanhope's shoe size.'

He reviewed another clue. A constable had picked up a blood-stained £20 note from the ground near the falls. Maybe the killer left them a sample of his own blood. Again, Nick thought of Charles. He'd put the young aristocrat at the top of his unofficial suspect list. However, he'd seen Charles's hands the day after Martin's body turned up at Stockgyll Force and hadn't noticed any cuts or scratches. The lab would find out what blood type had been left on the note.

Nick pulled his door closed behind him, headed for the lab.

★ ★ ★

Kate straightened her bed covers, then gazed out the window. She must stop thinking of Nick. She'd told him she didn't want to go out with him after learning he didn't want a relationship. Now, loneliness bore down on her. She needed someone who'd want to share her life, someone with whom she could build a future. It was wiser to stop seeing Nick before she cared too much.

After one bite of a cinnamon-raisin bagel and a sip of tea, Kate pushed back her chair, stuck her dishes in the sink, and climbed the stairs to find her shoulder bag. Glancing in the hall mirror, she stopped to dab on some lipstick, then locked the front door and strolled up the hill.

As she walked, she thought about Diane

and Chris. They exhibited all the signs of a couple in love. How lucky they'd found each other. She was fond of both of them.

She knew Diane from their days at the New York paper. Diane had a terrible track record with men. That was the main reason she agreed to re-locate to the U.K. and help Kate with the hotel, she needed to get away. Now Diane had a new life. She'd come to the Lake District and met Chris.

Chris, boyishly handsome with sandy hair and clear blue eyes, seemed familiar. However, Kate knew she'd never seen him until he applied for a position at the hotel.

Kate stepped onto the front porch. As she opened the door, she stopped. Diane's voice floated down from the next floor. Kate started up the stairs. Hurrying, she caught her heel on a ragged edge of wool carpet. As she stumbled, she grabbed for the railing.

One of the family portraits on the wall opposite her drew her attention, a faded print of Stephen and his younger siblings. Gazing at the portrait, it struck her. Chris Lewis resembled Stephen and his brothers. How odd. Kate shrugged and continued upstairs. Guided by Diane's voice, she tracked the two women to one of the undecorated rooms. Diane and Mattie sat, Indian style, on the floor surrounded by a stack of wallpaper books.

When Diane spied Kate, she held up a sample. 'Don't you think this room would be lovely in this rose moire?'

Kate marvelled at how they'd lugged the heavy books up to the second floor. Perhaps Chris had carried them. Eyeing the pattern Diane offered, she responded. 'That's beautiful, but we won't have funds to re-do these rooms for some time.'

Apprehension swept through Kate as she worried over how long her funds would last if they couldn't re-open.

That evening Kate sat on her sofa and flipped through a magazine, for some reason reluctant to undress and go to bed.

Walking to the half-open window, she inhaled the cool night air. When she closed her eyes for a moment, Nick's face flashed before her. Kate turned away from the window and thoughts of him. A second later a loud blast shook the room.

Terrified, she threw herself on the carpet. Every muscle in her body was taut. The air was full of exploding glass. Splinters flew over the floor and landed in her hair and on her dress. When all was quiet again, she pushed herself up. Shaken, she took hold of a chair. On wobbly legs, she staggered over to the sofa and collapsed. Her hands stung. Both palms were cut from fragments of glass.

'Mrs. Stanhope, are you all right?' The constable who served as night watchman yelled at her front door.

Kate managed to cross the room and let him in. Temporarily unable to speak, she nodded her head then sank into an arm chair. Her mind whirled. Someone had tried to kill her again.

The policeman wasted no time, searching the small apartment then rushing to her kitchen wall phone to dial the constabulary.

'This is Officer McClure at King's Grant Hotel. I need assistance right away. Someone just shot out a window in Mrs. Stanhope's apartment. She has some cuts from the glass. Yes, I'll stay with her. How long will you be?'

From his end of the conversation, Kate surmised Headquarters would send a patrol car to King's Grant right away. She found a handkerchief in her pocket and dabbed at the cuts on her hands. Then shock set in and she started to shake, her teeth chattered. Even wrapping her arms around her body didn't stop the trembling in her arms and legs.

Tires squealed. A vehicle raced through the hotel gates. It skidded to a stop in front of the gatehouse. Her front door flung open and Nick rushed in. He was unshaven, dressed

146

only in jeans, a sports shirt and loafers. Amazement and relief raced across his face as he stood still for a moment. Then he dashed to her side. An odd sense of homecoming swept over Kate as his strong arms engulfed her. She'd never been so glad to see anyone in her life.

'Are you all right?'

She started to speak but broke into tears. Nick sat on the sofa, cradling her in his arms. 'It's all right now, I'm here.' Once her sobs faded, Nick helped her to stand. 'I'll take you to the emergency room. Those cuts need a doctor's attention.' He kept talking.

She heard his words as from a great distance, Nick's presence itself reassured her more than any words he spoke. Everything would be all right.

'I'm going to put the guy who did this behind bars where he belongs.' Anger seethed under his soothing tone.

Nick yanked a light coat from her closet, stuck it around her shoulders and helped her out to his car, his arm around her. Just before they drove away, Nick rolled down his car window and called to the officer on duty. 'Constable, I'll take Mrs. Stanhope to the hospital. Please let her friends at the hotel know what's happened.'

At the emergency room, Nick spoke to the

nurse at the front desk. A doctor immediately appeared to examine Kate. He removed the splinters of glass and bandaged her hands.

'Should she stay overnight?' Nick looked concerned.

The doctor looked up and smiled, reassuringly. 'No, she'll be fine. She just needs to rest.' He scribbled on a pad, then tore off a page and handed it to Kate. 'That's a prescription for a painkiller if you need it.' He looked at Nick. 'You're her husband?'

Nick flushed. 'No, her friend.' He placed Kate's coat around her shoulders and guided her to his car. As he drove back to King's Grant, Nick talked quietly to Kate.

Sitting beside him in the darkened vehicle, his calm manner soothed her raw nerves. In the light from a traffic signal, he appeared calm, his large hands at ease on the steering wheel.

'That incident tonight may have nothing to do with Penmar's death. It could have been a prank that got out of hand.'

Kate glanced over at Nick. 'Is that what you believe or are you trying to make me feel better?'

'I don't know,' he admitted with a sigh. 'But whatever happened, we'll find out. And we'll keep watch on your estate, day and night. You'll feel safer staying up at the hotel tonight. At daybreak, a team will search your property and the woods.'

He slowed down to pull in front of the hotel. 'The best thing you can do is get a good night's sleep.'

All the lights were on. Through the front windows of the hotel Kate saw Mattie at the front desk.

Kate rested her head on the back of the seat and closed her eyes. She needed to go to bed. Nick walked around the car and opened her door.

Watching his face as she stepped out of the Rover, she acted on instinct. 'Would you kiss me?'

Nick hesitated for a heart beat, then he wrapped his arms around her and kissed her on the lips.

Kate liked the feel of his mouth on hers, tender but strong. This kiss was different. He seemed to be in no hurry. His heavy beard scratched her face. Nick tasted of mouthwash and coffee, his scent of citrusy cologne mingled with the soap he'd used to shower. She wanted to stand there forever locked in his embrace. The door squeaked open, they drew apart. 'Call me in the morning?' She needed to know she'd hear from him soon.

'I'll call you.' His voice was husky with emotion.

13

Next morning, Kate woke up and looked around, feeling lost for a moment. The room with its floral wallpaper and rosewood furniture didn't look like her bedroom, but one of the hotel guest rooms. Then she blinked sleep-filled eyes and the events of the previous evening flooded her mind.

Sitting up, she covered her eyes with one hand. The bright sunshine filling the room dazzled her for a moment. She lay her head slowly back against the pillow. When she touched her mouth, she remembered the previous evening. Most of all, she recalled a very tender kiss. Kate wondered what would have happened if they hadn't been interrupted.

A tap on the door then Mattie bustled in with a breakfast tray. Kate smelled oatmeal, Mattie's cure for all ills. What a pity her friend never married and had children.

'You'll spoil me. I just have a few cuts.' Kate held up her bandaged hands and smiled to reassure Mattie.

'The Inspector inquired about you earlier, but I told him to call back since you were still asleep.' Mattie poured Kate's tea. 'I don't think he called on police business. Is it possible he likes you?'

Kate shrugged and feigned indifference, then she broke into a grin. 'Who knows?'

Mattie cocked an eyebrow then she checked her watch. 'I'll be right back. I have a coffee cake in the oven.' As she walked out of the room, Diane appeared.

'We were all shocked when the police officer came in last night and told us someone had shot at you. It wasn't a hunter, was it?' Diane leaned in the doorway. She walked into the room and put a glass of wildflowers on Kate's tray, then she leaned over and hugged Kate.

'Was it a shot? All I know is the window exploded.' Kate frowned, trying to recall.

'Well, they dug a bullet out of the wall in your living room after you went to the hospital.'

Kate's stomach knotted. 'Whatever happened, I'd turned away from the window before it shattered. I just got some cuts from the glass breaking. It makes me feel like one of those proverbial cats with nine lives.' Her voice trembled a bit.

'Chris called about the window. I'm afraid the new pane won't be as ornate as the old minnowed glass, but at least it'll keep the rain out.' Diane paused, before continuing. 'Kate, there's something else which I . . . I mean Chris and I, need to tell you.' A smile covered Diane's tanned face.

'Go ahead, I'm all ears.' Kate dabbed at her oatmeal. Ugh. She sipped the tea then pushed the breakfast tray aside.

Chris strode into the room and gave Diane a big hug. He smiled at both women. 'Did you tell Kate about us?'

'Yes, Chris.' Diane tiptoed and brushed her lips against his before turning back to Kate. 'In case you haven't noticed, we're in love. Chris proposed a couple of days ago and I've accepted.'

'Congratulations!' Kate stretched out her arms to give Diane a hug. 'I can't think of much that would please me more than to see the two of you married.' Kate thought fleetingly of Nick and the feel of his arms around her. She grinned at Diane and Chris.

'Let's get Mattie. I want to share our news with her, too.' Chris left the room and reappeared shortly with the housekeeper in tow.

'What's going on?' Mattie's usually somber face lit up and her brown eyes sparkled with excitement as she looked from Kate to Diane and Chris. 'With the murders and Kate being shot at, this better be good

152

news for a change.'

Chris reached over and hugged the older woman. 'Mattie, I promise you'll be pleased with our news. Diane and I are getting married soon.'

'That's wonderful.' A smile spread across the housekeeper's face as she smoothed her apron. 'I'll bake the wedding cake.' She shifted her attention to Kate. 'We'll need to clean the house and prepare for the wedding.'

Kate laughed. 'With your daily cleaning, this has to be the most immaculate place in the country.'

Diane filled Mattie in on their plans. 'We want a small, simple wedding, Mattie, just the four of us and the minister.' She brought a small calender out of her jeans pocket. 'We'd like to get married on June 23rd.' She paused. 'Chris, unless I'm going to walk down the aisle alone, we need someone to give the bride away. This is just a thought, but what do you think about asking Nick Connor?'

'Fine with me. If it's all right with Kate.'

Kate knew Diane and Chris liked Nick. She was pleased that they'd want to include him. 'I'll inquire, but he may have to work that weekend.' Would he want to participate in the wedding? 'Why don't we have the ceremony in the rose garden?' Kate beamed at Diane and Chris.

As if on cue, Nick called. Mattie motioned for Diane and Chris to follow her. Chris picked up Kate's tray and the trio filed out of the room. She heard them chatting about wedding cakes as they walked down the hall.

'I know words are never enough but you took care of me last night.' Kate thanked Nick. 'I needed someone and you were there.'

'Enough, Kate.' He protested. 'I'm sorry you had such a bad experience. I wouldn't want anything to happen to you. We should get the creep who shot at you soon. Just called to see how you are. Would you like to hear some good news?'

'Good news?' Kate hesitated. She really yearned to hear him say he loved her. Too soon. They'd only shared that one kiss. 'You've caught the killer?' She held her breath.

'No, not yet. What's the next best thing?' She heard a smile in his voice. 'We can re-open the hotel?'

'Right. You've all been cleared of any possible wrongdoing. My Superintendent says you can re-open anytime you like. The investigation will continue until we find the culprit, so I may hang around your place for awhile. If you don't mind?' His voice sounded hopeful.

'I'll be happy to see you. We'll have a

Grand Re-opening as soon as possible. Consider yourself invited.'

'Great.' He sounded relieved.

'Before you go, I have an invitation for you. Diane and Chris just told us they're going to get married.'

'Good for them. Give them my congratulations.'

'I will. Ordinarily, the bride has her father or brother give her away during the ceremony, but Diane's father is deceased and she doesn't have a brother.' Kate hesitated. 'They'd like for you to give the bride away, if you would. It'll be a small service here on June 23rd.'

'I haven't attended a wedding in years. In fact, the last one was my own.' His tone became sad and pensive.

'We'll keep the occasion simple.' She tried for a light note. 'Of course, you'll have to take home a large wedge of wedding cake. And Mattie's cakes are considered the best in the county.'

He chuckled. 'Then I'd better come and help the rest of you with the cake. Let me know the time.' His voice was brighter now. 'Got to go back to work. I'll talk to you later.'

'This calls for a celebration.' Kate flashed a grin at her three friends later as they all relaxed in the living room. 'Let's go out to dinner. Things have definitely taken a turn for the better, first the wedding news, then our being able to re-open the hotel.' Privately, she added, and Nick. From the way he acted last night, she could have misjudged him. Maybe there was room for her in his heart and in his life.

'Let's take the limo, shall we?' Kate envisioned a future full of blue skies. Only one cloud loomed on the horizon now and that would vanish when the police put the killer behind bars.

Chris carefully drove the vintage Rolls around Windermere to a small Italian restaurant known for its Northern Italian cuisine. They arrived early, just as the owner unlocked the front doors.

A large smile spread across Antonio's face. He seated them at the best table near a window wall where they watched the last mauve streaks of sunset as the sun slipped below the fells.

Kate inhaled the mellow odor of chicken breast marinated in wine and baked, covered with Asugio cheese. 'There's nothing as spicy and tangy as Italian dishes,' she remarked, tackling her entree.

'I'll take canneloni and meat sauce anytime,' responded Chris. He eyed Diane's selection, a duplicate of his own.

'Keep your eyes and your fork on your own plate, please,' laughed Diane. She moved her plate out of his reach.

'No, my entree is the best', chimed in Mattie, busily eating veal tender and succulent, covered with tangy parmesan cheese.

Later, the owner rolled the cart to their table. 'Does anyone have room for a selection from our dessert cart?'

'Spumoni for all,' cried Kate. 'And let's have another bottle of wine. This is a celebration.'

Gazing across the table, Kate remembered her discovery. 'Chris, the funniest thing happened the other day. I caught my heel on the carpet on the front stairs. As I straightened up, that large portrait of Stephen and his brothers caught my eye. You look like the Stanhopes.'

A peculiar expression flitted across Chris's face. 'You have an active imagination, Kate.' He gave an uneasy laugh.

Mattie joined in the discussion. 'But she's right. You do bear a resemblance. You're blond with blue eyes and your nose and mouth are similiar to the Stanhopes.'

'Enough. You're embarrassing him.' Diane chimed in. 'We need to make reservations for our honeymoon. Chris has promised me we can stay in a hotel, and not camp out, so let's hear your suggestions on hotels.'

Later, they drove through the estate gates, Kate stared up at the hotel. 'We never leave lights on in the cellars, but they're blazing now!'

Kate caught the police constable before he started his nightly patrol and asked him to check out the cellars. Protectively, Chris led the women into the hotel.

The young officer cautiously crept down the cellar steps. A few minutes later he called, 'All right. You can come down. But don't touch anything.'

Walking through the cellar rooms, Kate saw chaos. Furniture had been overturned, drawers pulled out of chests, lamps lay on their sides and pictures heaped on the floor.

'A burglar must have broken in while we were gone. What a mess.' Kate sighed. 'It's all been turned upside down.' She shrugged to relieve the tenseness in her shoulders. 'We'll have to check to see what was taken. There's such a hodge-podge down here, I don't know if we can tell.' Kate and the others walked through the rooms. She shook her head in dismay.

The policeman again cautioned them not to touch anything.

'Don't worry, Officer,' Kate replied. 'We

won't disturb anything. I know your department wants to check for fingerprints.'

Kate sensed Mattie's impatience as she looked around her. A neatnit by nature, Mattie craved order. At the moment, her fingers must itch to sort things out. 'Who'd want to come in here, anyway? There's nothing but Stanhope discards.' Kate quipped.

In the kitchen, the officer found a broken lock on the outside door.

Kate turned to Chris. 'Please call a locksmith tomorrow.' She eyed the constable. 'Officer, could you wait and phone DCI Connor in the morning? I can't tell if anything was taken, but it's all family momentoes, nothing of real value.' She checked her watch. 'Besides, it's late.'

The constable raised both eyebrows, then he shook his head. 'DCI Connor ordered me to call him if anything happened. If I may use your phone?'

Kate gave in. 'Of course. I don't want you to disobey your orders. Here.' She pulled her cellular phone from her shoulder bag. 'Use mine.'

He dialed Nick's number. Nick didn't answer so the officer left a message. Next, Kate heard him ring HQ, report the break-in and ask for a team to dust for fingerprints the next day.

Kate turned to the constable. 'Now, if there's nothing else, it's getting late and I think we should get to bed.'

'If you'll all stay together here in the kitchen for a few minutes, I'll check the house and make sure it's secure. Then I'll escort you to your apartment, Mrs. Stanhope.'

'Fine, go ahead.' Kate and Diane sat down at the table and Mattie put the kettle on the stove. Chris roamed around the kitchen, restless to accompany the constable.

'Everything's fine as far as I can see.' The officer spoke from the kitchen doorway. 'The other rooms haven't been disturbed. If you're ready, I'll walk you to the gatehouse now, ma'am.' The young constable looked disappointed. Did he hope to find a burglar lurking in a closet so he could show his prowess as a law enforcement officer?

'Fine.' Kate smiled at the others. 'I'll see all of you at breakfast.'

The officer walked Kate to her door.

Once he'd inspected the small building and found it undisturbed, she breathed a sigh of relief. The living room and pullman kitchen on the first floor and her bedroom and bath on the second floor didn't give much space for a burglar to hide, anyway.

'It's just like I left it earlier tonight. Thanks, Constable. Good night.' Kate shut and locked her door. Knowing the policeman would patrol the estate grounds all night reassured Kate. Still, she got out of bed to check the front door and windows before going to sleep. And she slept lightly, on edge, braced for another late night telephone call, but none came.

The next morning, Kate, Mattie, Diane and Chris gathered around the kitchen table and shared a large platter of blueberry pancakes and Cumbrian ham.

Watching Chris consume two stacks of pancakes, Kate teased him about his large appetite. 'Chris, if you eat a few more pancakes, you may be eligible for Guiness Book of World Records.' She laughed.

★ ★ ★

Nick rushed into the kitchen. 'I just heard you had a break-in here last night. Ambleside lost its telephone service last night, and I didn't get the message until HQ sent a constable to my condo this morning.' He saw Kate sitting at the table. 'How are your hands?' It hurt him to see Kate's bandages. Nick burned to get his hands on the brute who'd wounded her.

161

'Fine, thanks.' She held them up for his inspection.

'Please sit down and join us.' Kate motioned to a vacant place at the table.

Nick hung his coat on a hook by the back door and pulled up a chair then accepted a cup of coffee from Mattie. 'Has the lab checked for fingerprints? I hope you didn't handle anything in the cellars.'

Kate smiled. 'Please relax. Nothing's been touched. We're waiting for the police to check for fingerprints.'

While they talked, a van pulled into the back yard. Nick looked out the kitchen window, then he pulled open the door. 'Good morning. Please come this way.' He led three uniformed officers downstairs to the cellars and stood by while they began their procedure. After a few moments, Nick left the men to their business and returned to the kitchen.

'I think it's great that you two are tying the knot. And I'm touched that you'd want to include me in the ceremony. I haven't been in a wedding in years.' Nick shook Chris's hand and beamed at Diane. He guessed some people had happy marriages. But he hadn't been one of them. Nick's stomach clenched tight at the thought of his ex-wife.

'Can you give us an update on the two

cases?' Kate gazed at Nick.

'There's really not much to tell right now, but I hope soon we can put all of the pieces together, and solve both murders.' Nick didn't mention his theory that the two murders were related. He didn't have any proof yet.

'All I can tell you is to be careful. Don't take chances and report anything unusual.' Nick glanced at Kate and reassured her. 'We'll keep a constable here until we catch the killer.'

'Do you have any leads on who shot at me?' Kate asked.

'No, not yet.' Nick frowned. 'We've checked the stolen goods database, but no guns have been reported missing.' It was possible that one person killed Penmar and Martin and also shot at Kate. Uneasy, he shifted in his chair.

'There's something else I should tell you.' Kate bit her lip. 'I've had several anonymous telephone calls late at night at the gatehouse. They're all the same, no conversation. But someone breathes into the phone.'

Frustrated, Nick let out a sigh. 'You should have told me about this earlier. What else should I know?'

'Only that I believe I've been followed.'

'Follwed? You'd better tell me about it.

163

Right now!' Despite his attempts to keep a cool demeanor, Nick heard his own voice grow louder. He inhaled sharply then pulled his chair closer to hers and continued, in a calmer tone. 'Where did this happen? Is it still going on?'

'Tuesday in the village and Wednesday while I walked in the woods.' Her voice trembled.

'How can I protect you if you don't tell me about things like this? Or do you think you can take care of yourself and don't need the police?' He balled up his fists and crammed them into his pockets. 'You could be in danger this moment.'

Hearing a gasp of alarm, Nick glanced around and saw Diane clinching the arms of her chair and Mattie with a scowl on her face. Kate seemed to be on the verge of tears waiting for what he'd say next. He better take a cooler approach.

'The calls could just be wrong numbers.' He spoke more calmly. No reason to scare them all to death. 'There may be no cause for alarm but we won't take any chances.'

'Sorry, Nick. I'll tell you if it happens again.' Kate bowed her head and bit her lower lip.

'I want your word you won't go in the woods alone.' What was he to do with her?

The bitter taste of fear in his mouth reminded Nick that she'd come to mean a lot to him. He didn't want to lose her.

'I promise, if it'll make you worry less about me. It's all right to go shopping, though, isn't it?' She raised her brow in question.

'I guess, as long as it's on Lake Road, and in the daytime. But tell the others where you're going, and how long you'll be gone. In fact, I'd prefer that you take Chris with you.' Nick glanced at Chris. From Chris's grave expression, Nick could tell the other man understood the gravity of the situation.

Chris nodded, slightly. His tone was casual when he replied. 'Diane and Kate often have some shopping to do. I'll just tag along and carry their packages for the next few days.'

An uneasy smile crossed Kate's face. 'The people who killed Mr. Penmar and Mel Martin could be in another country by now.'

'It's possible.' Chris's presence reassured Nick. He'd like to stay and watch over Kate himself, but that was out of the question with two murder cases to solve.

'We'll keep an eye on her,' Chris promised.

'I'll have a bug put on your telephone in case you get any more calls.' Nick's policeman's instincts throbbed. The killer was probably growing impatient.

14

'Hello, Kate. I'm setting up my calendar for next week. What time did you say your Open House starts next Friday evening, seven or eight o'clock?'

Her pulse rate increased, hearing Nick's voice. 'Eight o'clock.' Tucking the phone under her chin, Kate wiped her hands on a dish towel on the kitchen counter. She shook her head at Miles who stood on his short back legs, begging for a taste of the food she'd prepared. Mattie's old Scottie was a terrible mooch.

'We're hoping to have a crowd,' she informed Nick. 'The local paper ran an article on the party yesterday, and a lot of people have called, wanting to come. We've also booked a few hotel reservations for next week.'

'Why not have a raffle? You could give a dinner for two as the prize.'

'We are. The mayor called and asked me about having one. The proceeds will go to the youth hostels on the lake.'

'Hold on a minute.' Kate heard Nick speaking to someone in his office.

He returned. 'Sorry, but duty calls. I'll see you at the party.'

Kate turned and spoke to Miles, the only other occupant of the kitchen. 'He got away before I could ask about the case.' Giving up on handouts, the dog cocked his head and nodded before he hopped into his bed and curled up for a nap. Kate resumed stuffing mushrooms, one of the hors d'oeuvres they'd serve at the party.

She put the prepared food in the refrigerator, then walked down the hall to the living room. Watching Mattie and Diane set up tables for the food, Kate announced, 'Nick called to check on the time of our party. I wasn't sure he'd be able to attend.'

'How are things with you two?' Diane gazed at Kate.

'At this point, I don't know. I guess time will tell.' She'd developed a 'wait and see' attitude regarding Nick. He'd shown he cared the night the gunman shot at her. But she sensed he was reluctant to get involved.

★ ★ ★

June 8th arrived. Kate and Diane made a last minute check of the first floor of the hotel.

Kate eyed the arrangements of red dahlias, the streamers of bright blue crepe paper and the silver, blue and white balloons. 'I hope we have a large turnout,' she murmured before the guests appeared. As she turned on the stereo, the melodious tones of Mel Torme filled the air.

Kate got her wish. Throngs of people streamed in the doors, curious locals and prospective guests as well as her competitors. And many bought raffle tickets from Diane at the door.

'Good evening Mayor.' Kate smiled as a portly, graying man came in.

'Good to see you,' she called to a Canadian couple who'd just opened a new bed-and-breakfast down the road.

Going into the kitchen, she spoke to Diane and Mattie as they hurriedly popped hors d'oeuves into the oversize ovens. 'Will we have enough food?'

Mattie filled two empty platters with hot sausage rolls. Blowing the hair out of her eyes and wiping her hands on her apron, she grinned. 'Here's hoping. If we start running out, you can announce the mayor's sister is going to sing.'

'Right. That should empty the place fast.' Kate laughed. 'She's a lovely person but can't carry a tune in a bucket.' She picked up a platter. 'The response has been great. If I didn't know better, I'd say some of our guests are driving over from the next county.'

Weaving her way through the crowd, Kate placed the platter of appetizers on a table in the living room. She stood back, watching the party-goers descend on the food.

Kate squeezed between groups of chattering guests until she reached Chris's station. She eyed the large supply of white and rosé wine, as well as cans of soft drinks, stashed under the bar. 'Looks like we have enough drinks.'

Chris never missed a beat. He smiled and nodded at Kate while at the same time pouring glasses of wine and soft drinks for their thirsty guests.

★ ★ ★

Sighing, Nick stepped into the crowded room. Tonight he came as a guest, not a detective. It was relaxing to talk to others without having to interrogate them, but his idea of fun wasn't a room crammed with noisy people stuffing their faces and yelling at each other. He preferred just sitting and talking with Kate, or just looking at her. Nowadays he was often overwhelmed by his feelings for her. Was she what she seemed?

Scanning the crowd, Nick caught sight of Kate across the room talking to the mayor.

He felt a momentary twinge of jealousy when she laughed at something the mayor said then chided himself for being foolish. He'd give them a few minutes before he rescued Kate.

To get away from the crush of the crowd, Nick eased his way to the back of the mansion. Two young women were working in the kitchen. One carefully mixed a dip for a platter of fresh vegetables. The other took a tray of hors d'oeuvres out of the oven.

Standing in the hall, he noticed the back door open. A third girl entered the kitchen quietly. The two temps paid her no attention but concentrated on their tasks. The newcomer strode over to a shoulder bag which hung on the back of a kitchen chair. Unzipping her own handbag, she pulled out a bunch of keys and stuffed them into the shoulder bag, then she called out the name, 'Alicia,' and left. The temp at the stove replied 'Thanks,' and continued working.

Thinking about what he'd just seen, Nick stepped out onto the terrace. An idea came to him. He slapped his forehead.

'Are you all right?' another guest asked.

Nick smiled, sheepishly, and replied, 'Just thought of something.' Glancing through the french doors at the crowd inside, he saw Kate free at last. He opened the french doors and, catching her eye, waved for her to join him outside.

Weaving her way through the crowd, she stepped out the door. 'I've been thinking about the night Mr. Penmar died,' he said. 'Did you call the agency for helpers?'

'Mattie made the arrangements. She contacted Lakeside Temps and requested two kitchen helpers. I'm sure your department checked them out.'

'Yes, I interviewed them myself.' He remembered the girls now and their appearance.

'Have you found a new clue?'

He shrugged, 'Probably not. I shouldn't think of work when I'm off-duty. I need to learn to relax.' Nick realized his hunch could be dead wrong. Still, he'd send his sergeant to Lakeside Temps Monday morning with Kate's picture of Charles and Clarissa.

Did Clarissa or a look-alike visit King's Grant the night of Penmar's murder? He remembered Clarissa's suggestion that she might have a double.

Nick winced when a noisy guest full of wine staggered out the french doors onto the terrace. The man tripped, sloshing his drink onto the floor. Nick jumped back to avoid getting soaked.

Her mouth thinning with displeasure, Kate

stepped forward and steered the man to the group he had accompanied to the party. 'Please be sure he doesn't drive home.'

When Mattie called, Kate went indoors. A few minutes later Nick followed her.

Kate beckoned to him. 'The doctor who promised to help with the raffle prize had to go and deliver a baby. I don't suppose you could fill in for him?' Nick nodded, then watched as she stepped forward and beamed at the crowd.

'Ladies and Gentlemen, I'd like to thank you all for making this evening a success. As you know, the raffle proceeds will go to youth hostels on Lake Windermere,' she informed the crowd. 'These centers provide safe, inexpensive shelter for young people touring the Lake District.' Kate looked around the room. 'The mayor, assisted by DCI Connor from Windermere Constabulary, will announce the winner.'

The mayor smiled and inserted his hand into the large glass bowl Nick held. He pulled out one raffle ticket. 'The winning number is 45.'

Grinning ear to ear, the Canadian bed-and-breakfast owner stepped forward.

The mayor announced, 'I'm pleased to award you a certificate for dinner and one night's lodging for two in the Grassmere

Suite of the King's Grant Hotel.' He handed the paper to the winner and shook his hand. All of the party-goers applauded. The party resumed.

Later, the party began to lose momentum. Seeing a few slipping away, Nick eyed Kate beside him. 'Why don't we go out for a night cap? I'm sure you need to relax after this evening.'

'No, Nick. Not tonight.'

'Why not?' He wanted to be alone with her.

'It's been a frantic day. We've worked hard preparing for the party. Why don't you call me tomorrow? I need to help clean up the place tonight.'

'If that's what you want.' Since they'd met, he'd had to remind himself of his resolution to stay unattached. But his yearning for her grew greater every day whether they were together or apart. In spite of the fact that he found life simpler on his own.

Since he couldn't stop thinking of Kate, he tried again. 'Walk me down the driveway to my car?'

'All right.'

Nick and Kate filed through the front doors of the hotel, behind a group of party-goers. Car doors slammed, motors raced, and last good nights resounded, then the front driveway returned to its usual quiet state. The

173

cool air on his face refreshed Nick, as he gazed upward at the stars which sparkled in the night sky.

Arm in arm, they strolled down the driveway, the gravel crunching under their shoes. A slight breeze wafted the scent of wisteria and stirred Kate's short, sea-green chiffon dress. Nick noticed a bed of white dahlias, silver in the moonlight.

Kate stumbled. 'Careful,' He cautioned her and grasped her arm while she took off one green satin sandal and shook out a piece of gravel.

Reaching his Rover, Nick leaned against the side of the car and swung her into the circle of his arms.

'You're lovely.' He ran his hands over her bare shoulders.

'Thanks.' She stepped back and turned around to show off the dress.

As her skirt rippled, Nick admired long, slender legs.

'Do you like my dress?'

'I like you.' He smiled when she came closer. He inhaled roses and another sweet-scented flower. It suited her. His finger traced her cheekbone and continued to her mouth. When her lips curved into a smile, he bent and kissed her, at first lightly like the breeze, then deeper as her lips parted.

'I can't keep my hands off you.' Alarms exploded in his head. He ignored them when she moved into his embrace. Her arms pulled him closer.

'I've kept you too long. You better go.' He rubbed her bare arms, wishing she didn't have to leave him.

'Yes, they'll wonder where I am. Good night, Nick.' Before he could reply, she turned and darted uphill to the hotel. Nick watched her wave before she stepped inside. He climbed in his car and drove home.

★ ★ ★

The next morning, Nick looked up from his desk as Sergeant Kennedy walked into his office.

'Please go over to Lakeside Temps. Ask them to contact the two girls King's Grant Hotel hired for the night of Penmar's death. Let's find out if they can identify Clarissa.' Nick opened a desk drawer. 'Here's the picture.'

'I'll return these keys later today.' Nick spoke to the duty officer in the evidence room after he signed for the Bowness Herbalist keys. He wanted to take another look at Martin's shop. His team had found no clue as to who wanted Martin dead.

Driving down Lake Road, Nick reviewed the little he'd learned about Martin. The man was considered a local expert on herbs. And he opened his shop about four years ago. Not much to go on. Nick frowned, turning into the parking lot.

Searching through Martin's desk that morning, Nick found old bills, advertisements of new books on herbs, some marked 'Order,' as well as two prescriptions. He let out a sigh of frustration, finding nothing of interest. Spotting a glass paperweight on the corner of the desk, Nick picked it up. Turning it over, he read two words, Avon Gardens. The name was familiar. Avon Gardens was a large chain of nurseries. He'd once bought a ficus plant at their local store. Of course it died. He wasn't good with plants. He stood juggling the paperweight back and forth from one hand to the other, then replaced it on the desk. 'Did Martin work for Avon Gardens?' He muttered to himself. As a long shot, Nick dialed their corporate headquarters and reached the Assistant Director of Personnel.

'Can you tell me if a man by the name of Melvin Martin was an employee of your company?'

'I'm sorry, but we can't give personal information without confirming the legitimacy of an inquiry.'

'This is DCI Nick Connor with the Windermere Constabulary.'

'If you'll give me your badge number and telephone numbers where I can reach you and your constabulary, I'll call you back.'

He gave her the requested information. 'I'll be at the first number if you call within the hour. After that, you can reach me at my office.'

Ten minutes later, the phone on Martin's desk rang.

Dropping a book on herbs, Nick dashed back to the office.

'Inspector Connor, this is Mildred Jones, Assistant Director of Personnel at Avon Gardens. You asked about a Melvin Martin?'

'Yes, I need to know if he worked for your corporation, his position and years of employment.'

'If you'll hold on, I'll check our personnel files on my computer.' She returned to the phone. 'Mr. Martin was a salesman for twenty years. The last two years before he retired, he served as our Regional Sales Manager. He left the firm four years ago. I didn't know the gentleman since I just joined the firm two years ago.'

'I see.' Nick thought fast. He might find out more if he spoke to the Director. 'I'd like an appointment with the Personnel Director.'

'Let me check his schedule for next week. Just a moment, please.' Less than a minute later, she replied, 'The Director has an opening Monday morning at 11:00, if that's convenient?'

'That's fine. I'll be there,' he replied. 'Thank you for your help. Goodbye.' Nick wondered if a drive to Stratford was a wild goose chase. However, he did need to find out more about Martin. And he might find out more in person than on the phone.

★ ★ ★

Two days later, Nick parked the Rover outside Avon Gardens in Stratford-on-Avon. He observed the well-maintained condition of the aging limestone building as he stepped inside.

Jeremy Spencer, the Director of Personnel, waited for him. Spencer shook his balding head. 'I don't remember Martin. He must have retired before I joined the firm. Wait a moment.' He walked out of his office and came back with a manila folder. Leafing through its contents, he confirmed the data his office had already given Nick.

Nick noticed a frown on the other man's face. 'I'll treat any information you give me in confidence,' he offered, reassuringly. Sensing the man's hesitation, Nick persisted. 'Anything you can tell me might help solve the case I'm investigating.' He didn't reveal Martin had been murdered.

The Director looked sharply at Nick, then he wrote a name and phone number on a sheet of paper and handed it to him. 'This gentleman may be able to tell you more about Mr. Martin. As Sales Director, Edward Mercer was Martin's boss. Mercer now lives in a senior residence on the outskirts of Stratford.'

'Is there a telephone here I can use?'

'Certainly. If you'll excuse me, I must see my assistant.' He motioned Nick to the phone on his desk, then left the room, closing the door behind him.

Nick dialed Mr. Mercer. 'Good morning. This is Inspector Connor from Windermere. Avon Gardens Personnel referred me to you. I understand you supervised Melvin Martin while he was a salesman with the company.'

'Oh, yes. I knew him well, Inspector. Perhaps we should talk in person? You say you're in town?'

'Yes. I'm trying to collect information on the man. It may prove pertinent to a case I'm investigating. When can I see you?' He wondered if the elderly Mercer would be able to help.

'I'm sorry, but I'm tied up today. We're having a special music program this afternoon, then one of our residents celebrates her one hundredth birthday. We're planning a party. Why don't you come out here tomorrow morning? I'll be free after physical therapy.'

'All right. What time shall I come?'

'How about 10:30 a.m.?'

Nick hung up the phone and left the company building. He strolled around Stratford and managed to avoid the long lines of tourists waiting to tour Anne Hathaway's cottage.

When he located the hotel Avon recommended, the assistant manager found him a small, comfortable room at the back of the graceful, vine-covered, limestone building. Before Nick slept that night, he called Kate.

'I'm in Stratford, but I'll be back tomorrow. I have an appointment in the morning.'

'I haven't been to Stratford for years. Did you notice mobs of tourists mulling about in those charming little gift shops?'

'I try to stay away from such dens of iniquity. Do you want me to bring you a miniature replica of the Hathaway Cottage or perhaps a tea cup and saucer with

Shakespeare's picture?'

'No, thanks.' She sniggered. 'You may recall we already have a cellar full of Stanhope memorabilia.'

'Kate, what were you doing when I called?

'I just got into bed.'

'Another hard day toiling at the hotel?'

'Actually it's been quiet today, no guests. I thought I'd read one of Mattie's whodunits. They always put me to sleep.'

'Tell me what you're wearing.'

'Maybe I should leave that to your imagination.'

'No, really. I'd like to know. I wish we had one of those futuristic telephones where you see the person you're calling.'

She laughed. 'You'd be disappointed. I'm wearing a cozy, long-sleeved, high-collared, nightgown.'

'On you, it must look great.' What was he doing, talking to her like that? He hoped she didn't think he was getting too personal. 'Sorry. I didn't mean to be nosy.'

'It's all right.'

Then, as if they had a will of their own, words he'd never spoken in his life slipped from his lips. 'I miss you.'

There was silence on her end, then a faraway voice replied, softly, 'I miss you, too.'

'Go to sleep. I'll call you when I get back to the office.'

'Sweet dreams.' She hung up. Her soft voice echoed in his head while he prepared for bed.

15

Next morning when he strolled into the dining room, Nick inhaled the delectable odor of eggs and country ham. He indulged in a full English breakfast instead of his usual, black coffee. Later, he strolled along the River Avon, inhaling the cool, fresh air. Finding a seat on a wooden bench, he watched the canal boats navigating the locks. Two houseboats went by, their occupants on deck. A young couple stood alert as their boat cleared the locks. They waved to him and Nick responded. Then he spotted a small girl playing dolls on the deck of the other boat. A collie pup wearing a baby bonnet sat by the child.

How wonderful to be on holiday with your family. He thought of Kate and briefly imagined the two of them on holiday somewhere like Cornwall. They could lie on the beaches, climb to the top of Tintagel, and visit the beautiful, restored gardens.

Nick killed another hour in the quaint, Victorian hotel lobby, browsing through the local paper until time to see Mercer. Following the retiree's directions, he drove through the town. As Mercer had told him, the retirement residence wasn't far from Stratford. He slowed down and turned onto the long, curving private driveway, flanked by pines. The road led uphill to the residence. Rhododendrons in full bloom flanked the graceful stone building. As Nick parked the Rover, a fountain splashed out of sight.

Opening the door, he stepped inside the reception area, straightened his tie, and glanced around the spacious lobby. Spotting the receptionist's station, he walked across forest green carpet and stopped in front of an elegant antique desk.

'Good morning. I'm Inspector Connor from Windermere. I have an appointment with Mr. Mercer.'

The attractive, silver-haired lady smiled. 'If you don't mind waiting a moment, I'll let Mr. Mercer know you're here.' Nick sank into a comfortable armchair. Lulled by the soft music and muted ambience, he relaxed and thought of visiting his mother in a nursing home.

She had reappeared for his father's funeral. Nick never asked, and she didn't volunteer to tell him where she had spent those years away from them. When her health failed, Nick had put her in a nursing home. It wasn't a bad place, but nothing like this senior residence.

He recalled his last visits to his mother. Senile, she wanted him to visit daily but had to accept his weekly visits. The receptionist's tap on his shoulder broke his reverie.

'Sorry to keep you waiting, Inspector. Mr. Mercer finished his physical therapy and is expecting you. Please come with me.' As they walked down a quiet hall she asked, 'Is this your first visit?'

Nick answered, his words clipped short. 'Yes, I haven't been in a nursing home for years.' He pushed back his memories and followed the receptionist.

She knocked on Mercer's door, opened it and stood aside. A distinguished looking older man with white hair rested on a chaise longue listening to music. Nick recognized Saint-Saen, but not the particular work. The striking notes of the piano concerto filled the air. Seeing Nick, Mercer turned down the music.

Walking across the large room, Nick glanced outside and caught a glimpse of several bird houses and feeders hanging in the grove of birch trees. Pink rose bushes encircled the limestone fountain he'd heard earlier.

'Mr. Mercer, I believe you're expecting me.'

'Pleased to meet you, Inspector. Make

yourself comfortable. I don't have a lot of company nowadays.' Mercer struggled to sit up and Nick hastened to help him. He arranged the pillows so the older man could be more comfortable.

Nick pulled a wicker chair close to Mercer's chaise longue. 'I'm conducting an investigation into the murder of Melvin Martin, one of your former employees, sir.'

'I haven't thought about that fellow for years. Can't say I'm surprised to hear of his untimely demise!' The retired man looked Nick in the eye. His words rang clear and firm.

'I'm afraid I don't understand.' Nick clasped his hands over his crossed knee and waited for Mercer to continue.

'Just this, Inspector. I knew the man for years and found him to be a malcontent who continuously complained, especially about his salary. He told me numerous times he deserved more than the company paid him.' The older man shifted position.

Nick absorbed Mercer's words. 'Please go on.'

'Martin progressed to Regional Sales Manager. He was a good salesman, but not popular with the other employees. They avoided him. Right before he left, I heard something which caused me to question his honesty and integrity.'

Nick sat up straight in his chair, curious as to what was coming next. 'What did you hear?'

Mercer took a sip of water. 'The day before Martin left, I heard an ugly story. A retiree told his son that Martin had tried to blackmail another man.' Mercer gazed in Nick's direction. 'We had no proof. One of his victims was dead, and the other was senile. I talked to Martin the day he left and he said it was all lies. He retired with full benefits.' Mr. Mercer adjusted a pillow behind his head.

'For the past four years he's kept a low profile.' Nick shifted in his chair. 'No one says anything bad about him, but if Martin has one friend in our area, I can't find him.' Nick noticed the dark circles under Mercer's eyes as the old man reached for a pill.

'I won't take up any more of your time, Mr. Mercer. Thank you for your candor. Your description of Martin gives me a more clear picture of the man.' He rose to go, took Mercer's hand and shook it.

'I'm glad I could help you, Inspector. Good luck catching your murderer. No one deserves to end his life that way.'

★　★　★

Kennedy met Nick at his office door next morning.

'Inspector, before you ask, I've shown the picture to the temporary agency's employees.' She walked ahead of him into his office and took a seat across from his desk.

Nick hung up his coat, sat down and stretched his legs under his desk. 'Don't keep me in suspense. Did they identify Kate Stanhope's niece?'

Disappointment streaked across her face. 'No, they couldn't, but your hunch was right. There was a third girl. The first temp had just broken up with her boy friend, so she was upset and didn't pay attention. She'd forgotten the other girl until I asked.'

'I see.'

'The other temp didn't get a good look at the girl. But she'd lost her contacts that afternoon, and her vision was fuzzy. Her main concern was getting through the evening and going home to find them.'

'Then what do you make of it?' Nick frowned.

'The girl was there when they walked into the kitchen. The only description I could get was that she looked like them, tall, thin with long blonde hair. Since she wore a navy skirt and tailored white blouse, they assumed she also worked for Lakeside Temps. A couple of

188

minutes later, she told the others she was ill and had to leave. I called Lakeside Temps and they confirmed that they'd just sent two girls to King's Grant that night.'

'So who was the third girl?' Nick sighed. 'It's too bad the temps couldn't identify Clarissa, but the pieces of the puzzle are coming together at last.' He leaned forward in his chair and rested his elbows on the desk top.

'Tell me what you think of this. Charles wanted Kate to sell King's Grant when Clarissa and he sold their home. The hotel offered them a lot of money, much more than they would have received, listing the estates with a realtor. The catch was the hotel wanted both properties, not one. But Kate refused. He might have cracked and tried to kill her, poisoning Penmar instead.'

Kennedy shook her head. 'I can't see Charles losing his cool, can you? He strikes me as a person completely in control.'

'Perhaps, though even control freaks can break from too much pressure.' He put that theory aside and tried another. 'Okay, how about another motive? How about revenge? Their uncle promised them the property on his death then reneged and left it all to Kate. Charles considered King's Grant his legacy. And along came Kate, taking it away from

189

him. But did Charles hate his aunt enough to kill her?'

Nick loosened his tie then walked to the coffee dispenser and re-filled his mug. He sipped the hot coffee. 'I learned in Stafford that Martin was a malcontent. No matter how many raises he got, he always thought Avon underpaid him. And the day before Martin retired, another Avon employee told management that Martin had attempted to blackmail his father, but Mr. Mercer, Martin's old boss, said they found no proof. The employee's father was elderly and senile.'

Kennedy nodded and picked up where Nick had stopped.

'Martin could have heard rumors in the village that Charles was unhappy with the settlement of the estate last fall. Later, he would have met Clarissa in his shop asking for books on old herbs. If he'd figured out their scheme, Martin could have reverted to his old tricks and tried to blackmail Charles.'

'Correct.' Nick rubbed tired eyes. 'Now if we can just prove it.'

★ ★ ★

The June sun warmed Kate's head and shoulders as she stooped to weed her small garden behind the gatehouse. Her muscles tensed when a shadow blotted out the sun.

Looking up into the brightness, she squinted to see a tall, lean figure in jeans. Nick grinned down at her.

'I didn't know you were back from your trip. I didn't hear your car.' She took his outstretched hand and stood up, then wiped her dirty hands on her jeans. She blew a straggling lock of hair off her face.

'You really concentrate when you're working, don't you?' Nick's expression turned serious. 'I could have been anybody. You need to stay alert right now.'

'I know. It's just that . . . ' Her words trailed off.

'It's a beautiful, sunny day and nothing bad happens when the sun is shining and the birds are singing. Right?'

Kate flushed. 'Something like that. What brings you over here today? Don't you need to be in your office?' She tried to be nonchalant, though she was pleased he'd come to see her so soon after he got back from Stratford.

'I've been at the office to check on things, then decided to take the rest of the afternoon off. Don't worry, I'll be there early tomorrow morning.'

'I see.' She didn't, really.

'I'm driving down to Morecambe Bay to

see a man about a sailboat. Think you might like to ride along with me?'

'Give me time to clean up. I seem to have as much dirt on me as there is in this flower bed.' She wiped her hands on her shirt.

'If you can do it in five or ten minutes. After that I'm out of here.' He smiled.

Kate rushed indoors to wash her hands and face. She changed into a clean shirt and found jeans that didn't have muddy knees. In less than ten minutes, she stood by his car. He opened the car door for her. They drove at a leisurely pace down New Ferry Road toward the Bay.

She glanced over at Nick. Today he was acting like her pal or big brother. The man was as changeable as one of those little chameleons that change color according to their environment. Kate snickered to herself. Nick wouldn't appreciate being compared to a lizard, no matter how cunning. 'I take it you know all about sailing?'

'I've read a few books,' he replied, confidently. 'It can't be all that difficult.'

They rode a few minutes in companionly silence, then he asked, 'Have you been to Morecombe Bay before?'

'No, my husband was confined to bed most of the time we lived here before his death, and he didn't want me to leave him. Since then, I've been busy getting the hotel ready to open.'

'I see. Well I'll fill you in on its history. The Bay is dangerous to people who don't pay attention.'

'Really?' She raised an eyebrow.

'Right. At low tide, the water completely leaves the Bay, and you can walk out a long distance. If you walk too far, you could get caught when the tides come racing in. The local park service has set up flags, whistles and signs to warn walkers. Still, a few people are drowned each year. You can't out-race the tides.'

'Sounds like a place I'll want to avoid.'

'Wait, there's more. At low tide, you don't want to walk across the Bay without a guide. There are pockets of quicksand that shift about, so they aren't always in the same place. Guides will walk you across, but the best rule is to stay on shore.'

Kate swallowed hard. 'Thanks for telling me.'

'Here we are.' Nick pulled into a parking lot near a pier.

She breathed a sigh of relief to see the tides were in. The only sailboat tied up at the pier had a large 'For Sale' sign on its deck.

'Let's look for the owner.' Nick spotted a shed where a man was threading fishing lure.

He called to the man.

He came back to Kate, smiling. 'He'll take us on a sample ride out in the Bay.'

Kate eyed the small craft. 'You go ahead, I'll wait here. But don't take too long. The sky looks like a storm's coming.'

Nick studied the dark clouds. 'On second thought, I may come back later. Anyway, that sailboat doesn't look too good. My friend at work has one he'll sell me that looks better. Let's go. Maybe we can beat the storm.'

The rain poured down before they drove far up New Ferry Road. By the time the Rover stopped in front of the gatehouse, water pounded the earth.

'Want to come in?' She shouted so he'd hear her.

'Maybe until the storm passes.'

They ran into the gatehouse. By the time Kate unlocked the door and let them in, their clothes were plastered to their bodies.

'Take off your shirt. I'll get you a towel.' She went upstairs and stripped off her wet jeans and shirt and put on a terry cloth robe.

When she came back downstairs, Nick was kneeling in front of the fireplace. He struck a match and held it to some wood stacked in the fireplace until a flame sprang up.

Kate's eyes ran over his lean, wiry build. Too bad he only wanted her to be his friend.

Nick turned before she could look away. He smiled and dried his wet, matted chest with the towel she'd tossed him. 'You're shivering. Come sit by the fire and I'll dry your hair.'

'You don't need to . . . ' Kate protested, but in vain. Nick set her down on the hearth and unwound her braids. Taking a towel, he gently rubbed her hair. Kate relaxed. Then his hands moved to her shoulders.

'You're so tense. Relax. I'll give you a massage.'

She indulged his whim. His hands soothed her taut muscles. Closing her eyes, she felt herself unwinding.

'There. Isn't that better? There's only one thing more relaxing than a massage.'

By the tone of his voice as he stood behind her, Kate imagined he was smiling. Her heart pounded as he raised her to her feet and kissed her slowly, tantalizingly, until her lips felt swollen.

'Kate, I want you.'

Now it was her turn to smile. 'I thought you wanted us to be good friends, Nick.'

'I did but when I'm around you, friendship isn't what comes to mind. Come here.' He opened her robe. She was glad she'd removed all of her wet clothes earlier.

They stood chest to chest kissing before the

fire. Her skin became hotter where his body touched hers.

The doorbell rang.

Kate felt a moment's panic then they looked at each other in disbelief.

She slipped on her robe and tied it around her. Nick picked up his shirt and stepped into the kitchen.

She opened the door and found Diane and Chris on her porch.

Diane smiled. 'Hi. I saw Nick's Rover in front. We're on our way to the matinee of an old Harrison Ford movie, then out for pizza and thought you two might like to go with us?'

'Oh, thanks, but we already saw the movie. But thanks for the invitation.' Kate tried to look appreciative.

'No problem. Got to run to get those cheapie tickets. See you later.' Diane and Chris hopped in his old Volvo and splashed down the road.

Kate smiled and shut the front door. 'Come out, come out, wherever you are.' She peered around the doorway into the kitchen.

Nick was buttoning his shirt. 'Guess I better go. It's late.' There was a nervous expression on his face.

She bit her lip, trying to control her rage.

Nick put on his wet jacket. 'Our timing

wasn't too good today.' He peered out the window. 'Looks like the storm's over. I'll call you.'

Before she knew it, he'd driven out the front gates.

'I just don't understand him at all.' Furious, she muttered through clenched teeth. Angry tears wet her cheeks. She was growing weary of his behavior. He'd better make up his mind and soon.

16

Nick ached to turn the car around, go back and beg Kate to forgive him. He shouldn't have run away. Instead, he grasped the steering wheel firmly and headed for the constabulary. He'd frozen when Diane and Chris appeared at Kate's door. By the time Kate sent them on their way and found him in the kitchen, he'd convinced himself that making love with her would be a colossal mistake. Every time he became involved, he'd ended up disappointed. He'd made no commitment to Kate and respected her too much to treat her like a one-night stand.

The next morning, in his office, he pushed the memory of Kate's hurt, angry face to the back of his mind. Turning to Sergeant Kennedy, he inquired, 'What else did you find out while I was gone?' Nick sat the mug down on his desk and eyed Kennedy.

'We couldn't get a shoe store manager to identify the mold so our lab collected a pair of each brand of running shoes they could find in the area. After examining a lot of shoes, they determined Speedmaster, a new limited edition running shoe, made the footprint at the Falls. And Windermere Runner in Bowness is the only store selling the Speedmaster in this area.'

'Good work.' Nick grinned at his young assistant and waited for her to continue.

'Windermere Runner has only sold three pairs of that model so far. It's quite expensive. The store saves its sales information in a database so it wasn't difficult to get the names of the men who'd bought a pair. Here's a printout of the names of the customers.' Handing Nick the list, Kennedy smiled.

Nick quickly scanned the paper and laughed aloud on reading the third name. Charles Stanhope. He nodded for Kennedy to continue.

She shifted in her seat. 'I've already contacted the first two gentlemen. One of them returned Sunday from a three-week honeymoon in Spain. We have a call in to the hotel in Madrid, checking his alibi. The other man's motorcycle collided with a pickup truck last month. Luckily, he was wearing a helmet. He's in a body cast. So we can rule him out.'

'Which leaves the third man on your list, Charles Stanhope. We'll get back to him in a minute.' Moving on to other clues, Nick prompted his assistant. 'How about the bank note? What did the lab decide about the bloody £20 note found at the Falls? Was it Martin's blood?'

Kennedy consulted her notes. 'It could have been. The lab report said it was type AB, Martin's blood type.'

'There were no signs of a struggle, were there?'

'Not according to the reconstruction of the murder scene. From the dirt on the knees of Martin's jeans, he was kneeling when his assailant attacked him. The killer must have approached from behind and hit Martin over the head with a hard object. We haven't identified the murder weapon.'

Nick scanned a report from Dr. Walker's office. 'Autopsy indicates Martin died shortly after he was attacked. But why dump the body in the falls?' He paused. 'Did Martin's killer try to make it look like an accident?'

'I don't know.' Kennedy shook her head.

'We're missing something.' Nick frowned. 'I just can't put my finger on it. Never mind.' He moved on. 'There's another clue. The lab has identified a strip of newspaper found by the falls as part of a page from last Friday's Financial Times. But why would it turn up at Stockgyll Falls? That's a steep climb up to the top. I know, I've been there. You need both hands to hold onto the rocks. You don't take the morning paper with you.' Nick looked across his desk at the policewoman. 'Find the page that strip came from, fit the two pieces together, and we'd have a real clue. Right, Sergeant?'

Nick paced up and down. There must be a way to speed things up. Most of his cases had moved faster. This one dragged on and on. He sat back down. 'Here's an assignment for you. Visit Charles Stanhope and ask if you can see his running shoes. I bet he refuses. Then you show him your warrant and search the house.'

'Right, sir. You really think it's Charles?'

Nick nodded. 'I think so. It's possible, though not likely, he hasn't disposed of the shoes yet. They'd help us nail him. Let me know what happens.' He eyed a report he was writing for the Superintendent. 'We've got to catch him before he kills anyone else.'

Nick drove into King's Grant grounds that afternoon, hoping to see Kate, but when he knocked on the gatehouse door, the sound echoed through the silent apartment. She was probably up at the hotel.

Walking up the drive, Nick stepped into the kitchen just as Mattie lifted two hot, juicy apple pies out of the oven. His stomach rumbled as he inhaled the sweet cinnamon fragrance of the pies. 'Where's everybody, Mattie?'

'I packed Kate a picnic lunch and sent her down to the lake to get some fresh air.' When his hungry gaze stayed on the cooling pies, she moved them. 'I think Diane and Chris have gone shopping for groceries. Can I help you?'

'No, I wanted to see Kate. I'll walk down and find her.' He strolled down the hill to the lake glistening turquoise in the June sunshine. Kate sat at a picnic table near the beach. As he approached, several resident swans were begging her for a handout. The aggressive birds hissed and nipped at each other, competing for tidbits.

When Kate looked up, an uncertain look crossed her face. Then she smiled. Nick's throat grew tight with longing. She had no idea how she affected him.

'Hello, what a pleasant surprise! Come have some of my lunch. I've enough for a small platoon, thanks to Mattie.'

'Thanks, Kate. I missed lunch today.' His stomach growled, agreeing with him.

She scooted over on the bench to make room for him, filling another plate.

Nick made short work of the salty country ham, creamy potato salad and a piece of Mattie's fudge-like chocolate cake and washed it all down with a large glass of sweetened, minted iced tea. 'I've never tasted anything as good. Thanks for sharing.' Now he felt better.

'Are there any new developments on your cases that you can tell me about?' She leaned toward him.

Kate appeared more relaxed today yet Nick detected faint circles under her eyes. He hoped she'd been able to sleep the previous night. Nick knew he'd upset her. 'We're still examining evidence, but haven't made any major breakthroughs yet.' Maybe it wouldn't be too long before they caught the killer.

The last crumb of cake vanished, and Nick sighed in appreciation. 'Want to take a walk?'

'Sure, if you've got time.'

He carried the trash to a nearby bin while Kate packed up the glasses and containers. They strolled, arm in arm, back up the hill to King's Grant, dropped off the basket in the kitchen, then followed the fern-bordered path behind the property.

★　★　★

Kate remembered the cold, overcast day she'd last walked on that path. She'd been alone and left the woods when she sensed someone was following her. Was it only her

imagination working overtime, or did someone lurk in the woods watching her that day?
She'd been frightened in any case and glad to
see Nick when she returned home.

The sun warmed her face as they strolled.
Nick's arm brushed hers and Kate felt an
undercurrent of excitement.

Strolling through the unspoiled woods, she
noticed the blackberry bushes bent, full of
buds. Wild roses bloomed in the midst of the
tangle of trees and birds sang sweetly
overhead.

As they passed a glade off the path, Nick
suggested, 'Let's stop here for a few minutes.'

'How about over there?' Kate pointed to a
flowering pear tree. They sat and rested their
backs against the old tree's twisted trunk.

Nick stretched his long legs. 'What a
beautiful spot.' He looked around. 'Did you
know about this glade?'

'Why, no. I've walked on the paths but
haven't ventured back here in the woods.'

'I thought perhaps your husband and you
might have found this spot.'

'My husband wasn't interested in strolls in
the woods.' She could have added, 'Or in me.'
Someday she might tell Nick about her
pretense of a marriage, but why spoil a lovely
afternoon. They sat in companionly silence
for a few moments. So close to her, he filled

her senses. She could think of nothing else but Nick. His mere presence left her breathless. He put his arm around her, his hand accidentally brushed against her breast. She tingled head to toes when he cupped her face with his large hands and began kissing her. A gentle kiss which Kate sank into, enchanted by his touch. As Nick's lips slid to her neck and ears, a random breeze sent a gentle shower of wisteria blossoms down on their heads and shoulders. Kate sighed with contentment. The woods were quiet except for the birds chirping overhead. In the distance, a calliope was playing down by the lake.

'Kate, about the other day . . . '

'It's all right.'

'All this is new to me, you see. I've been alone most of my life. Now, you . . . ' He shook his head. 'You've taken me by storm.'

She waited but he said no more on the subject.

Kate felt his heart beat faster as she lay in his embrace. Nick's strong arms holding her, he kissed her shoulders and throat. His fingers touched her so lightly, she didn't feel him undoing the top buttons of her blouse. Kate sighed when he began kissing the v above her bra.

She didn't want him to stop stroking and

caressing her. In a dream-like state she unfastened the other buttons of her blouse and clasped him to her. Her skin burned where he touched her. Fascinated by Nick, Kate jolted back to reality when voices resounded through the woods. She quickly buttoned her blouse and smoothed her hair. A young man and woman burst through the ferns surrounding their glade.

Chris laughed. 'Someone else has discovered our hideout, Diane.'

Kate laughed. Relief washed over her, seeing two familiar faces. For a moment, she'd been frightened. After all, Nick and she were out in the middle of the woods. Stepping forward, she hugged Diane.

'It's a glorious day for a walk,' Kate smiled.

'Oh, yes,' replied Diane. 'We thought we'd get some fresh air while our guests are off on that Mountain Goat tour of the lakes. They'll be gone all afternoon. Let's all go walking.'

Kate glanced over at Nick and saw him nod, slightly. As they followed Chris and Diane back to the path, he murmured, 'Soon.' That one whispered word sent her heart soaring.

After they'd followed the path to its end, Chris checked his watch. 'Guess we need to go home and help Mattie with dinner.'

Kate laughed. 'That's right, I almost forgot we have a business to run. Those two couples staying with us will expect their dinner at seven o'clock sharp.'

Kate helped Mattie and the others serve dinner, then she sat with Nick on the terrace, watching the sun set behind the fells.

'Nick, why don't you come to my place for dinner tomorrow evening?'

'Thought you'd never ask. What time do you want me?'

'Shall we say seven?'

'Fine. I'll look forward to it. Now I guess I better go. I have a report to write this evening.' Leaning over, he traced the line of her cheek with his finger.

Kate's knees weakened as his lips descended, claiming hers. He kissed her once lightly on the mouth, then took hold of her shoulders and kissed her harder. Warming to his touch, she melted into the sweetness of his kiss. All too soon, he released her.

Kate sighed, watching Nick climb into the Rover and drive away. She stepped back into the hotel. Silverware rattling led her to the dining room and Diane setting the table for the guests' breakfast.

Kate eyed Diane. 'Do me a favor tomorrow night?'

Diane turned to face Kate, curiosity

streaked across her face. 'Sure. What is it?'

'Well, I've invited Nick for dinner . . . ' Kate hesitated.

'Are you telling me you don't want any interruptions while he's at your apartment?'

'Right. Just keep the others from calling or coming down to visit tomorrow night, would you?'

'All right. And if you have any calls for reservations, I'll take care of those, too.'

'Thanks, Diane.'

'That's all right. Anything for romance.' She rolled her eyes and smiled.

Kate returned Diane's smile.

Back in her apartment, Kate pulled out her recipe box and planned a dinner for two. Her heart beat faster at the idea of spending an evening alone with Nick.

★ ★ ★

Charles answered his front door that same afternoon and jerked with surprise, finding Sergeant Kennedy and a constable. He'd convinced Clarissa and himself that they'd seen the last of the police.

'Mr. Stanhope, I'd like to talk to you. There's a matter we need to clear up.' Kennedy's voice rang with authority.

'Sergeant, I'm beginning to find your

investigation a real nuisance.' Charles muttered and glared at the policewoman. 'You must have too little to do since you run around town harrassing people.' He sighed as if resigned. 'Oh, well. Come in and tell me what new lunacy the local constabulary has dreamed up.' After holding the door open, reluctantly, he stalked into the living room and slouched on a maroon velvet Queen Anne armchair. He didn't ask the police officers to sit.

Undaunted, Kennedy sat down opposite Charles while the constable stood behind her chair.

'We need to locate a pair of running shoes. The Windermere Runner records show you bought Speedmasters at their store on March 24th. May I see those shoes, sir?'

'I did purchase a pair of Speedmasters from the store you mention, but I haven't seen them for weeks. Why should I show them to you, anyway?'

'Here's a warrant to search the premises.' Kennedy pulled out the document and dangled it in front of Charles. 'Now, I'd like to see your closets.'

Charles shrugged. 'All right, but you're wasting your time. If you'll follow me.' He led them up the winding stairs then down a hall past several closed doors to a darkly paneled dressing room.

They followed Charles into the small room, sparsely decorated with a day bed, tweed armchair and a brass tent lamp. There were no other furnishings except for the floor-to-ceiling shelves of books.

Charles pushed a button and one wall silently slid open. He stood aside, revealing a closet full of shoes.

Kennedy and the constable knelt to examine the shoes. By the way her eyes widened, seeing his collection, Charles knew Kennedy was impressed. Neat rows of loafers and lace-ups in dark leathers, house slippers, rain boots, sneakers, shoes for all occasions filled the closet. In the back of the closet was one pair of running shoes.

Charles noticed again the old shoes' condition, shabby and worn. He'd given the new pair to Clarissa the day after the murder and instructed her to hide them until he could dispose of them. Now Charles hoped that Clarissa had hidden the shoes well. He'd told her little, just that he'd left the blackmail money for Martin. Neither Charles or Clarissa had mentioned Martin's murder. The less said, the better.

Kennedy and the constable quickly examined the closets, then expanded their search.

Charles sat in the living room while the

police combed the entire house, reassuring himself that he was too smart for the police, including this young officer. Connor was another matter. Charles fancied he might be a worthy opponent. On the occasions Connor and he'd talked, Charles had seen a speculative expression cross Connor's face. There was no doubt that Connor suspected him, but Charles had been careful to cover his tracks.

Breaking out of his reverie, Charles looked up at Kennedy standing before him. Relief flooded him, seeing her frown. 'If that's all, Sergeant?' He bit his lip to keep from laughing at her flushed, disappointed face.

'That's all for now, sir,' Kennedy retorted.

He heard anger and frustration in her voice.

Car doors slammed, then the motor started and the police car pulled out of their property. Charles walked to the staircase and called to his sister on the next floor.

Looking pleased with herself, Clarissa smiled down on him over the banisters. She cradled the Speedmasters in her arms.

'I hid them on the ledge outside my bedroom window while you were talking to that policewoman. Would you believe it? She actually asked if I knew where the shoes were?'

He chuckled. 'I can't imagine what I'd do without you.'

'What a nice thing to say. Now, let me tell you my news.'

Excitement flooded her voice. 'I've gone ahead with my plans to re-do the back gardens. This afternoon the gardener is moving the old gazebo. I've got to go out and see how he's doing.'

A few minutes later, Charles caught a glimpse of Clarissa through a window overlooking the gardens. A spring breeze played with her long hair while she talked to their gardener.

Charles opened the window and called out. 'Are you positive you want to rearrange the flower beds? I've always liked the gardens the way they are.'

Clarissa nodded. 'Don't worry. You'll like it.' She turned back to the withered old man in charge of their grounds for as long as Charles could remember.

Sitting at his desk, a wave of uncertainty hit Charles. As he picked up his favorite picture, a snapshot of two tow-headed children playing on the beach, their uniformed nanny in the background, Charles brooded. Clarissa had changed so much in the past few weeks. She seemed stronger, more sure of herself. She'd even talked of getting her own place.

He'd told her he wouldn't let her leave him. They'd stay together, no matter what.

His sister came in from the gardens. 'It's going to be lovely. Wait and see.'

Then a cloud of doubt crossed her pale face. She shivered and wrapped her arms around her body. In a low tone, she confessed, 'Charles, I'm frightened. What if the police find out . . . '

Embracing her, Charles felt her thin body tremble. 'Hold on, Clarissa. The police don't know anything. You don't think, seriously, that they can outsmart your brother, do you?' He plastered a big smile on his face in an attempt to exude a self-confidence he didn't feel.

'I've always taken good care of you, haven't I?'

She frowned. 'Yes, Charles.'

'Why don't you call Cook to bring us our tea. Let's forget about the whole police business for awhile,' he suggested and gave Clarissa a gentle nudge towards the kitchen.

★   ★   ★

Friday morning Nick glanced up from a report he was reading to see Clarissa Stanhope in his office doorway. Today she wore no makeup, her clothing was rumpled, and her hair messy. Not the well-groomed young woman he'd seen on other occasions.

She asked hesitantly, 'Can I . . . speak to you, Inspector?' Her voice trembled.

'Of course.' He motioned her to a chair.

'I've brought you something which may interest you.' She laid a box on his desk.

Nick leaned forward as Clarissa raised the lid.

17

Without speaking, Clarissa removed the lid from the box. Holding it at an angle, she exhibited the contents, a pair of mud-encrusted running shoes. 'May I?' She gestured to Nick's desk.

Nick nodded, speechless. His mouth went dry, then he sighed with relief, glad he'd refused to give up when his instincts pointed to Charles. It appeared he'd been right. Nick felt in his bones this evidence would lead to Charles's arrest.

Did she realize how much she'd helped move the case toward its conclusion? They'd spent days scouring the area for those damn shoes.

Nick pulled a pair of disposable plastic gloves from his desk drawer, put them on and then carefully picked up one shoe. Holding it, his fingertip traced the raised emblem of a runner on the heel, the trademark for the Speedmaster. A rust-colored stain on the toe of one shoe silently screamed for his attention. Blood? The lab would find out.

Peering inside the shoe, Nick saw size 12, the size of the footprint left at the Martin crime scene. Were they Charles's shoes? She'd just walked in and given them to him. Why was she doing this? Gazing at her across his desk, he let out a sigh of satisfaction.

'I've thought of coming to see you for awhile. I'm ready to help, if I can.'

'Who's the owner?' Nick gestured toward the shoes.

She replied in a flat, dispassionate tone, 'They belong to my brother, Charles.'

'And how did they come into your possession?'

'He asked me to hide them where they wouldn't be found.' She stared at Nick closely, as if trying to gauge his response.

Nick responded in a quiet, but firm manner. 'Please tell me the reason your brother asked you to hide his shoes.'

'He said the police wanted to incriminate him and might be able to do so if they had the shoes.'

'There's a stain on the toe of one of the shoes. Can you tell me about that?'

'I wasn't there at the time so I can only repeat what my brother told me. He said he cut his foot on a sharp stone running on the footpath behind our property.'

'Do you believe that, Clarissa?'

She shrugged. The shadows under her eyes suggested she wasn't as indifferent as she acted. When she tried to reply, her voice broke. Clarissa cleared her throat, then straightened her shoulders.

'My brother has always told me the truth in the past. At least, I believed he did. Now, I'm not so sure.' That was all she would say.

'Thank you for bringing them in.' His eyes scanning her face, Nick warned, 'Be careful. Don't let Charles find out you've been here today. If there's anything else you want to share with me, here's a number where you can reach me anytime day or night.' He handed her his business card. 'If you need to talk, call me.'

Minutes later, Nick watched Clarissa's Escort pull out of the constabulary parking lot, then he paged Kennedy. She dashed into his office and stood in front of his desk.

'Clarissa Stanhope just brought in these shoes.' Seeing the Sergeant's eyes widen with surprise, he added, 'don't jump to conclusions. Please carry them to the lab and ask the technicians to compare them to the mold. I've examined the shoes and one's stained. Let's find out if it's a blood stain and what type.'

'Do you think Clarissa was involved in Martin's murder?'

Nick shrugged. 'I don't know, Sergeant. She doesn't strike me as a cold-blooded killer.' Frowning, he put down his notes. 'But Charles is another matter. My impression is he's clever and devious. In my opinion, he could have killed Martin.'

'She hid the shoes while I searched the house, sir?'

'Yes, Sergeant. But today Clarissa's given them to us. It's possible she thinks we're closing in on Charles and wants to disassociate herself from him. But we can't assume she's entirely innocent. She may have played a part in the murders.

'We'll keep surveillance on them. If he discovers she's given us his shoes, Charles could lose control. We'll have to move quickly if he becomes violent. Judging by the closeness of their relationship, I don't think Charles would harm her, but we're not dealing with a totally rational person.'

Sgt. Kennedy nodded. 'Right. I'm glad I'm not Clarissa Stanhope, that's for sure.

★ ★ ★

Charles turned when Clarissa walked into his study later that morning. He sat at his desk, wrestling with a mound of bills. How was he to pay them all?

Straightening, he stretched and rubbed his tired eyes. 'There you are. Do me a favor and

218

get my checkbook. It's on the top of the bureau in my bedroom. That's a good girl.'

She returned shortly and handed the checkbook to Charles, then consulted her wristwatch. 'I'll check on lunch. It's such a dark, dreary day, I wouldn't mind eating a little early, would you?'

He nodded and concentrated again on finances. Where had the money gone?

Later, Cook served them a lunch of salads and cups of soup at the dining room table. The weather bureau had predicted thunderstorms, and right on schedule, one boomed its way into their area. Charles shivered when an accompanying wind rattled the windowpanes.

Rain pounded the roof with a mighty fist. In the distance, lightning crackled followed by rumbles of thunder.

Thunderstorms always got on his nerves. The muscles in his arms and legs tensed until Charles jumped up, pushed his chair back and walked to the window. He pulled aside a heavy brocade drape and wiped a peephole on the cold, fogged-up windowpane with his finger. An icy gust of air raised goose bumps on his arms as he stood by the drafty window. Sheets of water poured from the skies. Chilled, Charles was glad to be indoors. He regained his seat at the table.

'Charles, are you all right? You're so quiet today.'

He shook himself and made an effort to talk with her. 'This rain won't do the roof any good. I'll go outside after the storm passes and survey the damage.'

His mind jumped to the future. 'Soon, the police will move on in their investigation and no longer consider me a suspect. Then we can sell this place to the hotel chain and go far away, perhaps to another country where we aren't known. How about America?' He watched her face.

She shook her head. Anxiety rang in her soft voice. 'You don't really want to leave the Lake District, do you?'

'It would be all right if we're together. When we relocate, we can live together as man and wife. I'd like for us to have a child. We need to carry on the family name, don't we?' He gazed across the table at Clarissa, waiting for her approval.

She didn't reply, just looked sad.

★ ★ ★

That afternoon, Nick stood by his office window, watching the storm, then he paced the halls. Glancing at his watch, he called the lab. No news. They'd call him. An hour

220

passed and the Director phoned, asking Nick to come.

In the Director's office, Nick pulled up a chair by the other man's desk, eyeing the Director. He jumped right in, asking questions before the Director could tell him his news.

'What did your tests show about the shoes? Did they fit the mold?'

'Well, yes. We were correct when we estimated that a size 12 shoe made the impression at the falls.'

'And what about the rusty stain on one shoe? Was it blood?'

'Right.' The Director glanced at the clip board before him. 'Type B.' He held up his hand. 'Wait a moment. Before you ask, I can tell you that Mr. Martin's blood type was AB.'

Nick's face must have shown his disappointment because the Director apologized. 'Inspector, we've run the tests twice. One of my assistants ran the first test and I ran it again.' He took off his eyeglasses, wiping them on the sleeve of his white coat before he continued. 'It was type B, not AB which is Mr. Martin's blood group. If Mr. Stanhope is type B, he probably told the truth. He could have cut his foot on a sharp rock jogging. The hole in the toe of the blood-stained shoe could have been made by a sharp object.'

Nick's shoulders sagged. 'I see. I'd hoped, but we'll get our murderer yet. Thanks for rushing the tests.'

Nick walked out of the lab and down the hall to his office. He frowned, disappointed to find his hopes of catching the killer postponed.

Nick brightened up, thinking of Clarissa. He'd call her. It was possible she was ready to talk.

Clarissa picked up the phone on the first ring and spoke in a low voice. 'Yes, I'll be there within the hour. He's going out to run some errands.'

Thirty minutes later, Clarissa burst into Nick's office and sat down, breathless.

'You didn't take long getting here. Would you like a cup of tea or coffee?'

She shook her head. 'No thanks.' Clarissa removed her raincoat and pushed the hair out of her eyes, then she set the large paper bag she was clutching on his desk.

'What's this?' He eyed the young woman across from him.

'Open it and see.'

He gingerly opened the bag and found a worn leather briefcase. Baffled, Nick raised both eyebrows.

Clarissa leaned forward and explained.

'Charles left the house the night Mr. Martin was murdered with this briefcase. Martin tried to blackmail us. He thought we'd schemed to poison people at King's Grant. That's absurd, but Charles didn't want the notoriety. Afraid the tabloids would pick up on the story and smear our family name, he agreed to pay for Martin's silence.' She pulled a tissue from her purse and dabbed at her damp face.

'That's all I can tell you. I don't know what happened at the falls. Charles wouldn't talk about it next morning. But I'm cooperating and hope the police will remember.' She gave Nick a hard look and sat back on her chair.

Nick looked at the briefcase. Using his handkerchief, he returned it to the bag. Maybe there'd be fingerprints. 'We appreciate your help. I'll have the lab examine it.'

He eyed the pale young woman. 'Don't let down your guard for a moment, Clarissa. We can't predict what your brother will do if he suspects you're helping us.'

He wouldn't tell her about the police surveillance. She might let it slip to Charles. 'By the way, what's your brother's blood type?'

'I believe he's type B. Our physician, Doctor Wootten will have that information.'

Nick scribbled the doctor's name on a desk

pad. 'I'll call him, but thank you for your help, Clarissa. I realize how hard it must be for you to disclose this information. Be cautious.' In spite of her cool manner, Nick sensed Clarissa still cared for Charles. He hoped it didn't cost her her life.

Opening his desk drawer, Nick spotted the snapshot Kate had given him. In the picture, she stood on the beach at Lake Windermere with the wind ruffling her hair. A lump formed in his throat. He'd never burned with desire for any other woman. Only Kate. His feelings for her persisted, grew in intensity. Closing the drawer, he vowed to keep her safe no matter what happened. Nick shook himself. Back to business.

★   ★   ★

Later Friday, Kate shook her head in disbelief, seeing the time on the wall clock in her kitchen. Six thirty already? Her mouth went dry. Nick was on his way.

She walked around the kitchen bar into the dining area, she touched the flatware, ran her fingers over the dinner plates, and held the wine glasses up to the light . . . all clean and shiny.

The heavy Italian blue pottery went well with the red and white checked tablecloth.

Everything was in order. She wiped her hands on a dish towel.

Removing the lasagna from the oven, Kate turned the other oven to warm and placed the lasagna inside.

The wall phone rang. She jumped. Who could that be? 'Diane? No, everything's on schedule. I expect him in a few minutes.' She smiled. 'Remember, I'm counting on you to handle all possible problems and emergencies tonight. Thanks. See you tomorrow.'

Feeling hungry, she nibbled a slice of pastrami, then she stopped. Butterflies fluttered in her stomach.

She'd wouldn't offer second helpings tonight. She didn't want Nick so stuffed, he fell asleep over his spumoni and coffee.

Her lips curved into a smile, thinking of Nick. When they first met, she admired his handsome tanned face and wiry physique. Later, she learned to savor his dry sense of humor, his intelligence and his touch. A glance from those mesmerizing dark brown eyes and her heart raced. At his touch, her knees trembled, her whole body tingled and yearned for more. Just recalling his kisses, her skin grew warmer. She admitted it, she was in love with the man. But he remained an enigma to her.

Nick was continuously changing. In the

role of ardent suitor, he pursued her closely, eager for her embraces. But he also could be cool and wary. He'd made no definite committment to her or to a relationship. What had happened in the past to make him so skittish? Did another woman hurt him?

Kate knew she wanted him in her life but he needed to decide what his feelings were for her. Was he ready for love, the kind that lasts a lifetime?

Tonight she hoped to find out how he really felt.

Kate glanced in a mirror. Tonight she wore her hair smooth and sleek, twisted around her head. She hoped he'd like it.

Slipping on a cream and paisley silk blouse and matching long skirt, she eyed her reflection. Her finger trailed down the soft fabric as her gaze took in the provocative way the material clung to her breasts and hips. A touch of makeup, then a light spray of cologne on her throat and wrists. The roses and jasmine scent of Samsara filled the air.

Mmm . . . she still had fifteen minutes to kill before he got there. To calm down, she stepped outside. When she saw who waited for her, she laughed aloud.

'Miles. Did you come to visit?' Stepping indoors, she came back with a doggie treat. Kate handed it to Mattie's scottie and scratched him between his ears. 'Now, go home. I'm waiting for Nick.'

Miles wagged his tail and walked back up the driveway, his prize held carefully in his mouth.

The June sun hadn't set and a late ray of light reflected on the silvery wing of an airliner heading north to Glasgow Airport. It droned, passing far above her.

Hearing a car, Kate stiffened then relaxed as the car whisked by on the road outside King's Grant gates.

She paused to pluck a dead bloom off a potted red geranium on the porch and rubbed a fingernail over a rough-textured leaf.

'My dahlias are doing well,' she murmured, admiring scarlet flowers blooming on one side of the porch.

A slight breeze brought a minty fragrance to her nostrils from generations-old mint that encircled the foundations of the gatehouse.

Stooping, she sniffed each variety of mint, peppermint, chocolate mint and lemon, then she plucked a chocolate mint leaf and bit into it. Strange to taste chocolate in a leaf.

Moments after she'd stepped indoors, she heard a car drive up. A large scented candle filled the air with Samsara fragrance as she dimmed the lights in the living room. The soft tones of Shearing floated through the room, adding to the atmosphere of intimacy.

Nick stepped through the door clutching a long florist box of flowers.

'These are for you.' He spoke softly. 'I could only get red ones. Hope they're all right.' He cleared his throat and thrust the box at her. His dark eyes drank her in so completely she felt her cheeks burning. Damp black hair, combed smooth and a small cut in his chin. Did he hurry? Perhaps he was anxious to see her.

She opened the box and found twelve perfect red roses.

'They're lovely,' she murmured. Kate walked into the living room and picked up a tall Waterford vase. Filling it with water, she arranged the flowers quickly then buried her face in the flowers' velvety petals. After inhaling their sweet fragrance, she set the vase on a table by the sofa.

She could feel Nick watching her fuss over the flowers.

'It's just the two of us. Make yourself comfortable, take your coat and tie off.' He handed her his dark sports coat and she hung it in the hall closet, then he folded his maroon linen tie and laid it on the table by the sofa.

She gestured Nick to her living room sofa. 'Would you like a glass of wine?' She felt breathless and her knees trembled. Was this evening a good idea? She'd die if he laughed at her.

'Fine. Let me.' He uncorked the wine and filled their glasses, handing her a glass. Their fingers touched and she felt a warming shiver all the way up her arm.

Kate sipped her drink and watched him over her glass rim. 'Do you like the wine?'

'Yes, thanks.' He refilled her glass without asking if she wanted more. His hand was not too steady pouring the wine.

Nick crossed, then uncrossed his long legs. Seeing a smudge on the glass table where she laid her glass, she started to wipe at it with a paper napkin. The situation was ridiculous. She'd have to make the first move.

Putting down her glass, Kate turned toward Nick, the pulse jumping in her throat. 'Are you terribly famished?'

'Not really. Are you?' Nick raised an eyebrow.

'No.' She walked over to the floor lamp and turned it off, then stood in front of Nick.

'I think we've started something, the two of us.' He didn't reply. She blurted out, 'I've never felt this way before.'

Nick swallowed hard, then smiled. 'If you'd lean over for a moment?' When Kate obeyed, he gently unpinned her long auburn hair and let it cascade down her shoulders. She trembled.

'Come here.' He reached out and drew her onto his lap, kissing her slowly, softly on her cheeks, then her lips. He trailed light, butterfly kisses down her neck, then recaptured her mouth. His caresses felt familiar, yet deliciously strange.

With shaky fingers, Kate fumbled with the buttons on his shirt, then she reached inside and stroked his matted chest, learning the feel of him. His citrusy cologne drew her.

Kate gasped when his fingers slipped the soft material of her blouse over her shoulder. A ripple of excitement raced from her toes to the top of her head.

When he kissed her throat, she moaned.

Kate pulled his open shirt out of his slacks. Nick unbuttoned the cuffs, then she helped him take off the shirt. He tossed it across the room onto an armchair by the fireplace.

His fingers tugged on the back of her bra, looking for a way to remove it. She guided him to the front clasp, then he took it off along with her blouse.

Nick's eyes roamed over her. 'You're lovelier than I dreamed.'

As Kate rubbed her breasts against him, he growled, softly. His hand caressed her breast as his lips took possession of hers once more.

Heat simmered through her veins and she moaned with pleasure and rubbed her body against his, thirsty for more of his caresses.

'You have on too many clothes,' Nick murmured as he pushed up her long skirt, then pulled her bikinis down her legs until he could remove both the skirt and panties, tossing them away.

When she struggled to unbutton his slacks, he stood up and took them off. Then he pulled off his boxer shorts and returned to her embrace, as naked as Kate and fully aroused.

Nick kissed her on her lips, her shoulders, her breasts. He moved down to her stomach, kissing and caressing her all over. Kate ran her fingers through his thick dark hair and caressed his shoulders, his matted chest, then his thighs.

Her body yearned for more, much more.

Their bodies grew hot and slick with perspiration. Aroused, his caresses became more demanding.

She arched her back, pulled him to her, and ran her fingers through his hair, holding on to his back and shoulders. He buried himself in her.

18

Kate didn't move, wanting to savor the moment. Her body was tangled with Nick's, her head rested on his chest.

It was peaceful, lying there in his arms. She struggled to name the emotion that swept over her. Could it be contentment? Whatever it was, it was new to her.

They must have fallen asleep. Seeing discarded clothing all over the room, she chuckled softly. Her blouse lay on an armchair, her long skirt balled up on the floor by the sofa. She grinned at the bikinis perched on top of a lampshade.

God knew where they'd find his clothes.

Nick stirred, then stretched. Opening his eyes, he reached down and smoothed the hair off her face, then took a lock in his hand, playing with it.

When he smiled, her heart turned somersaults.

'I've wanted to make love to you since we met.' Nick kissed her soft white shoulders and ran his fingers down her arms.

Kate lost herself again in his warm embrace.

Later, she heard Nick's stomach rumble. They hadn't eaten dinner. She opened a sleepy eye and asked, 'Are you hungry now? There's food in the kitchen. If we don't eat, I'll have it around for days.'

Kate found his shirt under the sofa and pulled it on before walking into the kitchen. Opening the oven, she eyed the lasagne. A bit leathery but still warm. She popped it into her micro-wave then pulled the tossed salad out of the refrigerator. 'Dinner,' she announced, ten minutes later.

'This is really good.' Nick held out his empty plate for seconds of the lasagne.

Kate complimented him on his hearty appetite.

'Just a growing boy,' he laughed. 'Aren't you going to eat anything?'

'I'll have a little lasagne with you.'

Kate slid another large serving under his nose and heard a sigh of pleasure.

'Woman, I'm your slave for life if you always cook so well.' Before she could speak, Nick's fork attacked the lasagne.

★   ★   ★

'Sounds like you've been running with the wrong crowd.' She rolled her eyes. 'Maybe I'm old-fashioned, but I've always thought — .'

Laughing, he interrupted her. ' "The way to a man's heart is through his stomach."'

After they ate, Nick helped Kate put the food away. He walked around the first floor.

'In case you're wondering, my bedroom is upstairs.'

'Could we go up there? I'd like to spend the night, if it's all right with you, and I bet your bed is a lot more comfortable than that sofa.' He looked in the direction of the hideabed.

'Sounds good to me.' She'd hoped he'd want to stay.

Kate led him upstairs to her small bedroom where he helped her remove and fold up the quilted comforter. They collapsed on the bed and went to sleep.

Twice during the night, she woke up. Nick slept with his arm around her, and Kate missed him when he got out of the bed to close a window. He kissed her cheek as he returned to bed, then they dozed again. Once she dreamed he had gone and woke, her heart pounding. Blinking sleepy eyes, she was pleased to see his dark head on the pillow next to hers.

Nick raised his head. 'What's the matter?'

'Nothing. Guess I was dreaming.'

'Go back to sleep.'

When she shivered with cold, he found the

bedspread on a nearby chair and placed it over them. She cuddled up with her back to him. Nick began kissing the back of her neck, she turned and embraced him.

They made love slowly this time.

'Lie still and let me love you.' Nick kissed her from the bottoms of her feet, up her body to her breasts, finally her mouth.

Holding him in her arms, Kate felt the magic of being with someone you love. She hoped he loved her. He hadn't said so, yet.

Next morning, she opened the window, sucking in deep breaths of the cool, fresh air. 'Rain's coming. I smell it.'

'Don't guess this hotel includes back-scrubbing in its amenities?' Nick stood in the bathroom doorway, a towel wrapped around his narrow hips.

'Only for special guests. But I believe you qualify.' With a grin, Kate turned on the rain and stepped into the shower stall. 'Come on in. The water's fine.'

She'd read of people making love in showers, but had never experienced the pleasure herself. Now Kate was amazed how erotic a good supply of warm water and a bar of soap could be.

'Let me bathe you first.' He picked up her soap and began to lather her.

'Stop. We'll run out of soap before it's your turn.'

'Just one more spot.' He stepped back as if to admire his good work. Then he started kissing her, playful little kisses.

When he got a little rough, Kate called time. 'No beating with washcloths.'

They finished, rinsed each other off and stepped out of the small shower stall. He wrapped Kate in a large towel and carried her to bed. Again, she experienced the magic of his touch. Nick had opened up to her and shown her he could love.

Before he left, they stood inside her front door. Nick kissed her once more, a tender, gentle kiss. His lips felt firm and warm. He tasted of the freshly perked coffee she'd served him. She clung to him for a moment.

'I'll call you later,' he whispered.

Wishing he'd stay, Kate watched Nick climb in the Rover and waved as he drove slowly and quietly out the gates, before her guests stirred for the day.

★ ★ ★

Nick stepped into HQ with a light step, behind a constable who gripped the arms of two intoxicated men, leading them to the drunk tank. One man sang a sea chanty as he

236

weaved his way down the corridor.

Nick avoided close contact with the two but caught a whiff of cheap whisky mingled with the scent of tobacco and vomit as he passed them.

At the front desk, two sergeants yawned and sipped steaming mugs of hot coffee. One perused the sports section of the paper and the other chatted on the telephone.

When Nick walked by, the officer on the phone hung up fast.

'Good morning.' Nick spoke cheerfully.

The sergeant reading the paper looked embarrassed. Jerking, he shoved his newspaper into a desk drawer.

'Good morning, sir. Is it raining yet?' He turned his attention to paperwork.

Down the hall, a janitor hoovered the carpet. As Nick walked past the break room, two constables were loudly bragging about their snooker skills as they relaxed before their shifts.

Outside his office door, a young woman with orange hair and dangling earrings, in a purple jumpsuit and running shoes, swayed in time to the music coming through her earphones. She swished a dirty mop, cleaning the stained black-and-white linoleum. The sharp odor of ammonia burned Nick's nostrils.

Closing his office door, Nick sat down at his cluttered desk, smiling as he remembered Kate's kisses and caresses. It had only been a few minutes since he left King's Grant. He missed her already.

A blinking light on his answering machine caught his eye. He pushed the play button and heard Dr. Wooten's voice asking him to call when he got in.

Dialing the medical office number, he reached the doctor.

'Inspector, your message concerned Charles Stanhope?'

'Yes. I need to know his blood type.' Nick waited.

'I see. And you have a court order?'

'Yes sir. Standard procedure.'

'Under the circumstances, I believe I can tell you. Hold on. I have his folder right here.' The doctor returned to the telephone. 'My records show he is B blood type.'

'Thanks. I appreciate your cooperation.'

'I'll need a copy of that court order faxed, Inspector,' the doctor reminded Nick.

'It's on its way.' Nick hung up the telephone.

'Damn, I thought we had him this time.' He slammed a drawer.

Moments later, the police lab summoned him. Slipping on his sportcoat, Nick ran down the hall to the Lab Director's office.

The Director stood by his door. He ushered Nick into his office. With a self-satisfied expression on his face, he seated Nick at his desk. 'Look through this microscope. First, you'll see the piece of the Financial Times found at the Martin murder scene. 'What letters do you see?'

Nick leaned forward, looking through the microscope. 'I can make out the letters FIN.' Unimpressed, he frowned and glanced up.

'Right. But when I put the strip of Financial Times found in the briefcase hinges next to it?' Inserting the mentioned item and adjusting the lens, the pathologist stood back.

Gazing into the microscope for the second time, Nick found part of the top edge of one Times page. 'All right. I still see FIN and wait, there's an A right next to the FIN.'

The Director smiled and explained. 'That A was on the small piece of paper we found stuck in the briefcase hinges. The two pieces fit together. Believe it or not, they're from the same newspaper.'

'Bloody hell,' Nick exclaimed.

'I'll take that to mean you like our findings.' The balding pathologist smiled.

'You bet I do. According to his sister, Charles used this briefcase to carry the money to the drop-off at the falls. I don't suppose you found any fingerprints?'

'One set. We're checking those now.'

'They're probably Clarissa's. She brought me the case.'

Nick ran down the hall to his office and paged Kennedy.

She darted into the room.

He grinned and gave her orders. 'Sergeant, get a constable and a warrant. Pick up Charles Stanhope and Clarissa Stanhope on suspicion of the murder of Melvin Martin.'

'Yes sir.' Enthusiasm rang in her voice as she beamed at Nick. He closed his office door. He felt like dancing a jig, but instead, refilled his mug with coffee and waited for Sergeant Kennedy to bring Charles and Clarissa in.

★ ★ ★

Taken aback, Charles jumped as he again found Sergeant Kennedy and a constable at his front door.

The police officers stepped into the foyer.

'Mr. Stanhope, we need to see Miss Stanhope, also.' The Sergeant smiled.

'She's upstairs. I'll go and get her.'

'Constable Vaughan will come with you, if you don't mind.' Kennedy motioned to the young uniformed officer. He went upstairs, close on Charles's heels.

When both Charles and Clarissa stood in the living room, Kennedy pulled out two warrants and read them their rights. 'Charles Stanhope, we are arresting you on suspicion of the murder of Melvin Martin on the evening of May 27th of this year. We must inform you that you have the right to have a solicitor. Anything you say will be taken down and can be used against you.'

Charles sputtered, incredulous the police tracked him down. 'I'll call my lawyer,' he raged. 'You won't keep me long, I promise you.'

Looking at Clarissa, Charles saw a dazed expression on her face as Kennedy informed her of her rights.

★ ★ ★

'I can't believe I'm here.' Alone in his cell an hour later, Charles shook his head in amazement and paced the floor.

From childhood, he'd abhorred dirt in any form and had flinched earlier when the clerk rolled his fingers in ink.

Now he eyed the stain on his hands with disgust, then wiped them on the jail jumpsuit.

He waited for the Inspector's visit, bracing himself for the interrogation. He must take care in what he told the policeman. Charles sensed that Connor had suspected him from the first time they met. But how could he?

He'd tell the Inspector that, though innocent, he'd left the blackmail money at the Force to avoid a scandal. The police couldn't prove he'd done more.

He jerked to attention as a guard strolled by, gazing into his cell, then relaxed when the policeman continued his slow gait down the row of mainly empty cells.

Looking around, Charles saw another detainee who stood at the bars of his own cell. The man glanced at Charles then turned his back.

Charles's thoughts jumped to Clarissa. Closing his eyes, he saw again her dazed expression and teary cheeks as a jail matron led her away to the womens' section of the jail. He hoped she was all right. He didn't think the police would keep her long after they talked to her. He regreted getting his sister involved. At least, she hadn't participated in Martin's death.

He pushed aside the simple lunch of beef stew, hard rolls and chocolate pudding a guard brought him an hour later. But a few minutes later, his stomach growled and reason prevailed. If he didn't eat what they brought him, he went hungry. He didn't have

Cook here to prepare his favorite dishes. He picked up a plastic spoon and forced down a mouthful of soup. Not bad, but it needed salt. And he couldn't call for some since this wasn't the place for room service.

Later, when bond was refused, a wave of queasiness caused Charles to sit down on his cot. He rubbed his eyes and stared ahead, not seeing the bars around him.

★ ★ ★

Once he was informed the Stanhopes had been booked, Nick knew he must go and see them. But he'd call Kate first.

'I only have a minute, but something's happened you need to know.' He leaned back in his worn leather armchair.

'Nick? Are you all right?' She sounded anxious.

'I'm fine.' He hesitated. 'There's no easy way to say this so I better just tell you. Based on new evidence, we've arrested your nephew and niece as suspects in the Martin case. I thought it best that you hear it from me rather than on the news later.'

There was silence, then Kate replied. 'I've wondered for years what went on in Charles's mind, have never been at ease with him. He's only close to Clarissa, and I don't know if even she understands him. But murder? I can't vouch for Charles, but she's a gentle girl who doesn't have it in her to hurt anyone.'

'Charles is our prime suspect, but he may have coerced her into being his accomplice. Anyway, they've been booked and I need to go down and talk to them. That's all I can say now. I'll see you later.' He was glad Kate wasn't terribly upset. When did she become important to him? 'Kate, last night was special for me. Take care.'

19

'Inspector, I'm ready to tell you what I know about Penmar and Martin.' Clarissa sat across from Nick in an interrogation room later that morning.

He studied her pale features. Tangled hair and bleary eyes told him she'd slept little the previous night.

She fidgeted with her sleeve and looked at the floor.

'All right, Clarissa. We'll need a full statement. Do you want a lawyer?'

An hour later Perry April, Clarissa's attorney, sat beside his client.

Nick pushed the tape recorder 'on' button. He gave Clarissa a quick glance across his desk, then spoke. 'This is DCI Connor and I am interrogating Clarissa Stanhope.'

Addressing Clarissa, Nick spoke. 'You are the sister of Charles Stanhope and the niece of Kate Stanhope and the deceased Stephen Stanhope?'

'Yes, I am.' She shifted in her chair.

'Please tell me about your relationship with your uncle.'

'Both Charles and I were close to Uncle

Stephen. After our parents died, he was our only living relative.'

'This relationship continued until when?'

'Uncle Stephen died last October.'

'And he had no children of his own?'

'That's right. He loved us, I'm sure, and we reciprocated that feeling.'

Her lawyer smiled and nodded at her response.

'What were your expectations as to his estate?'

'One of my earliest recollections is Uncle Stephen walking my brother and me around his estate and telling us that it all would be ours one day. Later, he named Charles and me his sole heirs.'

'I see. And did that arrangement change?'

She looked at her lawyer who nodded again. 'Two years after he married, he changed his will and named his wife, Kate Stanhope, his heir.'

'How did Charles and you feel about this?'

'Well, shocked, at first. Then I realized it was the right thing for Uncle to do. We'd inherited a fortune from our maternal grandfather and didn't need Uncle's estate.'

'Can you describe your relationship with Kate Stanhope, your aunt by marriage?' Nick maintained a steadfast gaze on Clarissa.

'We became friends easily. She is much

younger than our uncle, only nine years my senior, and a warm, caring person. I think a lot of her.'

'And when they moved here, did their attention continue?'

'She was still friendly, but Uncle had changed. He seemed less interested in us. That was after his first heart attack and also when he changed his will. The last two years of his life, we rarely saw him. Charles blamed Kate for that. I believe it was due to Uncle's health.'

'When Stephen died, how did Charles and you feel?'

'Saddened, of course. Last winter, Charles began pestering Kate to give us the property. But Kate had other plans for King's Grant, as we discovered.' Clarissa twisted on the wooden chair, stood up and sat down again.

'Other plans?'

'To convert the property into a hotel.'

'How did you feel about that?'

'Well, horrified. Then she explained Stephen had left her the property, but not the funds to maintain it. Opening a hotel was a last ditch effort to keep King's Grant.' Clarissa sighed and dabbed at her eyes.

'You understood what she was doing. Did your brother feel the same way?'

'No, he still wanted King's Grant. Unfortunately, Charles has made many unwise investments on the stock market. He's lost our inheritance.'

Nick frowned. 'Excuse me, but could you clarify something? He's lost your entire inheritance?' Kate had mentioned Charles's losses on the stock market, but from the way she talked, Nick hadn't understood Charles had been wiped out, financially. So there was a motive other than revenge.

'Yes. All we have left is a lot of debt and The Folly. Fortunately, a large hotel chain has offered a premium price for the two properties, ours and Kate's. Our property alone won't accommodate their plans.

'But, Kate has refused to sell King's Grant so Charles used my new interest in herbs to get her to change her mind.' She sighed.

'How did he do that?' Nick began to see what had happened.

'He found a recipe in one of my herbal books and plotted to take a potion to the hotel, put it into Kate's herbal tea and upset her guests' stomachs.'

'For what reason?'

'I know this sounds absurd, but Charles reasoned if guests became ill at King's Grant, the hotel would have to shut down. Then

Kate would agree to sell.' Tears rolled down Clarissa's cheeks. Her attorney reached over and patted her on the arm.

'Please continue.' Nick kept his voice firm, but not harsh. Kate had desribed Clarissa as a gentle young woman who wouldn't hurt anyone. Kate was probably right. Talking to Clarissa, Nick didn't sense the cruelty displayed by her brother. Her only sin might be her blind devotion to Charles, also a meek spirit her brother used for his own selfish purposes.

Clarissa straightened and fumbled in her pocket. Pulling out a tissue, she wiped her eyes then looked at her attorney.

'At this point, I must advise you to tell the Inspector what you know of the situation,' her attorney told Clarissa.

In a husky voice she continued. 'Charles plotted everything and made me keep silent, but it was never meant to be murder.' Her gaze locked with Nick's. 'That was an accident. My brother didn't intend for anyone at King's Grant to die. He knew nothing about herbs and I refused to help him.'

The lawyer smiled and nodded again.

'By accident, Charles pulled a poisonous plant instead of one that can be used for a stomach purge. Using my recipe, he mixed up a potion. When I refused to be part of his scheme, he dressed in my blouse and navy skirt, the uniform Lakeside Temps wear at the hotels they service. We are about the same size, except Charles has larger feet. Wearing a long blond wig he'd bought at a garage sale years ago, he took the brew to King's Grant and put it in Kate's herbal tea.' Clarissa stopped for a sip of water and whispered to her attorney then continued. 'All I can tell you about Mr. Martin's death is Charles took the briefcase and money to Stockgyll Force. I stayed home.'

'Thank you. We appreciate your cooperation in this case, including the evidence you've brought us. That will be taken into consideration and should weigh in your favor. That will be all for now.' Nick turned off the tape recorder.

The forlorn look in Clarissa's eyes as the matron led her away tugged at Nick's heart.

Nick followed a guard to Charles's cell. His lawyer sat on Charles's cot talking to him. The guard unlocked the door and let Nick into the cell.

'Nice of you to visit me,' Charles sneered. 'Sorry about the accommodations, but I don't plan to stay here long.'

Ignoring Charles's rudeness, Nick said, 'I

have a few questions for you.'

'Ask away and I'll decide if I want to answer.'

Nick could hear uncertainty in Charles's voice despite his attempt at cockiness. And did he see the stirrings of fear in the other man's eyes?

'Your sister says you planned everything in the Penmar and Martin murders and tried to force her to take part.'

'That's rubbish. She wanted to ruin Kate's business by using the tea, but I opposed the whole idea, so she went ahead on her own.' Charles angrily balled one hand into a fist and hit his other palm, over and over.

'All right, who dressed as a temporary worker and took the poison to the hotel?'

'Clarissa, of course. I stayed home, waiting for her to return.'

'She says you wore her outfit and left the potion in Kate's tea pitcher.'

'That's ridiculous.' Charles frowned, tried to look indignant. 'I'll say this once more, she plotted and carried out the affair. It was all her idea, not mine.'

Charles's lawyer looked anxious. Perhaps he thought Charles was guilty, too.

★　★　★

Later that afternoon, Kate looked up when Nick slammed his car door in front of the gatehouse. She stood in her front yard, cutting dahlias. The scarlet flowers half filled the basket beside her.

The memory of his hard, eager body against her and his warm hands on her, caressing her, came to mind in a rush.

'Want to hear my news?' Nick came across the lawn, then he opened the front door for Kate and followed her into the gatehouse.

'I certainly do.'

'First I need a kiss.' His lips warmed hers for a few precious heartbeats as the entire world vanished, leaving just the two of them. Then, she shrieked and pushed him away.

'You didn't act like that last night when I kissed you.' He frowned.

Kate laughed, lightly and dropped the limp dahlias on her kitchen counter. 'No, but look. Between us we've crushed my lovely flowers. It's all right, I'll cut more later. Tell me the news.' Filling a tea kettle she put it on the burner, then perched on a bar stool, giving him her undivided attention.

Nick slid onto the other stool then checked his wristwatch. 'We've detained Charles and his sister. Bail was set low for her, so she may be out by now. Charles will be in jail until trial.'

Kate started to speak when the kettle whistled. She turned and took it off the stove.

'Put that down and come kiss me properly.' He sighed. 'Believe it or not, I've thought about you all day.'

She gave him a peck on the cheek and sat down. 'Have you?'

'You'd better believe it.' He smiled.

Feeling his eyes on her, Kate flushed. It could have been a lovely, erotic dream, the way they'd kissed and ravished each other the previous night.

'All right. Go ahead.' She handed him a mug.

'Clarissa brought me the briefcase Charles used to carry the blackmail money to Stockgyll Force. She's decided to help us. We were closing in on him so she may be trying to distance herself from Charles.'

'They weren't trying to kill anyone here, were they?' Kate looked at Nick for reassurance.

'No, both claim the poisoning was accidental.'

'And you put her in jail, too?'

'Temporarily. But, from the evidence and what Clarissa's told us, Charles is our primary suspect, so he'll stay behind bars until trial.'

The phone burred on the counter, and Kate answered it. 'I'll be right there.' She turned to Nick. 'Sorry, but one of our guests has misplaced a valuable necklace. Diane says the woman's throwing a fit and demands to see me.' Kate stepped toward the foyer. 'I'll be as soon as I can. This shouldn't take long.' She darted out the door and raced up the driveway.

Returning a few minutes later, she sat down in an armchair, though he patted the sofa cushion beside him.

'Sorry, Nick. I didn't mean to run out on you, but Mattie has gone to the store and Diane couldn't handle the guest. The silly woman misplaced a pearl necklace. She insisted I come and help her. She'd hidden it away in a secret compartment of her suitcase and forgotten where she'd put it.'

Kate paused, her heart aching for Clarissa. What she must be feeling right now. Kate would call her. Maybe Clarissa would want to come and stay with her. How could Nick assume that gentle creature had been involved in murder? 'You were saying Charles will be in jail until trial, but Clarissa is probably out on bail now.' She hesitated. 'You don't really believe Clarissa played a part in Charles's scheme, do you?'

'Depends on which story you believe,

Charles' or hers. The truth may lie somewhere in between.'

'I don't understand.' Kate raised an eyebrow.

'She says he did everything and forced her to keep quiet. He blames it all on her, and claims he did nothing.' He shrugged his shoulders. 'You really do care for the girl, don't you?'

'Oh, yes. We've become quite close, especially since Stephen and I moved up here. She's like the younger sister I never had.'

'I don't know,' he muttered. 'It's possible she's not the innocent she seems.'

A sinking feeling in her stomach, Kate kept silent as she waited for what he'd say next.

'I don't think she's more honest than most women,' he said.

She winced, hearing his words. Was this how he thought of women?

He added, 'Present company excluded, to be sure.'

'What does that mean?'

'Only that I don't think she's honest just because she's a woman.' Nick floundered.

Kate responded, abruptly. 'Why don't you go on and admit it? You wanted to say Clarissa's dishonest because she's a woman. Isn't that what you really believe?' She cast an angry glance in his direction.

'Of course not. Don't be unreasonable.'

Kate felt her blood pressure rise. 'Now I'm being unreasonable. Soon you'll say I'm dishonest, too.'

'Of course you're not, I mean . . . ' He punched the pillow by him on the sofa, obviously disgusted.

'Oh, go away. I don't know where you got your misconceived ideas about women, but you're dead wrong.' Enraged, Kate stormed across the room.

Nick followed her. 'If you say so. Guess I better leave before you put more words in my misconceived mouth.'

She opened the door and turned back to him, unspilled tears filled her eyes.

'I'll make it easy for you. If you don't trust women, you can't trust me. Goodbye!'

He walked, head high, to the Rover, climbed in, slammed the door shut. His vehicle raced through the open gates.

As the Rover sped away, Kate cried, her arms wrapped around her body. She'd thought she knew Nick. Wrong again, Kate. You didn't know him at all.

20

Gripping the steering wheel until his fingers ached, Nick sped down Kendall Road, away from King's Grant, away from Kate. He swallowed hard, his mouth dry. Her angry voice rang in his ears. 'You don't trust me, you don't trust me . . . ' Nick sighed heavily as he envisioned his future, dark and lonely without Kate.

Navigating a curve in the road, he swerved to miss a motor coach creeping up the hill. Its driver gestured with a finger to show his appreciation for Nick's reckless driving.

No way would he go home to his empty rooms. He needed to talk to someone. Misery loved company and he couldn't feel more miserable.

He drove by the White Swan, Nick glimpsed his friend, Pat Nolan stepping in the door. Two murder investigations and Kate hadn't left him time to join Pat for their weekly suppers and dart games at the old pub.

He drove home, parked the Rover and walked two blocks downhill to the pub.

Strolling into the smoky, dark pub, Nick

climbed onto a stool next to the nurseryman while a Country Western vocalist forlornly crooned of lost love on the radio behind the bar. 'A double scotch, bartender.' He turned and nodded to Pat Nolan.

The red-bearded man glanced sideways at Nick. 'You don't look too good.'

'I'm a fool.' Nick leaned both elbows on the scarred bar top.

'If you say so.' Pat grinned. 'Woman trouble?'

'Yeah. We had a fight.' His fingertips massaged the dull ache in his head.

'Why don't you apologize? That works sometimes.'

'Maybe. But I don't know if we can be together. We may be too different. She's not like any woman I've known before.'

'Sounds serious.' Pat flashed a sympathetic smile, then he reached over and thumped Nick on the back.

''Fraid so.' Nick tipped his glass up. The mellow, amber liquid burned a path to his stomach. 'Ready for another?'

Pat tilted up his mug and drained it. 'Yeah. This one's on me. Let's sit over there.' He nodded his head in the direction of a table just vacated on the other side of the room.

The bar shift changed and hard rock blasted the air for a minute until a customer complained and the new bartender turned down the volume.

Nick slumped in his chair while Pat pushed his way to the bar and ordered another round, a double scotch for Nick and a malt for himself.

At Pat's next request for refills, the bartender raised his bushy eyebrows.

'These are the last tonight. You've both had enough.' He wiped the counter with a damp cloth, then shook his head in a disapproving manner as Pat leaned into the bar.

The nurseryman brought the drinks back to their table and set them down. His unsteady hands sloppily spilled a little of each drink on the graffiti-marked table.

More customers jammed the pub. Glancing around, Nick could see only one unoccupied seat. The noise level increased until the timber-beamed room vibrated with the buzz of conversation, the beat of music.

'Don't feel like a game of darts tonight, do you, old mate?' Pat's weather-beaten face reflected his concern.

'Hell, no. I don't want you to pin me to the wall.' Nick barked a humorless laugh. A flash of loneliness stabbed at him as he thought of Kate. 'I haven't felt like this before. That's what's so scary.' Fear cut through an euphoria produced by too much of The Swan's best scotch.

Pat tried to help. 'You know what's wrong with you?'

'No. Tell me.' Nick slid down in his chair.

'You're in love. Happens to the best of us.'

'Don't know about love. That's tricky stuff.'

'You'll learn.' They finished their drinks in silence.

Pat pushed his chair back and glanced at Nick resting his head on the table. 'Think I better get you home.' Pat pushed open the pub's heavy oaken doors, then he pulled Nick aside as a couple darted into the pub. 'Let me drive.' He fished in Nick's jacket pocket to pull out his keys. They wrestled for the keys and Pat won. 'Where's your car?' Pat scanned the pub's small parking lot.

'I walked. It's only two blocks down the hill. I see your bike over there.' Nick flashed a smile.

'I'll get it tomorrow. Let's walk. Hit fewer pedes, pedes, you know.'

'People.' Nick smiled. 'You shouldn't drink so much.'

Pat chuckled. 'Right.'

They stumbled up the hill, arms around each other. Nick couldn't tell who held up the other.

At Nick's condo, Pat clumsily inserted the

key in the lock after several fumbling attempts. He opened the door and guided Nick to the sofa. Slipping off his shoes, Pat covered Nick with a comforter he found draped over the armchair by the fireplace. 'Get some sleep. I'll check on you in the morning.'

In a daze, Nick heard his friend bump into his umbrella stand and utter an obscenity, then Pat clicked the front door shut behind him. Nick closed his eyes.

He came to with a jolt during the night when he turned over and rolled onto the carpeted floor. Why the heck was he sleeping on a lumpy sofa when he had a comfortable bed? Grasping hold of the stair railing, he dragged his weary body upstairs. In slow motion, he struggled with his jeans, kicked them off and crawled under the bed covers.

Before dawn, a fierce headache woke him. Might as well get up. Before he could get out of bed, he had to untangle the covers he'd twisted around himself in the night. Nick yawned, scratched his head, and stumbled downstairs. A glance at the time on the hall clock brought a scowl to his face. Only five a.m.? You must be kidding.

His head felt the size of a house. Coffee and two aspirins would help. Delving into a kitchen drawer, he located a bottle of aspirin and took two. He fumbled in the cabinets in search of a clean mug. His cleaning service had missed that week. No wonder the place was a mess. He depended on them to keep the condo neat and clean.

Pulling the dishwasher open, he spotted a mug. Nick leaned on the stove and stared, blurry-eyed, until the pan of water bubbled and began to boil, then he poured the hot liquid into a black-and-white police academy mug. As he added a teaspoon of instant coffee, he inhaled the pleasant nutty aroma.

Some fresh air might clear his head. He opened the sliding glass doors then stepped onto the balcony. Standing there, he breathed deeply of the cool, crisp air. As he leaned against the wrought-iron railing, the night dew gradually soaked the sleeve of his shirt.

Sipping the hot drink, he felt it trickle downward, warming his stomach. A glance at the sky revealed no stars. Faced eastward in the direction of the dark lake, he waited for sunrise.

A slight breeze brought him the earthy scent of marigolds nesting in a neighbor's windowbox. A soft mew resounded in the quiet night as Lucky, the tomcat next door, announced his return from a night on the town.

Before dawn, the first riverboat of the day

rumbled. The crew was warming up its engines for another day of crowds of tourists taking a short trip on Windermere.

His headache diminished, Nick examined the dull ache inside him. Go on, he told himself. Admit it. You need her.

An unusual sensation, needing. He couldn't recall needing anyone since his mother left.

He'd built a wall around his emotions until he met Kate. Then, in spite of his best intentions, she'd pushed into his life until it was difficult for him to think of anything else.

His mind suggested a solution to his dilemma, just not see her again. But if he didn't see her, he'd regret it for the rest of his life. She'd touched him like no one else, and he felt the icy wall around his heart thawing. He found it unsettling but liked the sensation.

Nick wanted to apologize, but would he make matters worse? Would she talk to him if he called? He silently answered his own question. You'll never know if you don't try.

His mind made up, he watched a magnificent golden ball of sun slowly rising above the lake. In the first rays of sunlight, a pair of stately white swans led their offspring across the quiet waters.

Checking his watch, Nick groaned, swallowed, and dialed the hotel, full of dread and hope.

He recognized the sleepy voice at the reception desk of the hotel. It was early. 'Diane. It's Nick, please don't hang up.'

'I heard what you said to Kate.' At first, Diane's tone was cool, then her natural optimism broke through. 'But you didn't mean it the way it sounded, did you?'

'Of course not.' He lied. He did distrust most women, but not Kate. And not Diane, come to think of it. 'Anyway, I'm glad you answered the phone. I needed to check with you before I see her. What did she say about me?'

'Not much. She just told the three of us not to ever mention your name again.'

'I want to apologize, Diane. But will she see me?'

'Can I give you some advice?'

'Please do.'

'Send some flowers first. And not roses. You've seen the rose garden behind the hotel. She prefers bunches of flowers, try lilac, daisies, sweetpeas. Kate goes for flowers like that.'

'Great, thanks for your help, Diane.' Nick fidgeted in his chair, anxious to make amends. What was wrong with the clock? Had it stopped? He consulted his wristwatch. Both clock and watch showed the same time. In silence, he raged at the slowness of time when he was in a hurry, then he dialed a florist as soon as they opened.

'I want to order several bouquets of mixed flowers, lilac, sweetpeas, daisies, whatever is available right now.'

'Yes sir.' The young man at Bowness Florist responded. 'How much do you want to spend?'

'It doesn't matter, the sky's the limit.' Nick reconsidered the moment the words left his mouth. That could prove expensive so he added, 'Let's keep it to no more than £500.

'Deliver them to Ms. Kate Stanhope, Kings Grant Hotel on Kendall Road, the gatehouse, not the hotel itself. Can you guarrantee delivery today?' Nick waited while the florist checked the shop's supply of flowers.

'Yes, sir. I have everything in stock except the lilac and I can get that from our Lancaster store. How about roses? We have a special on yellow roses this week. Would she like some pale yellow roses?'

'No, she's got lots of roses. Be sure you get them there today. Call me when they've been delivered.'

All day her face flashed before him. And every time Nick tried to concentrate on the

Martin case, his mind played back another memory of Kate, the day at the beach, the evening she was almost killed, their night together in her narrow bed. Finally, he eased back in his armchair and closed his eyes, memories of Kate washing over him.

Once the florist called, he sighed with relief. The flowers had been delivered as promised. He pushed back disappointment every time the phone rang. Kate didn't call.

At the end of his workday, he drove to the gatehouse. Mmmm, no lights on. Was she up at the hotel, helping serve dinner to the guests? He'd wait for her. She'd come home sooner or later. Might as well get comfortable. Pushing back his car seat, he took off his jacket and loafers, stretched his legs, and lay back. The late afternoon sun blinded him . . . he'd rest his eyes for a minute. This time of year it'd be daylight until after 9 p.m. As he closed his eyes, the birds chirped in the trees above him.

A noise woke Nick later. He sat up with a start, amazed to find it was night. Rubbing sleepy eyes, he glanced over at the clock on the dashboard. 9:30 p.m. Did a door close nearby? Kate! He jumped up, bumping his head on the car ceiling.

Heart in his throat, he leaped out of the Rover and knocked on her door, then knocked again. The muscles in his arms and legs tensed, waiting for her to answer.

She opened the door a sliver and peered out.

'Kate, I'm sorry we quarreled.' Swallowing hard, he rushed on. 'I didn't mean what I said.'

'We can't talk out here, come in.' She opened the door wider for him to enter.

She watched Nick as he gazed at the apartment. She'd been pleasantly surprised herself at the lovely baskets of flowers. He'd gone overboard. The apartment resembled a florist shop. The first floor of the gatehouse overflowed with bouquets of flowers. Had he talked to Diane? He'd sent all of her favorites, daisies, delphiniums, lilacs, lilies and carnations. They covered the tabletops, the kitchen counters, the corners of the rooms, the stairs.

'You got a little carried away, didn't you?' In spite of herself, Kate felt her lips curving into a smile.

'I wanted to apologize. I didn't mean to upset you.'

'You don't really believe women are dishonest, do you?'

'Of course not. If we can find a place to sit, I'd like to explain.'

'Help me move some flowers.' She

motioned to the bouquets in vases around the living room sofa.

'Here, let me.' He picked up two arrangements and carried them outside to the front porch. 'Now, let's sit down.' He gestured to the sofa. 'I'll tell you my life story.'

'Make that the condensed version, please. It's been a long day, and I didn't sleep well last night.' Kate took a seat at the far end of the sofa.

'My experiences with women haven't been too great.'

She saw a hopeful expression on his face. Kate raised both eyebrows. 'I don't understand.'

'It all started with my first girl friend, Marigold. We were both sixteen and I thought I was in love. She swore that she'd love me as long as we lived.'

Kate glanced at her wristwatch. 'Could you get to the point?' When he'd appeared at her door, her first inclination was to throw herself in his arms. She fought down the impulse. For both their sakes, she must keep a cool head while she uncovered the reason for his distrust of women. Then, perhaps she could help him work through his problem. And they might have a chance together.

'I saved my salary from an after-school job

at the deli near our apartment and bought her an engagement ring. She showed that little ring to all of our friends in the neighborhood.'

'And you married this Marigold?'

'No. The owner of the neighborhood pawn shop called one night and told me Marigold had hocked the ring. I called her home, and her distraught mother told me Marigold had left after a fight with her Dad.' Nick stood and took off his jacket, looked for a place to put it.

Kate took it from him and draped it over a side chair. She sat down again, as far as possible from Nick.

'Later we heard she'd eloped with her real boy friend who used the money for a sure thing on the horses. When he lost at the racetrack, he dumped Marigold and left the area.'

When Nick paused, Kate walked into her kitchen and came back with two beers. He sipped the brew and gazed at her.

'So you got involved with the wrong girl. Does that give you the right to consider all women the same as this Marigold?'

'No, of course not. But another sweet young thing also took advantage of my naïveté. Do I need to give all of the details?'

'No, but haven't you learned that most

men and women are honest, even if there are exceptions?'

'Yes. Let me finish.' He raised his glass and took a sip of beer. 'Five years ago I was single and alone. The day I turned twenty-seven, I didn't have a special girl friend to help me celebrate.

'As if in answer to my prayers, Valerie, my ex-wife, came into the constabulary during a thunderstorm to report a stolen car. Several junior officers were down with the flu, so I helped her fill out the forms. Before she left, I'd asked for her telephone number. Three weeks later, we were married. Valerie had the face of an angel and a light sweet voice. But she wasn't what she appeared to be.'

Kate frowned. 'Did she have a criminal record?'

'No, but I married her without really knowing what kind of person she was. Her physical appearance fooled me. Anyway, our marriage was a disaster. We had nothing in common. After the divorce, I vowed I wouldn't get involved with another woman.'

He didn't seem anxious to elaborate on Valerie's problems, and Kate didn't feel right, asking. Obviously, it was painful for Nick to talk about his ex-wife.

Kate smiled and shook her head. 'You should have told me. But you don't think all women are like your ex-wife or the others?'

'I know you're honest. I'd trust you with my life. But can you understand why I've been wary of women?'

'I think so. But can we agree on one thing? Neither of us will keep secrets from the other. All right?'

'Right. No more secrets. Do you forgive me?'

'With all my heart.'

A deep breath, then he extended his hand. As she took it, he sighed with relief.

'I don't want to fight with you ever.'

'You don't know how good that sounds to me.' Nick slid across the sofa, took her in his arms and kissed her hard.

As he rested his forehead on hers, she gazed into the depths of his dark brown eyes. She saw no deception in them.

He kissed the corners of her lips and her auburn hair.

She inhaled his masculine scent, his citrusy cologne and the soap he showered with. As he kissed her throat and ears, she felt her heart race. Kate snuggled in his arms and gazed at the face she adored. What would she do without him? Smiling, he kissed her again. Her lips parted. His tongue teased hers.

While he kissed her, Kate couldn't recall enjoying a man's kiss as much as his.

He unbuttoned her blouse and ran his fingers over her lingerie. Under that, he touched her skin. Her heart beat faster when he unfastened her bra and lowered his head. He kissed her breasts.

'You don't know how wonderful you feel.' He pushed her long hair away from her face. 'I thought I'd lost you.'

Kate unbuttoned his shirt. She reached inside and ran her fingers over his chest.

Nick stood and pulled off his tie, then removed his shirt. He turned to her.

Kate shook her head.

'What's the matter?'

'Not here. Let's go upstairs.' Pushing aside flowers, they climbed the steep stairs to her bedroom and sank onto her bed, locked in each other's arms.

★ ★ ★

A few days later Kate glanced at her desk calendar. Diane and Chris's wedding was three days away. Nick had promised to give the bride away.

She was busily jotting down last-minute wedding details when Nick called from work with his own invitation.

'I want to cook dinner for you tomorrow night.'

'Nick, how sweet. I didn't know you could cook!'

'Well enough to keep body and soul together for many years. I won't be insulted if you turn down my offer, but please come. I want to see you.'

In a playful mood, she teased him. 'Would you classify that under business or pleasure, Inspector?'

'Use your imagination, my dear,' he growled softly.

'What time do you want me?'

'About seven p.m. And wear something comfortable. It won't be a formal evening.'

'Great. I'll bring a bottle or two from our wine cellars.'

Kate rang his door bell at seven p.m.

'Come in. Let me take your coat.'

'Thanks.' Slipping out of her jacket, she revealed a short black knit dress. Turning, she revealed the low-cut back of the dress.

'Now that's a neat outfit.' Nick leaned over and kissed her shoulder. Kate took a deep breath. Her skin tingled where his lips touched her and her knees went weak. He was the only man who affected her like this, and she wasn't sure why. Of course he was handsome, cocksure, intelligent. But why did a single touch from this man sizzle through her body with white heat?

'Stay there, I'll be right back.'

She took a seat on the sofa while he darted into the kitchen.

He returned shortly with a plate of appetizers, a big smile covering his face. The stuffed artichokes appeared too perfect to be edible food.

'I'm impressed. What do you call this dish?' She looked his accomplishment over as she held it in her hand. Carefully, she bit into one of the masterpieces. Her teeth hit bedrock.

'Ouch. Do you think you overcooked these a bit?' Her finger moved inside her mouth as she checked for breakage.

'They did turn out a little tough, didn't they? I haven't tried the recipe before.' Nick stuck his fork into an appetizer on his own plate and frowned. Picking up both dishes, he left the room.

Kate stepped into the kitchen in time to see Nick dump the whole mess into the trash container under the kitchen sink.

'Sorry about that.' His cheeks flushed with embarrassment.

'No problem. They looked great, anyway.' She wanted to encourage his efforts, but what other gourmet treats lurked in the kitchen?

'Well, on to the next course.' Nick led Kate to the tiny table in his dining area. Laughing, he bowed and seated her with a flourish, then he stepped into the kitchen and returned with a covered soup tureen. 'Try some split-pea soup. My neighbor shared the recipe, even let me help myself to leaves from her mint patch.' Ladling a lumpy green glob onto Kate's soup plate, he served himself a portion. Nick tasted the soup and watched her sample hers.

'Yuck. Maybe we'll pass on the soup.' He turned thumbs down on his concoction.

At his suggestion, she laid down her soup spoon. She could see him growing more annoyed by the minute. By this point, Nick's expression had turned grim. Searching for something consoling to say, Kate inhaled. Her nostrils detected the odor of burned food. 'What is that I smell?'

'The chicken,' he bellowed and dashed into the kitchen, Kate at his heels. Nick opened the oven door and released clouds of smoke. She stood back while he grabbed the fire extinguisher and zapped the burnt fowl.

Biting her bottom lip, she tried hard not to laugh at Nick. His face was red, his hair flopped in his eyes, and his shirt was soiled.

Kate touched his shoulder. 'Never mind. Gourmet cuisine just isn't your forte. I brought a dessert, if you'll look in my car.'

Nick walked back into the kitchen, with a covered cake plate. As Kate removed the lid, she displayed a beautiful lemon sponge cake and a small covered container. She eyed the messy kitchen. 'Now, if we can find a clean pan?'

'Here's one.' A relieved expression flitted across his face as he unearthed a small saucepan from the cupboard and handed it to her.

'Good. We'll heat up this sauce I've brought. And we can have a glass of wine with it.' As Kate heated the cinnamon sauce and poured it over the moist cake, the spicy aroma of cinnamon filled the room. It masked the odor of the burned fowl.

They consumed every crumb of the cake, washing it down with the fruity white wine. Nick liked it so much, he took a spoon and scooped up the crumbs stuck to the bottom of the cake plate.

'Why don't we take the rest of the wine and go upstairs?'

On the next floor, Kate walked around his bedroom. A kingsize brass bed covered with a dark blue duvet dominated the room. Obviously a man's room. No pictures of family or friends. One watercolor of a schooner, the wind in its sails. A bookcase held numerous books on a wide range of subjects, psychology, history, poetry, mysteries, also several books on sailing.

Kate picked up one book. 'You do enjoy sailing, don't you?'

'I used to with that friend I told you about. Since you and I went to Morecambe Bay, I've been too busy at work to think about sailing. I guess I should go ahead and buy my friend's boat, if he hasn't sold it. Windermere is great for boating.'

'I'd like to learn.' She walked to the front of the room, opened the glass doors and stepped out onto the balcony.

Nick followed and put his arms around her as she leaned on the railing. Through the trees she could just make out the lake. He nibbled her ear until she turned.

'Enough sight-seeing.' His deep voice whispered into her ear.

A shiver of anticipation rippled through her as Nick lifted her into his arms and carried her inside.

He laid her down on the bed, then crossed the room to shut the curtains.

Waiting for him, Kate raised her head and murmured, 'Can we leave them open? The moon will shine in.'

Later, as they lay quiet in bed, her head on his chest, she made a suggestion. 'I'll give you cooking lessons, all right?' She kissed him to soften her criticism of his cooking prowess.

'At least I don't have to worry that you like

me for my cooking, do I?' He played with a strand of auburn hair, then he tucked it behind her ear.

'Heavens, no.' She sat up in bed and poured them each a share of the last of the wine. Before Nick, she'd wondered how it would feel to make wild, reckless love with a man. In the last few days she'd found out.

It was breathtaking, sensual fun. Yes, fun was the best way she could describe it. But much more than that to her. She was in love with Nick. But did he love her? He hadn't said.

He kissed her shoulders, then his lips moved lower to her breasts. Her nipples grew hard. His mouth continued down her body, tantalizing her with the touch of his tongue.

Soon her entire body vibrated and her legs went limp. He kept at his art, planting light, playful kisses everywhere his lips touched. By the time he slid into her, she was moist and throbbing with desire.

Later, Kate sighed with contentment as he cradled her in his arms, gently brushed the hair off her face and dozed. Why couldn't she have met Nick years ago? She should never have married Stephen. But if she hadn't married him, she wouldn't have come to the Lake Distict, wouldn't have met Nick.

Half-asleep, he murmured, 'I love to make love with you.'

'I love you.' Kate offered words she longed to hear him say. She waited for his response.

He opened one eye. 'You mean a lot to me.' Then he went back to sleep.

That's a start, anyway. Kate blew the hair out of her eyes and climbed out of bed, pursuing the top sheet. 'Did someone have a fit in this bed?' Locating the sheet on the floor, she threw it over Nick and crawled back into bed. She claimed her share of sheet, fluffed up a pillow and placed it under her head.

Lying on his back, hands folded on his chest, Nick snored, oblivious to her efforts.

Kate lay awake a few minutes. She'd accepted his apology the other night, but now a thought returned to nag her. What did he really think of women? Had he only told her what she wanted to hear?

She pushed back the thought, unwilling to be disloyal to the man sleeping beside her. If she loved him, she must take him at his word. She closed her eyes and drifted off to sleep.

Before daybreak, the telephone rang. Kate reached for the phone on her nightstand, then realized where she was.

Half-conscious, she felt the mattress move as Nick got out of bed and grabbed the noisy machine. He talked softly into the cordless phone as he walked out into the hall and closed the door behind him.

When he called her name, she sensed immediately there was trouble. 'What is it?' She raised up on one elbow and pulled the sheet to her to ward off the cold breeze coming in the open windows.

'It's Charles. He pretended an attack of appendicitis and got away when two constables took him to the hospital. He killed one officer and the other's in critical condition.' Nick shook his head. 'He's out there somewhere right now.'

She shivered with dread. 'Will he leave the area?'

'I don't know. A sane man would get out of here as soon as possible. But Charles?' He put his arms out to embrace Kate.

'He's coming after me, isn't he?' She looked into Nick's eyes and saw her own fear mirrored there.

21

'Did you know I live with a trio of nervous wrecks?' Trying for a casual tone, Kate smiled at Nick, while they sat in the hotel library the next afternoon.

She pushed back her fear of Charles. Nick was right. With no sightings of her nephew, Charles must have escaped the police dragnet and be far away from the Lake District by now.

'I guess Diane, Chris and Mattie are a little excited over the wedding.' Nick raised an eyebrow.

'That's putting it mildly. Mattie's cleaned the place five times in the past week. She even barked at a guest yesterday after the woman wrinkled a chair cushion. And Diane trims and trims the rose bushes. I've hidden the clippers so we'll have roses left for the ceremony.'

'Stress can cause people to act in peculiar ways.'

'That's the understatement of the year.'

Kate turned at a light tap on the door, then Chris walked into the room.

'Excuse me.' Fidgeting on one foot, then

the other, Chris stood in front of Kate and Nick. 'How do you think this looks?' He wore a dark summer suit, white shirt and paisley silk tie, not his usual casual attire.

Kate glanced at the handsome man with deep blue eyes and sandy blond hair. How odd, his resemblance to the Stanhopes. 'Great, but what happened to the dark pinstripe?' She spoke in a calm tone, attempting to soothe Chris's pre-wedding jitters.

'Changed my mind.' Chris grinned, sheepishly, turned on his heels and left.

'See what I mean?' Kate glanced at Nick.

'You're right about Chris. He's a bundle of nerves.' Nick shook his head.

'I hope he holds together until the 23rd.' She frowned. 'If I didn't know better, I'd say he's concerned about more than the wedding.'

'Like what?'

'I don't know.' Kate paused in reflection. 'Well, for one thing, I've caught him staring at the family portraits a lot as he goes up or downstairs. And twice, I've caught him sitting on the stairs, gazing at the large portrait of Stephen and his younger brothers.' Kate shook her head, puzzled.

'Maybe he's interested in old photographs,' Nick said.

'It could be pre-wedding jitters. Besides trying on suits, he polishes the Rolls. He's almost worn a hole in the finish.'

'Didn't you say they plan to take the train to Skye?'

'Yes, but I'm driving them to Windermere station.' Kate stepped to the door, heard no one, then returned to her seat.

Rolling her eyes, she hissed, dramatically, 'Mattie's threatened the rest of us.'

'Why in the world?' Nick grinned.

'She said if Diane, Chris or I lay a finger on the cake before the wedding luncheon, she'll boil the guilty wretch in oil.' She laughed and leaned over to give Nick a light kiss. 'You don't really mind giving the bride away, do you?'

'I'm flattered they'd ask me.' Nick's dark eyes beamed with pleasure, then he hugged her.

That afternoon, Kate and Diane sat in the library reviewing the wedding plans.

'You did check with the pianist?' Diane chewed on her fingernails, a sure sign she was nervous.

'Oh, yes. Meant to tell you. I called Miss Rose. She'll contact you tomorrow so you can give her your selections. She's coming an hour before the ceremony to try out our piano.'

Diane smiled. 'She'll love playing the old baby grand. I like your idea of opening the doors so the music floats outside to the garden.'

'I've arranged for the piano-tuner to come two days before your wedding.' Kate ran a finger up the keyboard. She winced when a sour note resounded. 'It needs a good tuning.'

The bridegroom strolled by on his way to the garage. Sticking his head in the door, Chris jumped into the conversation. 'Has Dr. Nash become a tad hazy? During church on Sunday, he kept staring at me. And after the service, I had to tell him my name twice and remind him of our wedding date. I hope he doesn't get muddled and forget to come.'

'I'm sure he's circled that day on his calendar, but if you like, I'll remind him the day before the ceremony.' Kate patted Chris on the arm, reassuringly.

*　*　*

Light rain was falling the next morning as Kate drove Diane and Mattie down the motorway to a small, exclusive shop in Lancaster to shop for wedding dresses.

'How lovely.' Kate admired the ambience, parking in front of a small, pink frame house. They strolled through a gate in a white picket fence up to a door flanked by earthen pots of fragrant pink geraniums.

Inside, she eyed the floral wallpaper, plush mauve rugs and burgundy velvet loveseats. Welcoming her first customers of the day, the white-haired proprietor, in a long floral organza gown, motioned them to the loveseats.

They sipped raspberry tea from shell-thin china cups and nibbled on a selection of dainty sugar cookies.

Mattie muttered under her breath and shook her head at each selection the proprietor picked out for her.

'I know you'll want to look your best.' Kate whispered in Mattie's ear. 'You can't wear one of your dark winter wools to Diane and Chris' June wedding.' Kate resolved to find her frugal friend an attractive outfit that day. Later, when Mattie reviewed the wedding pictures, she'd see how pretty she appeared at the wedding.

'Oh, look.' Diane sounded excited. Kate turned her head as the owner glided out of a back room. She held a pale peach silk dress.

'Go and try it on,' Kate urged. 'It's perfect for you.'

Diane walked out of the dressing room a few minutes later.

'That's the dress for you.' Kate thought

how well the peach color went with Diane's blonde hair and hazel eyes.

The proprietor brought out another dress in a larger size for Mattie.

'Try that one. And don't argue.' Kate spoke in a firm voice.

The tall, large-framed woman came out of the dressing room. She stood before them, her body stiff-postured but handsome in a sky-blue silk dress.

'This'll do, I suppose.' Mattie looked down at the dress. She fingered the material. Then she twirled around, not at all like their sedate, serious Mattie. Her dark eyes shone.

'That's you, Mattie. Two down, one to go.' Kate picked a size eight jade green organdy off a rack and carried it to a dressing room. Mmmm . . . perfect fit, and it accentuated her green eyes. She winced, seeing the price tag but bought it.

That afternoon Mattie knocked on Kate's door. 'Can we talk? I have to tell you something.'

'Let's sit down. Diane and Chris have gone to the grocery store so we have time. Would you like a cup of tea?' What in the world was worrying her friend? Was she ill? Kate motioned Mattie to the sofa in her living room and sat down near her.

'No, thanks.' She swallowed hard. 'You

know I was twenty when I came to work for the Stanhopes?

'Yes, and over the years they came to consider you part of the family, dear. As I do now. I hope there's no trouble?' Kate studied her friend's face.

'No. This happened a long time ago. I'll just say it out plain. Stephen was older but his brothers Alex and Charles were closer to my age. We were all shaken by Mrs. Stanhope's death. Stephen was more upset than his younger brothers. He was always his mother's favorite.' She took a deep breath then continued.

'The day of the funeral, the family retired after dinner. I woke up hungry during the night and went down to the kitchen to heat some milk for cocoa. Stephen called to me when I walked by the open library door. He was slumped in an armchair, a decanter by his side. I stood in front of him, smelling the brandy on his breath. He pushed himself up from his chair and gave me a brotherly peck on my cheek. He did that sometimes so I wasn't alarmed at first.'

Her grim expression warned Kate what was coming. 'You don't have to tell me.' Kate reassured the older woman.

Mattie gripped the arms of her chair. 'Yes, I need to talk about it. Stephen started to make love to me. I pleaded and cried, but he wouldn't stop. Afterwards, he went to sleep on the sofa. I ran to my room and threw up. Then I sat on the side of the bed and cried. I could scarcely believe what happened.'

'I'll never forgive him for this.' Kate's head reeled from the shock. How could he have been so brutal? She recalled her husband's coldness and the nights he'd come to her bed drunk. Now she ached for the woman who'd filled the void left by her mother's death. Kate put her arms around Mattie.

Mattie sent her a ghost of a smile then patted her hand. 'The next day he apologized, but the damage was done. Two weeks later, I missed my period, then another the next month. I lied to the family about an ill sister, packed my trunk and took the train home to Scotland to have the baby.'

'I'm so sorry. You must have been terrified.' Kate's heart went out to the older woman for the pain Stephen caused her. Damn him to hell, anyway. He'd hurt Mattie, too.

'My sister lied for me,' Mattie explained.

'She told her husband and the rest of the family I'd married a fisherman who was lost at sea during a storm. She helped me through the whole ordeal.'

'And the child?'

'I never saw my child. In fact, I told the

nurses not to bring the baby to me. I don't even know what sex it was. I guess I was afraid once I held the baby, I wouldn't be able to give it up. The day I gave birth, I signed papers giving up all rights to my child. It was put up for adoption right away and I heard a couple adopted the baby.' Mattie dabbed at a tear with a tissue.

'I wish I could have been here for you.' Kate embraced her. 'What about Stephen? Did he suspect you had his child?'

'No. He believed my lies about an ill sister like the rest of the family. I returned to the household and two years later became housekeeper for the Stanhopes. Stephen and I avoided each other. I retired when Stephen's father died. You know the rest. Stephen and you re-opened the estate two years ago and asked me to return as housekeeper.'

'Mattie, thank you for telling me.' Kate thought of the child. 'Have you ever wondered what he looks like?' An idea occured to Kate. Had her comment about Chris resembling the Stanhope men stirred Mattie's memories? Surely Mattie didn't think Chris could be her child . . . and Stephen's.

'Yes, I've wanted to see him, but not while Stephen lived. Recently, I've been corresponding with the orphanage.' Her face lightened into happiness.

'And I can tell by your smile you've found out something, haven't you?'

'Yes, the orphanage administrator has promised to give me a name and address when I visit there next Monday.'

'That will be wonderful. And he'll be part of this family. When you find him, please invite him to visit, won't you? Tell him he's welcome anytime.'

Kate and Mattie hugged each other, their cheeks wet with tears.

After Mattie left, Kate heard her phone ring and ran to pick up the telephone in the kitchen, thinking it was Nick. There was no one there, only the sound of breathing. Replacing the receiver, she tried to stay calm.

It was the first such call in awhile. Could it have been a wrong number? The call was too short to be traced, even if the police still traced calls to her number. She should ask Nick. But in the back of her mind, Kate thought of Charles. Did he still lurk nearby? And even if he did, why would he call her? Did he really hate her so much? Kate remembered Clarissa's remark. Charles blamed her for all of his troubles. That wasn't rational.

★ ★ ★

'Connor, I'm pleased with your work, solving the Penmar and the Martin cases.' Nick's Superintendent Vaughan beamed at him across his huge mahogany desk at Windermere Constabulary.

'Thank you, sir. It won't be long until Stanhope's trial.'

'I don't guess he's confessed yet?' Vaughan looked hopeful.

'No sir, but I expect the evidence will send him to prison for a long time.'

Nick walked back to his office, his ears ringing with his superior's praise. The Superintendent obviously liked him but tried not to show favoritism.

He had the next evening off. What better way to spend it than with Kate? He didn't see as much of her as he liked. He dialed her number. 'How about a picnic supper on Sunday?'

'Sounds good to me. We didn't take any reservations for the weekend, and all of the wedding arrangements have been made.'

'You mean Diane, Chris and Mattie have calmed down and are acting like normal human beings?'

'Not quite, but I'd love to get away for a few hours.'

'I have to check on a couple of details at work, but there's a spare key under the geranium pot on my front porch. If I'm not home when you arrive, go inside and wait for me.'

He chilled two bottles of pale gold chardonnay. What would his 'Little Red Riding Hood' bring in her basket?

* * *

When Kate entered her apartment Sunday afternoon, the light blinked on her answering machine. Hitting the play button, she heard Nick's voice apologizing. 'Sorry, but I'll be at work later than I hoped. Make yourself at home, see you later.' Kate hoped he wouldn't be too late. She made a mental note to mention the latest anonymous phone call when she saw Nick.

Her picnic basket loaded with roasted chicken, rolls, salad and Mattie's lemon chess pie in the trunk, Kate drove her small car to Nick's. She parked near his front door and set her picnic basket down on his front stoop.

Now where did he say the key was? Oh, yes, in the flower pot. A search in the pot, then by the pot, even under the pot, revealed a few dead insects, but no key.

Kate was rubbing her ear, deep in thought, when the door swung open. Surprised, she glimpsed a small woman peering out at her.

Was this the wrong condo? The rows of shingled, weather-beaten condos that crested the hill overlooking Windermere seemed identical, and Kate had been there only once before. Glancing at the condo number, she confirmed it was Nick's.

Gazing at the woman, Kate noticed the over-size maroon silk robe she was wearing greatly resembled Nick's robe. She stood for a moment, uncertain what she should do.

'Were you looking for someone?' The sweet, light voice rang like the wind chimes outside Kate's bedroom window. She flashed a smile in Kate's direction and looked younger, reminding Kate of a pretty china doll her mother had given her one Christmas long ago, all blonde ringlets, rosy cheeks and baby blue eyes.

'Excuse me, but I'm meeting DCI Nick Connor here. I hope he's all right? Would you be his younger sister?' Kate racked her brain. Hadn't Nick told her he was an only child?

'Nick doesn't have any sisters. I'm sorry, I should have introduced myself. I'm Valerie, his wife, I mean ex-wife, but we're going to remedy the situation soon. You can be the first to congratulate us! What is your name, dear?'

22

'Kate Stanhope, a friend of his,' Kate replied, amazed at how nonchalantly the words slid out of her mouth. Inside, her heart hammered against her ribs and her mind whirled. Why would Nick's ex-wife appear in his condo, wearing his robe? Was the woman speaking the truth? Had Kate caught him lying?

She knew Nick had been married, but he'd told her that it didn't last long. From his abrupt manner, speaking of Valerie, Kate assumed he didn't communicate with the woman. But he did.

Kate's heart insisted he hadn't betrayed her. But had he? She reeled inwardly with apprehension. What did Valerie say? They'd remarry soon?

Taking a deep breath to calm herself, Kate straightened her shoulders held her chin high and determined to appear indifferent to the obnoxious woman whose words had just smashed all of her dreams. She focused on Valerie.

'If you like, I can give him a message. But don't expect him to get right back to you.' A smirk flitted across her face as Valerie toyed with the sash of Nick's robe.

Biting her bottom lip, Kate fought back the urge to scream. 'That would be nice, if you don't mind. When he comes home, tell him Kate Stanhope came by. He doesn't need to call me. In fact, I don't want to hear from him. And you can give him this picnic basket. I won't be needing it.'

Her foot nudged the basket toward the other woman, then Kate walked to her car, a smile pasted on her face. As she drove away, she sensed Valerie watching her.

Nick heard the rumble of thunder in the distance when he pulled into his parking space in front of the condo. Kate's Ford Escort wasn't in sight. She must have parked around back. He unlocked his front door, stepping into the condo as the first raindrops splashed on his small front porch.

'Sorry I'm so late.' A quick glance informed him the living room was empty. Listening a moment, he heard no response to his call, no sound broke the silence. Where was Kate? 'Where are you?' He'd expected to find her absorbed in the evening news on his television. At the sound of a noise upstairs, he looked up.

'I'm up here, Nick.'

That didn't sound like Kate, but who else

could it be? The voice was muffled. Was she playing coy, hiding in his bedroom? A smile crossed his face as he envisioned a romp with Kate. A flick of his finger turned on the hall light, then he took the stairs two at a time. Peering into the dim bedroom, Nick spotted a figure under his bed covers. He grinned. Two could play this game. He dove across the bed.

'Surprise, Nick!' A small hand threw back the covers. Jerking back, his horrified eyes fell on his blonde, blue-eyed ex-wife. Her breath reeked of alcohol.

'What the hell? Valerie? You're the last person I expected to see. Where's Kate?' Turning on the lamp on the nightstand, Nick sat down on the side of the bed, fighting the urge to throttle his ex-wife. Disappointed, he controlled his temper. He'd never struck a woman in his life and wouldn't start now, no matter what she did to aggravate him.

'Who?' Valerie lifted the covers and playfully peered under them. 'There's no Kate here, just you and me.'

'How did you get here?'

'I rode the train from Manchester, then waited for you all afternoon. You know we've needed to talk face-to-face for ages.' Valerie wagged her finger at him, listing his crimes. 'You ignore me. You don't answer my letters and you won't talk to me but a few minutes each time I call you. Fortunately, I recalled where you keep the spare key.' She smoothed her hair with her fingers and looked pleased with herself.

'Come on, admit that you're glad to see me. Give me a kiss?' She puckered her mouth and closed her bleary eyes in anticipation.

He turned his head to avoid her dragon breath, then picked up an empty bottle and frowned. 'The only thing I'll give you is lots of hot black coffee, then we'll drive to the station and get you on the next train to Manchester.' He tried to sound as gruff as possible, glaring at her. She stopped smiling and drew back against the bed headboard.

'I'll call and get your father to meet your train. Now, tell me the truth.' Nick clutched Valerie by the shoulders, resisting the impulse to shake her. 'Are you sure another woman wasn't here this afternoon?' His eyes scanned the room. A discarded sweater and jeans lay on the floor where she'd dropped them, also his robe.

Valerie shook her head but didn't reply.

Nick thumped downstairs and into the kitchen. A picnic basket sat on the table. The label on its side read 'King's Grant Hotel'. He unloaded its contents onto the kitchen counter. Any other time he would've picked up and nibbled on a drumstick. He'd had a good appetite on the way home, and not just for food. Finding the wrong woman in his bed had quenched his hunger. Nick climbed the stairs again and slammed the empty basket down on the bed. 'What happened when Kate came over here, Valerie? Tell the truth, if you can.'

'All right, all right. Don't get so upset.' She pushed the hair out of her eyes, climbed out of bed and stood for a moment, nude before him.

Her body appeared as perfect as ever. His eyes flicked over her figure, but she didn't arouse him as she had in the past. Now she just appeared ludicrous. After a moment, she retrieved his robe from the floor where she'd tossed it, wrapping it around her.

'What did Kate say?' He persisted, determined to force the truth out of Valerie.

'Not much . . . You don't need to call her. She prefers you don't.'

'Damn you, Valerie. Get yourself in shape while I make some coffee. Then I'll drive you to the station. Now move.' Nick loomed above her. His stern words commanded her.

'No, I won't. Why can't I stay here with you? We can be happy again. Don't you want me at all?' She whined and burst into tears, clinging to the bed rail.

Nick remembered how she'd cried to get her own way while they were married. Now her tears didn't move him. Prying her slender fingers off the bed, he took hold of her shoulders and marched her toward the bathroom. Turning on the cold water full blast in the shower, Nick pushed her in, robe included. She yiped as the cold water hit her.

Rain pounded down on the Rover while Nick drove to the station an hour later. That and the whish, whish of the wipers moving back and forth contrasted with the silence inside the car.

'Couldn't I just stay for the weekend?' Valerie's voice broke the quiet. She wheedled and coaxed, trying one more time to change his mind.

Nick frowned and shook his head. He had nothing to say to her. How did he ever delude himself into thinking he loved her? At Windermere, he pulled into a space near the moss-covered limestone station.

Ignoring the downpour, Valerie climbed out of the car, then slammed the door and marched into the building. Nick followed her.

'You didn't buy a round-trip ticket, did you?' Did she think he'd let her stay? 'One to Manchester, one-way, please.'

The stationmaster handed Nick the ticket. 'That'll be £20, sir.'

'When does the shuttle to Oxenholme leave?' Nick pulled £20 from his wallet, sliding it under the wire enclosure. Through the dirty window, he viewed the train on the eastbound track.

'You've got about five minutes.'

'And she'll reach Oxenholme in time to catch the next train to Manchester?' Nick would drive her to Oxenholme, nearest stop on the main line, if necessary. His instincts screamed for him to get rid of her as fast as possible. He must see Kate.

'Right.' The stationmaster pulled out a worn pocket watch and checked it. 'That train's fifteen minutes late.'

With a firm hand on her arm, Nick led Valerie outside. He opened one of the coach doors and stood aside as she climbed aboard.

She turned to him as if she wanted to speak.

'Please go back into therapy. It'll help you straighten out your life if you give it a chance.'

'You're sure you won't change your mind about us?'

'I'm sorry, but that's not possible. I'm in love with a woman I met recently.' He smiled. 'And I bet there's a guy in your future who'll love you if you give him the chance.'

Through the train window, he watched

Valerie sit down beside a woman holding a fretful baby.

With one shrill whistle, the train left the station. Nick turned and walked away.

Jumping in the Rover, Nick raced up the narrow, rain-slicked road. Ten minutes later, he drove through the gates at King's Grant. No lights at the gatehouse. Would he find Kate up at the hotel? He couldn't talk to her with her friends around. What should he do now?

He yearned to see her, to hold her and explain. Thinking of the trouble Valerie had caused, his heart ached. It was his fault, too. Why hadn't he told Kate his ex-wife was mentally unstable, a pathological liar? He should have prepared Kate in case she ever met the woman.

He drove to the nearest pay phone and called Kate. The phone rang several times, then her answering machine cut on. Should he leave a message? At least she'd know he wanted to talk to her. But what could he say? He slammed down the receiver.

His beeper went off. Nick answered. 'Connor.' He heard his Sergeant's voice. She sounded excited. 'What's going on?'

'I took a call from a man ten miles from here and he saw Charles, or someone who looks like Charles. He gave the guy a ride into the town where he lives.'

'Great. This is the first report we've had on Charles since his escape. I want a patrol car up there right away. Call me if you find out anything.' He paused. 'Yes, you can go with the other officer.' He turned off his beeper. Where was Kate?

* * *

Kate had kept her composure until she was out of sight of the condo. Around a bend, she pulled over on the side of the road. With the heavy sweet fragrance of honeysuckle filling the air, she laid her head on the steering wheel and wept.

One thought raced through her mind. Did Nick toy with her while planning to remarry Valerie? Did he just consider her a brief episode?

A few minutes later, Kate took a deep breath, wiped her eyes with a hanky she found in her pocket, and drove home to King's Grant. The gatehouse loomed dark and still when her car lights shone on the front windows. Not able to stand being alone, Kate headed up the drive to the hotel. Relieved to find Mattie in the kitchen, she called out, 'Are you busy right now? I need to talk to you.' Kate sat, bent over with grief, at the kitchen table as Mattie prepared supper. Thank goodness they didn't have guests that night.

'Didn't expect to see you again today. Didn't you take a picnic supper over to Nick's?' The housekeeper's back was turned while she chopped ingredients for a salad. Putting them into a large bowl, she turned then stared at Kate, wiping her eyes. Mattie reached over and gave Kate a big hug.

Seeing the love and concern on her friend's face, Kate's reserve broke down completely and she sobbed against the other woman's shoulder. A few moments later, Kate took a deep breath to get a rein on her emotions, then explained the reason for her upset state. 'I didn't expect Nick until later. He left me a message. While I searched for his key, a woman came to the door, in his maroon silk robe. Nick's described his ex-wife as blond and petite, so I knew it was Valerie even before she introduced herself. You should have seen her expression. She looked like the cat that swallowed the canary.' Kate wiped at her eyes with her soggy handkerchief, then she took the tissues Mattie offered.

'Didn't you tell me he was divorced a few years ago?' Mattie's calm voice soothed Kate.

'Yes, and I assumed they didn't see each other.' Kate blew a sagging lock off her face.

'But today, Valerie informed me I should congratulate them since they're back together. Nick hasn't said much about his marriage, but I got the impression he had no feelings for his ex-wife.'

'Shouldn't you talk to him, get his side of the story?'

'I suppose I should, but I'm almost afraid to hear what he'll say.' Kate's heart ached, thinking of Nick. She'd fallen in love, and believed he felt the same way. Was she too eager to escape her loneliness? It was difficult for her to accept the idea he'd used her. The man she'd fallen in love with wasn't like that.

Diane and Chris walked in a few minutes later and appeared surprised, but pleased to see Kate.

Diane chatted while she set the table for four. 'Of course you'll stay for dinner, Kate. You can't turn down Mattie's beef stew. We have plenty.' Diane patted Kate's arm.

Kate observed Diane take Mattie aside and ask what happened.

Kate stared, bleakly, out a kitchen window while the rain poured down in a steady stream. Tiny rivulets flowed into a ravine until they made a lake around the rose garden.

Well, better to know than to wonder. She made up her mind. 'Go ahead and have dinner, don't hold it for me. I'm going down to my place to call him.'

'Are you sure? Would you like me to walk down there with you?' Chris's blue eyes showed concern and genuine affection.

'Thanks, but I'll be all right. One way or another, I've got to find out what happened. I'll see you all later.' She grabbed an umbrella from the stand in the front hall then ran down the driveway. The rain beat down on her, soaking her legs and feet. The phone was ringing as she unlocked the door. Kate rushed inside, dropping the drenched umbrella in the kitchen sink. She hesitated, then took a deep breath and picked up the receiver.

'Kate, where've you been? I've called several times. You did come over here this afternoon, didn't you?' Nick's voice sounded worried.

'I sure did.' She took a deep breath and tried not to cry.

'I know my ex-wife upset you. This is the first time I've seen her since the divorce. I had no idea she was coming today. Please believe me.'

'I don't know what to think. Where is she now?'

'On the evening train to Manchester. I should have warned you about her.'

'I didn't want to pry. We only met last month.'

'I feel as though I've known you for years. You have the right to know about her. I want you to know.' He paused. She didn't reply so he continued. 'I'm sorry she upset you with her lies. Can I come over? I stopped by the gatehouse earlier, but you weren't home. I figured you'd gone up to the hotel.'

'Yes, I did. Perhaps it would be best if you came over.'

Fifteen minutes later, Nick drove up. When he stepped inside the door, she saw him stare at her. She must look a fright after crying so much. Her eyes felt sore and puffy. Kate took his wet jacket and draped it over a chair.

Nick tried to embrace her but she stood frozen, then stepped away. He followed her into the living room and took a seat on the sofa. The spicy fragrance of pine began to fill the room from a fire crackling in the fireplace.

'Kate, please come and sit by me.' He patted the floral sofa. 'I want to tell you everything so you'll understand.'

Ignoring his plea, she sat down in a chair across the room.

He cleared his throat, then he took out a handkerchief and wiped his wet face. Nick eyed his shoes. 'Do you mind if I put these by the fire? They're soaked.' He gestured to his soggy loafers.

'No, of course not.'

She watched him slip off his loafers and set them on the hearth. In the momentary silence, Kate heard the rain clattering against the window panes.

Nick began to speak, and she couldn't help seeing the pain on his face. It dawned on her that he was in the past, reliving his marriage.

'I've told you I met Valerie five years ago. I found her charming and a delightful change from the others I'd dated. We married three weeks after we met. A month later, I caught her in a lie. A trivial matter. She lied about how much she'd spent on a new dress. Next, she lied about taking money from my wallet. Little by little, I noticed more lies. The worse came the day I walked into our kitchen after night shift while she was having breakfast with a friend.'

Kate frowned. 'From your expression I assume you mean a male friend?'

'Right. Hoping there was an innocent explanation, I asked her for an introduction. She immediately insisted the man was her brother, trapping herself. Early in our relationship, she'd told me she had three sisters, no brothers. Right away she tried to wiggle out of the situation with more lies, then she broke down and cried, admitting she was a liar but couldn't help it.'

'Why not?' Kate leaned toward Nick, concerned.

'Lying is a way of life for her. She'd rather lie than tell the truth. I guess she prefers her lies to reality.' He stood and paced, back and forth in front of the fireplace, then stopped and looked in her direction. Kate didn't comment so he went on. 'Her father confirmed her story. Two doctors have diagnosed her as a pathological liar. To those not close to her, she seems normal. For instance, she's employed as an assistant interior decorator. It's just in close, personal relationships that she is flawed. She has started therapy numerous times but always discontinues treatments before the doctors can help her.' He rubbed his eyes.

Kate kept her silence. He needed to talk about Valerie.

'I tried to convince her to resume treatment, but she put me off. After awhile, she argued that I was the one needing help.

'After two years, I couldn't take any more. Worrying about her affected my work. I couldn't think of anything else. At last, I gave her an ultimatum . . . get professional help or I'm leaving. With reluctance, she began therapy again, this time with a new doctor, but soon dropped out and refused to go back. I couldn't take any more, so I arranged for the divorce. Before I moved out, her father promised to keep an eye on her and try to get her back in therapy.' Nick grimaced and rubbed his forehead.

'So what happened? Did she get help?'

'Not for long. She continues her pattern, find a doctor, keep appointments until the doctor tries to help, then she stops the therapy. She blames everyone else for her problems. Now she appears to be drinking. She wasn't feeling any pain when you met her. I found two empty wine bottles in the condo.' He ran his fingers through his tousled hair.

'Sounds like she's given you a bad time.'

'She was drunk when I got home today so I tossed her in a cold shower, clothes and all, filled her with lots of coffee, and put her on the train to Manchester. And I alerted her father to meet her train, so she'd get home all right. Before I left her, I encouraged her to go back into therapy, even offered to pay for it, if needed. I can only tell you how sorry I am that she upset you. I promise you, it won't happen again.'

Now Nick stopped and gazed at her. She could see his heart in his eyes, begging her to believe him, to forgive him. 'You say it was her own idea. After what you've told me about your ex-wife, I believe you. But if you saw how she stood there in your robe and how she talked to me, you would understand why I'm upset.' Her voice broke and a tear trickled down her cheek in spite of her effort to stay calm. 'If you'd told me about her, I'd have been prepared.'

'Kate, I couldn't tell you about Valerie. I didn't dream she'd come up here. I wish I'd warned you now. Then you'd have known what she is.' He rubbed his eyes. 'Can you forgive me? All I want is for us to be together. The past month with you has been the happiest time of my life.'

'Nick, do you love me?' She waited for his reply.

'You know I do, Kate.'

'No. How could I? You haven't told me.' Kate heard her voice become higher, almost shrill.

'Then let me make it clear.' He leaned forward. 'I love you more than anything in this world. But how do you feel?'

'Right now I'm numb, hurt and disappointed. I thought I knew you, but I don't.'

'It's the shock of meeting her. It will pass.'

'No. Love doesn't mean the same thing to each of us. If I love someone, I trust them completely. That's where we differ. Love and trust can't be separated as far as I'm concerned. I don't believe you love me since it's obvious you don't trust me. If you did, you'd have told me about your marriage and Valerie. It's just as well that I found out now.' She started to tear up and took a deep breath.

'You don't mean that, you're just over-wrought, and it's no wonder, Valerie appearing out of the blue. I admit I was shocked to see her, myself.'

'I'm sorry. It just won't work, the two of us.' Kate fought to control the ache in her heart. She couldn't think straight with him so near. Rising, she handed him his jacket and opened the door.

'I can't believe this is happening.' Pain and anger flashed across his face as he stood before her. 'You understand . . . if I leave now, I won't come back?'

'Yes.' Her eyes filled with unshed tears.

'Think a moment. You'll change your mind . . . '

'I won't.' She sighed. 'Goodbye. Take care of yourself.'

Nick marched out into the storm, then she closed the door behind him and leaned her forehead against it. A moment passed, and Kate heard his car start up, then the Rover splashed through the gates, and the sound of the car's engine faded away.

Kate looked in the direction of the fireplace. 'Oh no. He forgot his shoes.' She picked up the soaked loafers and hugged them to her chest. Would he come back for them? She doubted it. Chris would have to take them to Nick.

Tears came in a torrent and she sat down, burying her head in her hands. His words echoed in her mind, 'I won't be back . . . I won't be back.' If hearts could break, hers was breaking now.

23

'She's a lovely bride, isn't she?' Kate whispered. Mattie and she sat beside the photographer's wife watching Diane, a vision in peach silk and antique lace veil. Carrying a bouquet of pale pink Cecile Brunner roses, Diane walked, smiling, toward the altar where Chris and the silver-haired minister waited.

'Yes, and look at Chris. He's positively beaming.' Mattie smiled, fondly, in Chris's direction.

Kate relaxed, lulled by the June sun on her face and arms. She inhaled the heavy sweet scent of the roses surrounding them, pleased they were having the ceremony in the garden.

The simple service didn't last long. A few minutes passed, then Kate nudged her friend. 'Here they come.'

Miss Rosa burst forth with the Recessional as if inspired by the beauty of the occasion while the radiant newly-weds walked, arm in arm, down the path bordered by antique rosebushes. They climbed the steps to the terrace, Chris supporting his new bride so she wouldn't trip on the flagstones.

'Doesn't the baby grand sound mellow?'

Kate decided to call the piano tuner the next day and thank him again for doing such an excellent job. The music floated out to the garden under a cloudless sky. A perfect day, except for one thing. Nick didn't stand beside her. Closing her eyes, she saw once more the disappointment and pain on Nick's face. How hurt he'd looked when he realized it was over for them. Kate pushed back her regrets and focused on the wedding.

'Aren't you glad I talked you into a new dress for today? You look gorgeous.' Kate smoothed a ruffle on Mattie's sleeve and admired the older woman.

With amusement, Kate noticed that Mattie kept an eye on the luncheon preparations. She didn't need to do so since they'd arranged for Lakeside Temps to serve luncheon. 'Thank goodness the weather's holding.' Kate watched as two girls brought a table and chairs out to the terrace. She eyed the dishes they'd have for lunch. 'The star of the show will be your gorgeous wedding cake.'

Mattie grinned. 'I had to threaten all of you so you'd keep your fingers off until today.'

Luncheon was announced. Kate had invited the minister and his sister, also the photographer and his wife to join them. The small group sat, talked, ate and toasted the bridal couple. Kate sipped her champagne, the golden bubbles tickling her nose.

After Kate, Mattie and the pastor took turns toasting the bride and groom, Chris stood and proposed a toast. A mysterious smile flitted across his boyish face.

He raised his champagne flute. 'Let's drink to Anne and Alex Stanhope. Without them, this wedding wouldn't have been possible!' He lifted his glass and gazed at the party seated round the table.

As one, all of the attendees lifted their glasses.

Baffled by his odd toast, Kate spoke up. 'Chris, forgive me for being oblique, but why toast my husband's deceased brother and sister-in-law? It must be nearly thirty years since they died.' Kate frowned. What did she miss?

'Sorry, Kate, everybody. I thought this might be a good way to break the news. I'm toasting Anne and Alex because they were Arthur Stanhope's mother and father. If Arthur hadn't survived their plane crash in the Amazon, I wouldn't be here at King's Grant marrying Diane this morning.'

Mattie moaned and slid off her chair. She crumbled onto the terrace, her blue dress billowing around her, before Kate and the others could move.

315

'What on earth!' Kate knelt by the other woman and cradled her head in her lap. 'Some water, please.' The photographer's wife hastily poured a glass and handed it to Kate.

Less than a minute later, Mattie regained consciousness. The moment she opened her eyes, she asked, 'What happened?

'You seem to have fainted, Mattie.' Chris looked worried. 'Are you all right now?'

'Of course. I just felt light-headed all of a sudden. How odd. I can't recall fainting in my entire life.'

'Perhaps you should go inside and lie down?' Kate wrinkled her brow.

'Nonsense. I'm fine now, probably a combination of too much sun and champagne. And Chris's toast . . . surprised me.' Her words trailed off into the air as she stood up and brushed off her dress.

Chris reseated her at the table. Kate stepped into the kitchen and came out with Mattie's sun bonnet which she insisted her friend wear. 'Chris, you were about to toast Alex and his wife,' Mattie reminded him, her eyes shining with excitement. 'I always liked him best of the three Stanhope brothers.'

'Yes, I'm curious, too. What did you mean? You couldn't be their son . . . or could you?' Kate held her breath.

'No, afraid not. I met Art in the Navy last

year. He told me an amazing story of how he survived his family's plane crash. A Foreign Service couple adopted him. Later they hired a series of private investigators to hunt for Art's natural parents. An investigator finally uncovered Art's true identity last Fall. He was Anne and Alex Stanhope's son. After his Navy stint, Art was coming up here to meet his family.' Chris paused.

Looking at Chris, Kate wondered at the sad expression now covering his face.

'I'm sorry to have to tell you but Art died in an accident on maneuvers in November.' Regret rang in Chris's voice.

'You came to King's Grant to tell us, Chris?'

'Yes, but I got here this Spring, after Art's Uncle Stephen died. Then I saw your ad for help in the paper and needed a job so I applied.'

'But why didn't you tell me you were Arthur's friend?' Kate wrinkled her brow.

'I know I should have told you, but I didn't want you to feel obligated to give me a job. You hired me, not knowing who I was. And you were all so friendly, I began to think of this place as home. That's why I stayed at first.' He hugged Diane and kissed her cheek. 'Later, wild horses couldn't have moved me. These last weeks, I've felt I belong here. I've never had quite that feeling before.'

'Now, shall we have that toast? To Anne and Alex Stanhope and to Art.' He gathered Diane, Kate and Mattie into one big bear hug while the others raised their glasses and the photographer clicked his camera. Kate saw the photographer's wife wiping her eyes, apparently touched by the moment.

'We really have grown together and become family.' Kate replied, then she stood on tiptoe to kiss Chris's cheek.

They lifted their glasses and toasted the Stanhopes.

A few minutes later, Kate set down her glass and glanced at her watch. 'Whoops. If you want to connect with the evening train to the coast we ought to leave soon.'

'I'm ready. My bag's just inside the kitchen door.' Mattie was riding Chris and Diane's train as far as Glasgow where she'd visit relatives and talk to the orphanage director. 'I'll call you Monday night, Kate, after I visit the Little Sisters of the Poor.'

Mattie looked hopeful. Kate knew she yearned to find her long lost child.

'Our reservation's at Tigh Osda Eilean Iarmain on the harbor of Skye's southern coast. The phone number's on the kitchen counter if you need us. I wish you weren't going to be alone here while we're gone.'

Chris cast an anxious glance in Kate's direction.

'Don't worry about me, just have a wonderful time. It's your honeymoon.' Kate knew she'd have lots of time to think, maybe more than she wanted. She must try not to brood about Nick. That was easier said than done. Ordinarily, the guests would keep her busy, but they'd closed the hotel for the week Diane, Chris and Mattie would be away.

At Windermere Station, Kate watched her friends board the shuttle bound for Oxenholme and waited for the small train to pull out of the station.

At the last minute, Mattie opened her window and called to Kate. 'Are you sure you won't come to Glasgow with me? My sister has lots of room now that the kids are grown.'

Kate shook her head and reassured her she'd be fine. 'Miles will keep me company.'

★ ★ ★

From the woods near the mansion, Charles watched and saw no signs of life. Where were they? Did they all take a day trip? Cautiously, he crept out of the woods and approached the back of the building, ready to jump behind a tree or dive into a hedge if Kate or the others appeared. The kitchen door was unlatched.

He clicked his tongue at Kate's carelessness before stepping inside.

A brief sense of homecoming filled Charles, entering the mansion he'd expected to own someday. Watching the estate, off and on, for days, he'd noticed people running in and out. It had been late afternoon when he arrived today and found the place deserted. He'd come to say goodbye to King's Grant before leaving the country.

He listened and didn't hear a sound. The place was desolate. Good. He'd hide there that night. Then he'd leave the area before the police got lucky and tracked him down.

Standing in the kitchen, Charles debated where to hide in the house and decided he'd be safer down in the cellars, the least used place. But first he needed to eat something. Hiding in the woods for several days, he'd stolen food whenever he found the opportunity. It didn't come often, so he was faint with hunger.

He pulled open the refrigerator and eyed a pot roast. Even cold, the slices he cut tasted delicious. His hunger abated, he cleaned up after himself. Perhaps they wouldn't miss it. Charles crept down to the cellar, the old stairs creaking under him. He wandered through the lower level, eying rooms full of Stanhope furniture, pictures, old toys and other items his ancestors couldn't discard. Then he burrowed down behind a stack of boxes, in a corner of the last room, his bed two dusty sofa cushions. As he dozed off, the walls of the old mansion soothed him. He'd rest and leave before daybreak, resigned to leaving the place he loved best.

Footsteps resounded on the cellar stairs and he jerked into consciousness. What? Where was he? Then he got his bearings. For some reason, he recalled the last time he visited here. On that occasion, he'd sat in the living room. Today, he lurked in the cellars, afraid someone would find him. It was hard to believe how much his life had changed.

Through a crack in the wall of boxes shielding his hideout, he watched surreptitiously and was rewarded by a glimpse of auburn hair when Kate passed by in the narrow hall. Imagine her surprise if he rose up and moaned. He fought down a chuckle at the thought. Then he heard her enter the next room. Why was she down there? Perhaps she was making plans to use the space for the hotel? He'd remain out of sight and wait. Kate would go back upstairs shortly, he was sure.

24

Kate drove back to the hotel and parked the Rolls in the garage, then stood on the back driveway watching the Lakeside Temps girls pack up their company's station wagon.

As the girls climbed into the car, Kate called out, 'Wait, I'll get you both a piece of wedding cake.' She dashed indoors and ran back out with foil-wrapped cake.

Soon, she found herself alone in the hotel, except for Miles who followed her everywhere. In the silent mansion, his toenails clicked loudly on the hardwood floors. 'I guess you miss Mattie, don't you, Miles?' Kate stooped to rub his black head. 'Never mind, you can sleep on the foot of my bed tonight.' He gazed up at her as if he understood.

Nick hadn't called for a week, since they fought following his ex-wife's surprise visit. Kate hoped, for awhile, that he'd call or come to see her. Hope died slowly, bit by bit. Now it seemed unlikely she'd see him again. He'd told her he wouldn't be back. Several times she started to call him, then hung up before he answered. It wouldn't work unless he changed.

She took a deep breath, blinking back the tears that tried to form in her eyes. It wouldn't be easy, not seeing him. She missed his company and their talks. And she ached to feel his arms around her, his lips on hers. If only he'd learn to trust, to confide.

She took off her 'wedding dress' and slipped into a pair of jeans and a shirt. Changing clothes, she thought about Charles and Clarissa. Despite strong evidence, Charles had never admitted to killing Martin. Now he fled from the law. Was he hiding in another country, using an alias?

Confident that Clarissa wouldn't hurt anyone, Kate hoped the courts wouldn't consider the young woman an accessory. Clarissa should have a chance to live her own life, free from the shadow of her brother's crimes. In a day or so, Kate planned to visit Clarissa. But she hoped never to lay eyes on Charles again. She admitted, privately, that Charles had always frightened her.

The telephone rang. 'King's Grant Country House Hotel. May I help you?' Kate picked up the reservations book on the front desk and turned to the desired date. 'We've named our best room The Grassmere. It's available then. It's spacious, furnished with antiques, and has a beautiful view of the lake.

May I book it for you? Fine, if you'd give me your name and credit card information?' Hanging up, she resumed her prowl through the hotel.

The phone rang again. 'King's Grant Hotel.' Kate listened to a tour guide's cry for help. The woman's hotel reservations had gone awry. 'No, I'm sorry, but we're a small hotel and can't handle a large group.' She grinned, imagining fifty tourists in her small hotel. 'You might try the Waterside Hotel on the south end of the lake. Wait, I'll tell you how to reach them.' She found the larger hotel's telephone number for the caller.

Kate admitted she needed time off. The strain of the last few weeks had taken its toll. How long was it since she'd slept all night? She couldn't remember. Since the silent telephone calls began, she dozed every night, leaving a light on. At least she hadn't received any of those calls recently. And she didn't get hungry, anymore. Even Mattie couldn't tempt her with specially baked cookies or cakes, her favorites. Kate felt her loose waistband and resolved to gain a few pounds. She decided to rest for a few days, then she'd create two or three new menus, read a good book, picnic by the lake, even go shopping.

Why did she feel so restless? Maybe she should have gone with Mattie to Glasgow.

Too late now. She envisioned the three of them rolling along, happily, heading for their destinations. Well, she'd use her free time wisely. She picked up her notebook. She found her best ideas came while she walked. Today she decided to compile a list of projects they might take on to further improve the hotel.

What did Diane suggest? Oh, yes, mini-cooking classes for interested guests. That might work. How about one on soufflés? And each class member would take a soufflé dish and recipes home with her.

Kate looked around her, strolling through the storage rooms. Thanks to Mattie and Diane, they were well-organized with the Stanhope antiques. Chris had helped by removing a few pieces.

Kate resolved to keep the same overall ambience in the hotel since guests found that pleasing. She'd focus on making the public rooms more comfortable. For example, she jotted herself a note to look into a new sofa for the living room.

Maybe they'd paint the gazebo and add two or three cushioned lawn chairs. Guests might sit out there if they had a perch more comfortable than the top of the stone wall edging the terrace. Kate had noticed several times guests took their drinks outside on the lawn and terrace to watch the sun set behind the fells.

Perhaps when the hotel was better established, she'd include plush terry cloth robes in each room. That was a nice touch the upscale hotels were using. She remembered the hooded maroon robes that Thornbury Castle put in its rooms and suites. Hadn't a local store advertised a special on robes?

The front door bell chimed and her heart raced. Could Nick have come back? Then, reality took hold and her spirits fell back to earth with a thud. It wasn't Nick. She'd seen the last of him.

Who was it? She didn't expect company. She'd checked earlier, and Chris had put up the closed sign on the front door before they left.

The bell rang a second time. Her caller seemed persistent. She'd have to answer. Cracking the door, Kate spotted the round, weathered face of Dolly, the owner of a new bed-and-breakfast down the road. Kate had sent the older woman business on two occasions. Unlocking the door, she swung it open.

'Kate, I know you're alone with your friends in Scotland, so I brought you something for your supper.' The older woman smiled and held out a covered dish. 'Here's a bowl of my Vermicelli Salad.'

'How thoughtful, Dolly. Won't you come in?' For a moment Kate felt the cathedral-ceilinged rooms of the first floor looming vast and empty behind her.

'Sorry, but I've four hungry guests to feed. I've taken your suggestion and offered breakfast and a light supper and now I'm booked up for weeks.' Dolly looked tired, but pleased. Kate knew the widow needed a successful business, also.

'Well, thanks again.' Kate closed the door, carried the dish to the kitchen and placed it in the refrigerator. She spied a half-bottle of champagne on a shelf, also the wedding cake she didn't freeze.

An unexpected burst of 'sweet tooth' caused Kate to stick her finger into the luscious creamy topping. She caught herself looking over her shoulder, like a naughty child, half expecting Mattie to inform her, 'You're going to ruin your appetite. Dinner is almost ready.'

Why not be frivolous and have a glass of champagne with the vermicelli salad and a slice of wedding cake for supper? And Diane had left a new peach bath gel for her to try. She'd take a bath, then get in bed with her supper tray and read the whodunnit Mattie lent her.

Kate and Miles wandered through the mansion. From a second floor window, she gazed downhill and caught a glimpse of the lake through the evergreens covering the fell. Overhead, Kate noticed several dark clouds now marring what had been clear blue sky. She felt chilled as she stood by the open window and watched the wind playing with the curtains. Had the temperature dropped since she went out? Perhaps another cold front drifted through the area on its way west to the Irish Sea.

Back downstairs, she inspected the kitchen. Didn't the Lakeside Temps personnel do a good job? The counter-tops were spotless and the copper-bottomed pans shone, hanging on their racks over the stove. Spying one lone smudge on the counter, she took a cloth and cleaned it. It looked almost like a dirty handprint.

Checking the dining room, Kate found the Haviland china they used that day neatly stacked in the china cabinet and the multicolor arrangement of rosebuds she'd assembled for the luncheon set in the center of the dining room table. She'd save a rosebud or two and dry them for Diane as a memento.

She probably ought to check the cellars since the help had gone down there to get the champagne for the luncheon. Anyway, she'd looked over the rest of the house. Why not be complete and take a quick look downstairs? Then she'd fix a supper tray to carry to the gatehouse.

Kate turned on lights on her way down the steep stairs to the cellars, Miles close behind her. She couldn't help but think of the night they'd come home to find the lower level of King's Grant ransacked. A shiver ran up her spine then she muttered, under her breath, 'Stop trying to scare yourself. This isn't a good time to think of burglars.'

Stephen and she had rarely visited the cellars. Well, she didn't have a time schedule for the next week. And they needed to tackle the Stanhope discards. If the hotel expanded, the cellar space could be used for better purposes, maybe for rooms.

Why not try to find a few items they could use upstairs?

Miles wandered off to investigate. Kate heard him sneeze as he snooped through the other rooms. She let him go since he couldn't hurt himself in the cellars. 'Have fun, Miles, but remember you're getting a hot sudsy bath with dog shampoo before you sleep on my bed,' she called after him. She reminded herself to take a box of Doggie Yummies to the gatehouse to lure the Scottie into the bathroom for his bath. Miles strongly objected to soap and water.

Kate examined one object, then another. Feeling lonely, she talked to herself. 'Mmmm . . . maybe I'll clean up this tall cut-glass pitcher with matching glasses for a bedroom. And this set of blue-green pottery.' The rough clay felt cool under a coat of grime. She picked up a plate and held it up to the light coming in the windows. 'We can use this on the breakfast table.'

On and on Kate foraged. She put aside a handsomely framed autumn scene of hunters in the first room, a few more vases in the next. Tired, she stretched and rubbed her shoulders, sitting down on an old bar stool to rest. Gazing at the walls, her eyes traveled up to the ornate borders. The first time she missed it. A second glance, and her eye snagged on an irregularity in the border. Or was it the light? Curious, she pulled the bar stool to the wall and climbed up. Then she stretched to reach the top border. Her muscles tensed as she jumped and almost fell from her perch. 'Whoops.' The second time she again missed. The stool wasn't tall enough. Looking around, she found a stepladder in a far corner. Manhandling the ladder, she dragged it to the wall. Good, now she could reach the top of the wall.

There was a hole, a small space in the top border, probably the home of a spider. She shuddered. 'No spiders, please.' Then she scolded herself. 'Don't be a sissy.' Getting up her nerve, she stuck a hesitant finger into the hole. Bolder, she probed further into the small space. Hitting something smooth and cool, her fingers slowly pulled a small object out of its hiding place. At last she held a small tin coffer in her sooty hands. It rattled as she shook it. What fun . . . a mystery.

Climbing down from her perch, she moved under the high, narrow windows to get a better look at her prize. Sitting on a convenient armchair, she placed the coffer on a small table near her. She eyed the coffer for a few seconds, then she took hold of it with both hands, trying to pry it open. At first it stuck, then it creaked and flipped open. Seeing its contents, her eyes widened with surprise.

★　★　★

No sound came from the next room. Charles jerked at the screech of furniture dragged across the floor. Again there was silence. Next, he heard the sound of clapping, then Kate's laugh rang out loud and clear. What was she up to? Curious, he stepped out of his

331

hidey hole. He had to see what was going on. Stiff-jointed, he stood and crept toward the light that spilled through the doorway of the next room.

Kate had found a floor lamp to supplement the meager rays which filtered through the small, high, dusty windows.

Moving with care, Charles reached the doorway. Navigating around stacks of Stanhope castoffs, he tiptoed into the room. Kate sat facing the windows with her back to him. As he approached, she stared at an object on a small table in front of her.

Silently, Charles gazed over her shoulder at a stack of what appeared to be gold coins. On top of the stack was a large ruby ring.

'Hello, Kate.'

25

Kate jumped up and whirled around. Seeing Charles, she froze in place, her heart racing in her breast. She struggled to think. What was he doing there? He should be far away from the Lake District by now.

'Sit down, Kate.' He glared at her until she obeyed. Charles pulled up a chair. Straddling it, he sat in front of her. He had her cornered. 'What have you found?' Ice cold eyes bored into hers for a moment, then he reached over and picked up the ring.

Kate could see the ruby's facets twinkling blood red in the light as he examined it.

Charles fondled the piece of jewelry. 'This is beautiful, just beautiful.' He jumped when an unexpected crack of lightning struck nearby in the woods followed by torrents of rain. The abrupt change in weather seemed to distract him since he stared out the window at the storm.

Perhaps she should take the offensive. With her hands on her hips, Kate feigned outraged indignation. 'How dare you. That doesn't belong to you. I found it by accident while I was hunting for a few items to use upstairs in the hotel.' She grabbed the ring out of his hands.

A puzzled expression flitted across his face, so Kate spoke in a more pleasant, conversational tone. 'Who do you think hid it, Charles?' Examining the ring, she pretended interest in his opinion.

'I couldn't say but . . . ' He stopped and shook his head. 'You know it's all your fault, don't you? Clarissa and I would own King's Grant now if not for you. Instead I'm hiding in the cellars, a fugitive from the law.'

'That's unreasonable. You can't blame me for everything that's happened to you. After all, you're an adult and responsible for your own actions.' If she kept him talking long enough, she'd figure out a way to escape.

He shrugged. 'True, but your appearance in Uncle's life threw a monkey wrench into my plans. This estate was meant for Clarissa and me.'

His cold glance grazed her face and Kate fought to keep calm. She was lost if he realized he frightened her. 'No one forced Stephen to marry me. I didn't meet him until he turned up at my mother's funeral.' Kate looked down at the floor. 'If I knew then why he wanted me . . . ' She tried to stir Charles's pity.

'What are you talking about?' He leaned forward.

'Your uncle told me on our honeymoon why I interested him. My mother turned him down for my father. When we met, Stephen saw his chance to make up for the past. If he couldn't have my mother, he'd settle for her daughter. But he soon learned that Mother and I were two different people. Also, I was less than half his age and had my own interests. For example, I wanted to own a small, elite hotel. While Stephen lived, he wouldn't let me convert King's Grant into a hotel, though we could have used funds the last year of his life.'

A bitter laugh slipped through Charles's thin lips. 'At least you have King's Grant now. You survived Uncle. On the other hand, Clarissa and I ended up with nothing. I'm running away from the law and she'll have to sell The Folly to pay debts.'

Kate nodded, trying to keep a sympathetic expression on her face. Keep talking, she told herself. I'll find a way out of this yet. She ground her teeth.

'I wanted to go away somewhere with Clarissa. She owes it to me. I've taken care of her all our lives. We could have a child together, one with two parents to love it. Not like us. Mother and Father weren't suited for each other. I can remember their quarrels. There'd be a lot of yelling and door slamming, then Mother would pack her trunks and go home to Milan for weeks, leaving us with a nanny.'

'But you were so small when you lost your parents, Charles. Five or younger, weren't you?' Kate tried to keep a consoling tone in her voice as she surreptitiously glanced around the room looking for a weapon, anything she could use to overpower the man. Her cold hands gripped the table edges.

'I do remember. Don't you dare tell me I don't.' His pale face flushed with rage, then he pounded his fist on the table between them. 'When Clarissa cried at night, I'd pick her up from her crib and rock her. She was only an infant when both of our parents vanished from our lives. I realized then Clarissa was all I have in the world. And I've always taken care of her. Our nannies didn't love us. Minding us was just another job to them. When we outgrew nannies, Uncle arranged for tutors. I wouldn't even leave Clarissa to go off to college.'

'Yes, you've always been close.'

'And I won't let anyone separate us, Kate.' He looked at her with ice-cold eyes. 'I know you've encouraged Clarissa to go away, but she won't. I have to leave now, but I'll come back for her.'

Kate saw a muscle jump in his cheek. She nodded.

He smiled, grimly. 'Oh, by the way, in case you're curious, we weren't trying to kill you.' He spoke casually of her life.

'What did you intend to do?' Kate strived to sound mildly interested.

'Just to ruin your business. The herbal tea was the ideal place for us to put a 'purge' to upset your guests.' He leaned forward, looking pleased with himself. 'At least that's where we started. Next, we would have put something in your guests' meals. As soon as people started getting sick after dining here, the word would be out. Your hotel business would go down the tube, and you'd be forced to close.' Now a smug, tight smile perched on Charles's pale face.

'And then what?' Kate sat there, his captive audience, stuck between fear and the desire to learn how his twisted, yet ingenious mind worked.

'Oh, you'd give the estate to us, then hop on a plane back to the States. We'd sell the properties to the hotel chain and leave the Lake District with enough funds to live well for the rest of our lives.' He rocked the small chair back and forth until it creaked in protest at his rough treatment.

'So you pulled a poisonous herb by mistake and killed my guest, Mr. Penmar.' Anger flooded Kate until it became difficult for her to sit there quietly. She wanted to scream.

'Yes, that was too bad.'

Kate heard no trace of regret in his emotionless voice. What had Clarissa told her? Charles only loved her and Kings Grant. 'Just for the record, I suppose you killed Mel Martin?'

Charles shrugged. 'Oh, him. That busybody figured us out. My dear sister goofed when she asked Martin to order medicinal herbal books for her. Stupid little sister. It's a good thing I'm here to take care of her. I guess Martin discovered her identity, then heard about your guest's being poisoned. He called me, demanding £50,000 or he'd inform the police. Of course I couldn't let him blab his theory. Who knows, the police might have taken him seriously.'

How incredible that two men had died and the killer sat before her, coolly chatting, in his maddeningly calm voice. How was she to get away? And stop Charles from hurting anyone else?

'Now you know the entire story, except for the ending.' He stood and leered at her. 'But you won't be around for the ending, will you?'

Miles appeared, dusty from exploring a room down the hall. Hard of hearing, the old Scottie hadn't heard Charles's voice until he padded back into the room.

'Get out of here, you mangy mutt.' As usual, Charles kicked at the little dog.

Miles barked ferociously and lunged, attaching his still sharp canine teeth to Charles's pant leg.

Kate took advantage of the disruption. She tossed a handful of coins at Charles and turned the table over on him. Then she escaped by darting into the next room.

Screaming like a banshee, Charles kicked the Scottie loose and pursued her like one possessed. Determined Miles followed his foe, barking hysterically.

'Damned dog.' Charles roared.

Kate winced, hearing a yipe from Miles. The barking ceased, abruptly. What did Charles do to the little Scottie? At the moment, she couldn't stop to find out. She darted through the connecting rooms, upsetting stacks of boxes and books on her way to slow down his pursuit. Turning off light switches as she passed through each room, she made it as difficult as she could for him to catch her.

Charles cursed and bumped into furniture. China and glass shattered in his wake.

For a minute or two, as she worked her way toward the stairs, Kate thought she'd escape. If she could lock Charles in the cellar, the heavy oak door would withstand his fury for a few minutes, and give her time to barricade herself in the library and call the police.

Unfortunately, she tripped over an antique foot stool and fell, sprawling, on her stomach. The air knocked out of her lungs, Kate lay dazed.

Close on her heels, Charles pounced and yanked her up by her long hair until she cried with pain.

'Now what shall I do with you?' He panted, winded from their chase. His cold hands seized Kate's shoulders, then they slid around her throat. He began to choke her.

She struggled, but her strength faded fast. Charles proved stronger than his thin body indicated.

Just then Nick's voice resounded from the top of the stairs. 'Kate, are you down there?'

Both Charles and Kate froze in position. Then he loosened his grip on her and muttered, 'Go ahead, call him down.'

'I won't.' She glared, panting.

'Call him.' He stuck a knife under her chin.

'Nick, I'm here. Come down.'

Charles pushed her onto a stool. He put his finger on his lips, ordering her to stay quiet.

'Kate?'

She heard concern in his voice as Nick entered the room.

'I called but got no answer at your apartment, then heard Miles barking. When I came in the back door, I noticed lights on down here. Are you all right?'

She stared at a spot behind Nick with fear in her eyes. Nick turned just as Charles smashed a vase over his head. He fell with a thump on the cellar floor. Kate jumped up to go to him.

Charles stepped over Nick's unconscious body. 'Stay right there. I figured he'd be around. What a pest your Inspector is.' Holding his knife, Charles gazed at Nick with bright eyes.

'Please don't hurt him, Charles. I'll do anything you say.'

'Oh, all right. But you'll have to find some cord or rope so I can tie him up.' He looked annoyed.

'I think I saw some curtains boxed up over there.' She pointed to a stack of boxes. 'I bet there's some curtain pulls if you open one of the boxes.'

Charles tore open a box and found two tired curtain cords which he used to tie Nick's hands and feet. He confiscated her handkerchief and stuffed it in Nick's mouth as a gag. 'All right, let's go, Kate.' He waved the knife in the direction of the stairs. Once in the kitchen, he pushed her out the door to the garden, and on to the garage.

What would he do with her? She saw him frown and sensed his confusion. He appeared unsure of just what he should do. Kate held her breath. Would he take her with him or leave her behind? She watched him covertly while he eyed the three cars parked side by side.

'What is that old nursery rhyme? Eeny, meeney, miney, moe . . . ' Chuckling, he added, 'which car shall I take?'

Kate stared at Charles, babbling like he'd lost his mind.

'No. This car's low on gas.' He rejected Chris's old Volvo after turning on the engine and checking the gas gauge. He next eyed the old Rolls. 'Uncle's car is handsome but too heavy and slow for the route we'll take today.' That left Kate's Ford Escort. 'We'll take your car.' Locating a spare set of keys on a peg inside the garage door, Charles walked over to the car and unlocked the trunk.

'After you, madam.' He bowed deeply, then waved his arm toward the open trunk.

'Please, Charles, not the trunk. I get claustrophobia.' That was no lie. Since childhood, she couldn't tolerate small spaces.

'Too bad. Hop aboard.' Charles half-pushed, half-lifted her into the small compartment. 'It won't be for long. Relax. Take a nap, read a book.' Giggling, he slammed the lid and left her in the dark, cramped space.

Kate swallowed hard, forcing herself to relax. She breathed slowly. You'll be all right. Fumbling in the darkness, she touched the softness of an old blanket kept in the car for emergencies and bunched it under her head as a pillow.

The car lunged forward and Charles drove out of the garage, down the sloping driveway onto the main road. Where were they going? A few minutes later, Kate heard the car tires beating on wooden planking. A bridge? They must be crossing Newby Bridge, the high, one-way drawbridge that spanned the southern end of Lake Windermere. Nick and she had taken the same route the day they drove to Morecambe Bay.

Thoughts of Nick brought anxious tears to her eyes. She wiped them away with the backs of her hands. 'Please, God, let him be all right,' she whispered.

Crouched in her small, dark space, Kate realized Charles might escape. Living in the area most of his life, Charles knew the back roads. She felt the car slow down, then a thump when he drove off the paved road onto sand. Where were they?

'I'm taking you on a ride you'll never forget,' he called to her in the trunk. His troubles apparently forgotten for the moment, he sang in a shrill voice. 'On the sea, on the sea, on the beautiful sea . . . '

After a minute or two, the car wheels ground to a halt, stuck in the sand. Charles turned off the engine, then he got out and opened the trunk. The light momentarily blinded Kate as he hauled her out and set her on her feet. Feeling light-headed, she leaned against the car. Charles slapped her.

'All right.' Kate muttered, stepping back out of his reach. Her anger revived her and she suppressed the urge to slap him back. 'Enough is enough.' She gritted her teeth, knowing she mustn't panic if she wanted to survive.

A quick glance told her they stood on the edge of Morecombe Bay at low tide. The view was desolate, just a darkening sky and wet sands. As she watched, a lone seagull perched on a piece of driftwood with the remains of a fish. He gazed at them then squawked and flew away toward the sea.

Did Charles want her as a hostage? And what would he do when he no longer needed her? She shuddered, knowing the answer.

His next words answered the unasked questions plaguing Kate. 'You're going to lead me across the Bay.'

So that's how he thought he'd escape. There was no way she'd help him.

As if he'd read her thoughts, Charles gripped her shoulders and spun her around until she stood with her back to him. Then he pulled his knife out of his pocket and pressed the blade against her back. It prodded her. 'I can kill you with this. Or you can help me get away. It's up to you.'

The chill in his voice convinced her he was serious. Kate took a deep breath of the salty air and straightened her shoulders. She wouldn't let him see her fear. 'All right. Let's move before it gets dark.'

They stepped, hesitantly across the sands. On the other side of the Bay, Kate detected movement. She squinted her eyes and thought she'd caught a glimpse of a figure. When she looked again, there were only the sands, with the embankment on the far side.

Charles didn't appear to notice. She wouldn't call it to his attention. She concentrated on survival — one step at a time.

His knife at her back urged her to go faster. Hesitantly, she increased her speed. She was lost if her feet hit quicksand. Charles wouldn't hesitate. He'd abandon her and take another route.

They approached the embankment. Kate could see it just a few yards away. Her heart raced faster with each moment, her one thought the danger surrounding her. If she survived, Kate vowed she wouldn't walk on a beach for a long time. All she wanted was Nick's arms and his voice saying she was safe.

26

Nick regained consciousness. He struggled free from the cords, and placing a hand to his throbbing head, he felt a lump already forming, then he pulled himself up and staggered through the small, gloomy rooms. 'Kate? Are you down here? Kate?' His voice rang through the cellar. Who hit him on the head? Nick remembered coming down the stairs and finding Kate. Then, lights out. Was it possible? Was Charles lurking in the darkness of the cellars? If so, he must have taken Kate with him.

Nick crossed the room, heading for the stairs. A whimpered cry stopped him in his tracks. Looking into another cellar room, Nick found Miles. The old dog wagged his tail when Nick ran his hands gently over him. 'You're all right, fellow. I don't feel any broken bones or ribs. You may just be badly bruised. You tried to protect Kate, didn't you?' He carried the Scottie upstairs and laid him in his bed in the kitchen. 'I'll be back as soon as I can. We'll have a vet look you over.' He left a bowl of water where the dog could get to it. Miles's bowl was full of fresh food.

Kate must have fed him today.

Rubbing the lump on his head, Nick walked outside. He peered into the garage and spotted the Rolls and Chris's Volvo. Kate's Escort was missing. Nick called for help and gave a description of Kate's car. 'I want road blocks at all roads out of this area. That includes roads heading west to the sea. We don't know where they're heading, but Charles Stanhope has taken Kate Stanhope as hostage. You can assume he's armed and dangerous.'

Minutes later, Nick stepped into the Rover and gestured for the patrol car now parked in the driveway to follow him. They headed south toward the Bay. As they approached Morecambe, Nick spotted Kate's car. It sat abandoned, doors and trunk lid open, a short distance onto the seaweed-covered sands.

Squinting, Nick detected movement in the middle of the Bay, at low tide a desert of sand across to the other side. He pulled a pair of binoculars from his car's glove box. After he adjusted the lenses, two thin figures came into focus . . . Kate appeared to be walking ahead of a man. Nick zeroed in on the man's face. Even unshaven, Charles was recognizable.

'The crazy fool. He's got Kate out there with him and they could step into quicksand at any moment.' Nick jumped into the Rover

348

and raced off, followed by the patrol car. As Nick drove he prayed silently. 'Please, God, keep her safe. Don't let me lose her.'

Parking on the opposite end of the Bay, Nick and two other policemen positioned themselves out of sight behind the embankment. He eyed a stack of life preservers and waited. He'd toss one to Kate if he got the chance.

A few harrowing minutes later, Kate and Charles approached. Nick's team sprung into action. One officer imitated the high, shrill call of a loon.

The odd sound tore through the silence, Charles jerked and dropped his knife onto the sand. Kate kicked it away.

Nick seized the opportunity and tossed Kate a life preserver. While Charles scrambled for the knife, Kate slipped on the life preserver and tied it around her.

Nick pulled her to safety. As she hit the embankment, they both rolled down to the beach. Giving her a quick hug, he helped her to her feet.

'You're safe now.'

At the sound of his voice, she burst into tears and clung to him.

The police officer tossed a life preserver to Charles. He panicked and stepped into the quicksand he'd avoided with Kate as his guide. Charles started to sink, then stood still. That slowed down the process. But a moment later the sands resumed their merciless pull on his body.

The officer tossed a rope to Charles. It didn't reach him.

Charles stopped fighting, shuddered and closed his eyes. He appeared resigned to die.

Nick held Kate's face against his chest so she wouldn't see Charles sink, then disappear in the quicksand. Soon he was out of sight. A few air bubbles floated on the surface but they soon dissipated.

'We need to get you to a doctor, Kate.' His voice choked with emotion, Nick helped her to his car and drove to Windermere Hospital. They parted a few minutes later after she checked in at the hospital. 'I'll be back as soon as I tell Clarissa.'

Kate's color was better now. She managed a faint smile when he kissed her.

Nick drove over to the Constabulary. Stepping out of the Rover, he inhaled deeply. The air was washed clean and fresh by the thunderstorm which had rolled across the area earlier.

Walking into HQ, Nick found his assistant sitting at his desk with a stack of paperwork.

Sergeant Kennedy looked up as he came in the door, and smiled a welcome. 'I'm glad to see you. Constable West came in and told me what happened. Is Kate Stanhope all right?' Her face mirrored her concern.

'Yes, no thanks to Charles. He almost killed her out there in the Bay.' Nick wiped his hand across his eyes. It seemed like a lifetime since he'd driven to King's Grant. He'd almost lost Kate that day, might still lose her. She'd wept in his arms. Was she glad to see him or was it from shock?

'My guess is he'd been lurking in the woods for days.' Charles had been the first prisoner to escape from the new jail with its state-of-the-art security systems. Nick found a mug and poured himself coffee so hot he had to sip it.

The sergeant vacated his chair and he sat down.

'It was clever of him to pretend an attack of appendicitis. That was the only way he could get out of the jail. And because those two constables tried to help him, one is dead and the other is in critical condition.' Nick sighed. He blamed himself for not requesting more experienced officers to watch Charles.

Kennedy seemed to read his thoughts. 'You had no way of knowing what he'd do. Maybe we would've caught him if he had tried to leave the area.'

'I walked right into a bad situation today at

the hotel, but I needed to see Kate. We all assumed Charles had left the area right after his escape. He should have left town. Maybe he wanted one last look at King's Grant.' Nick shook his head and leaned back in his armchair. Again he said a silent prayer, thanking God for her safe recovery. 'Kate was able to tell me a little. After she got over the shock of Charles appearing in her cellars, they argued over a ring she'd found. I wonder where it went?'

'Maybe it sank with him?' The sergeant shivered and pulled her jacket closer around her.

'Well, I have to make a call. As next of kin, Clarissa needs to be informed about her brother's death.' Nick drained his coffee mug, set it on the desk and reached for the telephone.

A few minutes later, he parked in front of the graceful brick mansion. He detected the slight movement of a curtain next to a front window, then Clarissa opened the door. It was obvious she'd been waiting for him.

'Come in, Inspector.' She preceded him into the living room where they sat down on a sofa.

He felt her eyes watching him, intently.

'How did he die?'

'In the sands as Kate and he crossed

Morecombe Bay. If it's any consolation, he didn't suffer long. I'm sorry.' Not for the first time in his life, Nick felt the inadequacy of words at the moment of grief.

'Why would he do something stupid like that? He knew how dangerous it was.' Though her voice remained calm, her eyes filled with tears.

'I guess he thought he could escape if he reached the other side of the Bay. Fortunately, Kate survived. She's in hospital under observation.' He wouldn't forgive Charles, not in this lifetime.

'My brother blamed her for his problems. Do you think he lost his mind?'

'He could have suffered a nervous breakdown. We'll never know what his thoughts were.'

'It'll take me a while to get used to life without him. He had such dreams, such fantasies these last months. I suspected he wasn't well, mentally, but didn't know what to do to help.' She sighed.

'You'll miss him?'

'Yes, of course. But I also feel free for the first time in my life. He controlled me, or tried to control me. He didn't even want me to date. He feared I'd find another man to love.' She flushed, looking at Nick. 'You knew, didn't you?'

'I wondered when I saw how close Charles and you appeared.' Nick felt no repulsion, only pity.

'I was thirteen the first time. He convinced me that our relationship was special, meaning we could do as we wanted. But as I grew older, I realized it wasn't normal for brothers and sisters to act as we did. I've locked my bedroom door the last few weeks and would have moved out soon.' She straightened her thin shoulders and gazed directly at Nick.

'You should rest.' He turned to go.

'I know you're anxious to get back to Kate, but later can we talk? It's about Martin.' Clarissa's tone became urgent.

'All right.' Would she confess to the murders, also? He hoped not. Nick drove back to the hospital. The doctor attending Kate reassured him she was all right. Her only injury was to her throat. She'd be hoarse for a few days. He suggested Nick come back the next morning. If all went well, she'd be able to go home.

The next morning, he got up early after a night filled with nightmares of Kate and Charles on the sands. He'd rescue Kate but as he pulled her into his arms, her figure would change to that of Charles who leered at him. Nick checked the clock on his nightstand. It wasn't time to go to the hospital. He drank a mug of coffee and dialed Clarissa's number. 'Is it too early to talk?'

'No, I'm ready. Come now.'

Clarissa opened the door at his first knock and stood there, pale and tired. Judging by her red eyes, she hadn't slept well.

Again they sat in the living room. He waited for her to tell him what bothered her.

'I've thought all night about this.' Her expression could not have been more serious.

'What is troubling you?'

'I didn't know Charles would kill Martin, but I saw it.'

'I thought you said you fell asleep waiting for Charles to come home.' Nick frowned.

'I lied. Charles wouldn't let me go with him to the Falls. After he left, I followed him and hid in the ferns near Stockgyll Force. I saw him kill Martin with a rock.' She stopped and looked at Nick. 'After Charles left, I crawled out of my hiding place. I could tell Martin was dead. My only thought was to get rid of the body. So I pulled Martin to the edge of the Falls and pushed him in.' She looked down for a moment. When she raised her face, Nick saw her eyes overflowing with tears.

In a ragged voice, Clarissa struggled to gain control. 'Are you going to arrest me for the murder, too?'

'No, let me ease your mind. We'll need your statement on your actions and you may face a smaller charge, but Martin died from the blow to his head.'

'My one thought was Charles and how I could help him. Later, I realized he was beyond help, but I might be able to save myself.' Tears ran down her tired face. She looked relieved. 'I was afraid I'd spend the rest of my life in prison. Thank you for telling me.' Apparently comforted by his words, Clarissa slumped into the sofa and wept quietly.

'Call your lawyer and tell him what you've told me. We'll talk again later. And I'm sure your Aunt Kate will be in touch.'

Now Nick only wanted to see Kate. At the hospital a nurse told him that Kate's doctor was in her room but would be out in a moment. He waited impatiently, pacing the halls. As he checked his watch for the second time the doctor came out. 'How is Kate, Doctor? I'm a friend, Nick Connor.'

'No harm done, Mr. Connor. I've discharged her if you want to take her home now? She has a prescription for tranquilizers to help her sleep the next few nights.' He paused. 'You're the detective who's investigated those two murders recently?'

'Yes, I am. But that's all over now. Thank

you, Doctor. I'll see that she gets home.' He tapped on Kate's door.

★ ★ ★

Kate took his hand in hers and smiled wanly. 'You saved my life out there. I'm sorry Charles whacked you on the head. Has a doctor looked at it?'

'The Windermere doctor checked me out. It's just a bad lump, no concussion.' His eyes scanned her face.

'I've never been so glad to see anyone as I was to see you yesterday. But I was afraid he'd kill you. Charles wasn't rational. While I was with him, his moods kept changing. One moment he'd be friendly, then he'd flip and be hostile. I think his mind snapped. Clarissa said that Charles had two loves, her and King's Grant. He may have felt both of them slipping out of his grasp. Let's go home, Nick.' Kate left the hospital room.

They drove back to the gatehouse. He didn't appear to want a conversation so she remained quiet.

When he parked the Rover, she spoke. 'Come in.'

Nick took her keys and unlocked the door. Once inside, Kate removed her jacket and went into the kitchen. She returned in a minute or two with two steaming mugs.

'Can we talk now?' He appeared anxious.

'Yes, go ahead, Nick. All I need to do the next couple of days is rest, so we've all the time in the world. Diane and Chris heard about Charles on the news and called me from Skye. They wanted to come back, but I told them you'd bring me home.' She relaxed on the sofa and gave him her full attention.

'Let's see . . . where to begin?' She could feel him gather his thoughts.

'I'll start with my parents, Kate. They didn't have a happy marriage. My father never talked much and told my mother little, even after he returned from a long trip. Mother apparently grew weary of his behavior and after ten years of neglect, she found happiness with another man and left. Father blamed her for the failed marriage and became embittered. He told me, over and over, that women couldn't be trusted.' Nick stopped and sipped his coffee.

'So he taught you not to trust women?' She could imagine what happened. An angry man left with a son to raise by himself. Surely, Nick missed his mother, and if he looked like his mother, he'd have been a constant reminder of what his father had lost.

'I guess so. Also, I can see now that I didn't use good judgement picking my friends.'

'Could that have soured you a bit, Nick?'

He nodded. 'By the time I reached 25, I'd learned to avoid people, especially women. Five years ago, I was so solitary I could almost taste my loneliness. Then Valerie appeared out of the blue, and I convinced myself that I cared for her. Actually, I was starving for love.'

'So you've been lonely?'

'Yes. When I met you, I'd given up on love. You struck me as hard as a bolt of lightning.'

'I think I know what you mean.' She smiled.

'But I couldn't let my guard down and trust you. I was afraid you'd turn out like the other women I'd known. Now I realize most people, men and women, can be trusted. Finally, as to how I feel about you, let me make it crystal clear. I love you more than anything in the world.' Then he got up his courage to ask the question he'd longed to ask. 'Is there a chance we can start over? However long it takes, I'll wait if you just say the word.'

She suppressed the urge to embrace him at that point. This time would be for keeps. He needed to be aware of how she felt. She leaned toward him. 'Nick, first you couldn't decide how you felt about me and later, we fought. I felt hurt and confused.' She stood, walked to the window and looked out. She turned to face him. 'My marriage wasn't a happy one and I vowed not to rush into another relationship with a man. Then you came along and changed my mind. Even with your ambivalence and our fights, I hoped. But I felt deserted when you shut me out and wouldn't confide in me.'

'That's over. I promise you. We'll talk about any topic you like. But let's talk about us a lot.'

'Come here and kiss me, then. We'll make a new start. I haven't ever loved anyone the way I love you.'

'Kate, I love you . . . always.' They kissed and gazed out the window at the lake, sparkling blue under the summer skies.

Epilogue

Six months passed before Kate married Nick. She wanted them to spend more time together and be dead sure (no pun intended) about each other. Also, she needed time to get the hotel established.

The Christmas Eve Kate's pastor married them, it was too cold for the rose gardens. Instead, they used the living room for the ceremony. Again it was a small group, Kate and Nick, Diane and Chris and Mattie. Miss Rosa played Christmas music before and after the ceremony.

That night Nick and Kate slept in her gatehouse for the last time.

'Just think, tomorrow we'll be in your condo, Nick. I'm sure you'll be more comfortable sleeping in your king size bed.'

'True, but I'll keep fond memories of this apartment. And in the spring, our new home will be ready. Those gold coins you found in the cellar will help pay for it. You never found the ring, did you?'

'No, Charles must have taken it down with him.' She sighed. 'It's been a year of changes. I'm sorry Clarissa couldn't come for the ceremony. She wrote from Devon that she wasn't ready to come back for a visit yet. And she'll never live at The Folly again. There're too many unpleasant memories there. She wrote that her agent has a buyer for The Folly.'

'Diane and Chris looked happy tonight, didn't they?' He stood behind Kate and watched her brushing her long hair, then he took the brush and brushed her hair himself.

'Yes, she's blooming. She has what is referred to as a 'pregnant glow' that some women get. I wonder who the baby will look like? Both Diane and Chris are so blonde.'

'It could look like its maternal grand-mother.'

Kate smiled. 'Didn't that work out well? Mattie thought Chris could be a Stanhope.'

'It goes to show woman's intuition isn't always right. You were as surprised as everyone else when we got Mattie's news.'

Kate turned to face him. 'I remember Mattie's coming back from Glasgow. She handed me a piece of paper with a name on it. I can still hear Mattie fretting over how long it might be before she could locate the woman. After all, the orphanage was only able to give Mattie her daughter's last known address in the States.'

He grinned at his bride. 'That's the first

time I've heard you cluck like a hen that's found its missing chick.'

'But, Nick. You can't blame me. As soon as I saw Mattie's paper, I knew. The name the orphanage gave Mattie, Diane Turner, was our Diane's maiden name. She kept her married name, Diane Frasier after the divorce.

'Poor Mattie was so impatient over getting in touch with her daughter. And all I had to do was call Diane out of the kitchen. Then I left them alone for awhile. I've never seen such smiles and tears in my life. Diane already knew she was adopted, but didn't dream Mattie was her mother. Now, as she says, she has two mothers.'

Nick stopped brushing her hair to kiss the nape of her neck. 'Just think, Kate. Last winter, we didn't know each other. If it weren't for your hotel and Mr. Penmar's death, we wouldn't have ever met.'

'I'm not so sure about that. I believe that some things are meant to happen. I know I was meant to love you, though I must say you didn't do well on your clues.'

'My clues? Are you questioning my sleuthing abilities as a police officer? As the new Superintendent of Windermere Constabulary, I could have you put behind bars for that remark.'

'You misunderstand. I referred to your clues to love.'

'Oh, I see. Well, you must admit, once I got on the right track, I did well.'

'Very well. I need a kiss.'

He obliged.

Other titles in the
Ulverscroft Large Print Series:

PLAIN DEALER

William Ardin

Antique dealing has its own equivalent to 'insider trading', as Charles Ramsay finds out to his cost. Offered the purchase of a lifetime, he sees all his ambitions realised in an antique jade cup, known as the 'Loot'. But as soon as the deal is irrevocably struck he finds himself stuck with it like an albatross around his neck — unable to export it without a licence, unable to sell it at home, and in a paralysing no man's land where nobody has sufficient capital to take it off his hands . . .

NO TIME LIKE THE PRESENT

June Barraclough

Daphne Berridge, who has never married, has retired to the small Yorkshire village of Heckcliff where she grew up, intending to write the biography of an eighteenth-century woman poet. Two younger women are interested in her project: Cressida, Daphne's niece, who lives in London, and is uncertain about the direction of her life; and Judith, who keeps a shop in Heckcliff, and is a divorcee. When an old friend of Daphne falls in love with Judith, the question — as for Cressida — is marriage or independence. Then Daphne also receives a surprise proposal.

SEARCH FOR A SHADOW

Kay Christopher

On the last day of her holiday Rosemary Roberts met an intriguing American in the foyer of her London hotel. By some extraordinary coincidence, Larry Madison-Jones was due to visit the tiny Welsh village where Rosemary lived. But how much of a coincidence was Larry's erratic presence there? The moment Rosemary returned home, her life took on a subtle, though sinister edge — Larry had a secret he was not willing to share. As Rosemary was drawn deeper into a web of mysterious and suspicious occurrences, she found herself wondering if Larry really loved her — or was trying to drive her mad . . .